THE SAND DIGGER'S SKULL

EAST TIMOR CRIME SERIES №2

Chris McGillion

coffeetownpress

Kenmore, WA

coffeetownpress

Coffeetown Press books published by Epicenter Press

Epicenter Press
6524 NE 181st St. Suite 2
Kenmore, WA 98028.
www.Epicenterpress.com
www.Coffeetownpress.com
www.Camelpress.com

For more information go to: www.Epicenterpress.com

This is a work of fiction. All characters, events and village names are creations of the author's imagination.

The Sand Digger's Skull
Copyright © 2023 by Chris McGillion

ISBN: 9781684920532 (trade paper)
ISBN: 9781684920549 (ebook)

LOC: 2022936037

Printed in the United States of America

Dedication

For Raji

Acknowledgments

Thanks to Raymond Harding and Bill Blaikie—partners in crime (writing)—long-suffering witnesses to my schemes Milton Cockburn, Alan Mitchell, and Ross Gittins, my Timorese accomplices Francedez Suni and Silvano Rodriguez, and the folks at the Esplanada—the best little hideout in Dili.

1

A little while longer and that would have to do it. The sun was now above the hilltops to the city's east and leaching color from the sky. Heat was reflecting off the sand like light from a mirror. It had been a long, hard night. His arms and back ached and could not be pushed much further if he wanted to come back and work again this evening.

Beto Correira was working a stretch of the Comoro River, south of the old bridge that carried traffic from the sleepy airport district of Timor-Leste's capital, Dili, to the congested commercial and administrative sector in the city. During the rainy season, the monsoons drench the Comoro catchment in the mountainous regions to the south; the run-off becomes a huge wall of water that roars through the city and can sweep people and vehicles off the bridge along with it. But in summer, the Comoro presents a much thinner, more placid flow snaking through eighty yards of dry sand and river pebbles on either side of the main channel. This is what brought sand diggers like Beto to work each night. In the cool dark hours, they shovelled sand through make-shift wire filters for use in the many construction and re-construction sites around a city emerging from the turbulent birth of the nation a decade before. Each morning, trucks would drive down to gather the piles of sand and tally what each digger was owed.

A few more shovelfuls and Beto Correira would be done. He wiped the sweat from his forehead, replaced the rag in his trouser pocket and sliced the shovel back through the sand.

That's when he found it.

1

At first Beto thought it was a piece of driftwood washed down from the mountains. When he noticed the eye sockets and the teeth on the upper jaw line, he knew it was a skull. He dared not touch it for fear of exciting the spirit of the dead person whose skull it had once been or inviting another evil upon himself. He called over to a fellow sand digger who was also packing up for the day and the two of them stood over the skull without speaking. Eventually Beto muttered that they should call the police and he looked down at the cell phone in the other's hand. The man nodded and made the call.

Investigator Vincintino Cordero of Timor-Leste's elite Scientific Police for Criminal Investigation unit was at home, tying the laces on his new black leather shoes, when his cell phone rang. He finished a knot, looked at the result with satisfaction, and only then answered. It was a dispatcher from police headquarters.

"*Bondia maun, diak ka lae?*" the voice said, greeting Cordero with a polite inquiry into how he was feeling this morning.

Everyone in law enforcement knew everyone else in a small city like Dili and Cordero recognized the voice as Officer Arao Beixo of the regular Timorese national police force. "I was doing fine until you rang, Arao," he replied. "Do you know what time it is?"

"Well, that's the problem, you see," Arao said and laughed. "It's peak hour, there's been a big traffic accident in Vera Cruz and there's not one available police officer to deal with this in the entire city. Not one. That's why I—I mean we—called you."

"Deal with what?" Cordero asked with little interest.

"Down on the Comoro. East side of the channel roughly in line with the back fence of the Ministry of Agriculture and Fisheries compound. A sand digger rang in to report a skull he found this morning." Arao was rushing to finish before Cordero became angry with him for calling. "Well, the man who called didn't find it; another sand digger did a"—there was a pause and Cordero could hear the ruffling of paper—"a Belo Correira. No, wait a minute. Beto Correira. Yeah that's it. *Beto*. That's who found the skull. There's no one else we can send."

"What about Lucas Rama or Manuel?" Cordero said, trying to hide annoyance. The two men shared his office in the special police unit. "Why am I the one who's always asked?"

"Lucas isn't answering his cell and I'm told Manuel is away sick," Arao said. "Anyway someone needs to get down there and secure the scene until we can free up officers to attend. It shouldn't take too long." And with that Arao hung up rather than have to argue the case any further.

Cordero swore to himself and gazed through the window at the purple bougainvillea that had grown into a kind of shrubbery shield for his small house against the dust and grim of the street outside. His car—an old SUV supplied by the office but only kept serviceable with the help of several innovative mechanics who owed him favours—was parked in the concreted front yard between his porch and the fence. He checked his wallet quickly for money, checked it again more thoroughly in the forlorn hope of finding more, and put it, his cell, and the police badge he rarely had occasion to show in his trouser pocket. He felt in his jacket for a notebook and pen and picked up his car key from his bedside table. He let out a deep breath of frustration, ran a hand through his hair, and walked to the car. He lived alone but never bothered to lock the door because burglary was rare in Dili and especially for houses owned by police.

Cordero worked his way through the tangle of cars, motorcycles, brightly painted microlet buses and assorted trucks coughing diesel fumes along the main artery through the city—*Avenida Nicolau Lobato*. The *Avenida*, like the airport, was named in honour of Timor-Leste's first prime minister who held office for less than two weeks before Indonesia invaded in December 1975. After that, Lobato took the title of acting president for three years while he led a guerrilla campaign against the invaders in the countryside. Eventually, Indonesian forces ambushed and killed him. Lobato was only thirty-two years old when he died. On most estimates, Indonesia was responsible for the deaths of one hundred thousand Timorese—ten percent of the entire population—through warfare, repression, and policies that resulted in mass starvation. Cordero was reminded of that recent history as he took this untypical route to work. He compared it to his own years growing up in a relatively comfortable exile in Australia. As always, he soon ceased to feel angry about the jobs he was sent to do in a country that was now independent and relatively peaceful.

Consequently he was in a brighter mood when he pulled the SUV up on the bank of the Comoro. Below him was a small group of curious onlookers—women going to or returning from the market, clumps of children, an office worker unconcerned about the time—who stood around two men leaning on shovels he assumed were sand diggers. A man who might have been the driver sent to collect the sand was arguing with one of the diggers and pointing to a truck parked nearby.

"*Para lao hela. Sees ba sorin*," Cordero yelled from the river bank as he exited the car, ordering the group to stop walking around the area where he took the skull to be and move aside. "*Ajente polisia. Ita halo laran-susar fatin nee*," he said, adding that they were disturbing what was a police scene.

He jumped down onto the riverbed. For a man of forty years of age, he was exceptionally fit and agile, but he was also fussy and he cursed as dust took the shine off his new shoes. He waved the group to move further back as he approached and asked for Beto Correira to come forward. The sand digger edged toward Cordero who was bending down to get a closer look at the skull. "You have nothing to worry about," Cordero assured Beto, gesturing him to stop coming any further forward. "You've done nothing wrong. I am Investigator Cordero. I just need to know how you came to find this skull, when, and whether you moved or touched it in any way."

Beto looked this way and that before explaining that he didn't own a watch but said he had smoked four cigarettes since finding the skull. It was a common way for Timorese who'd moved to Dili from the rural districts to calculate time and Cordero worked it back to approximately 7am. Beto said he was completing his last pile of filtered sand when he felt the thing on the end of his shovel. He pointed to the spot. He had moved the skull about two feet from where it lay to examine it and determine what it was. When he saw it was a human skull he dropped it immediately from his shovel and hadn't touched it since. Neither had anyone else, Beto added, but Cordero could see footprints in the sand telling him the onlookers had completely corrupted the area around where the skull had been found.

"All right, *maun*," Cordero said, addressing Beto by the customary title of 'brother'. "I will have to take your details, then you can go home." He rose to address the others. "Unless you know about this skull and why it is here, I want everyone to leave in a straight line from here to the river bank," he said and gestured with his arm so there'd be no confusion.

The people looked at each other and started to peel away, first the women, then the office worker, and finally the children. Cordero took down Beto Correira's details. "What about me?" asked the man Cordero took to be the truck driver. "I'm supposed to drive further up the riverbed and collect all the sand. I can't drive my truck in a straight line to the bank."

"Then you'll have to leave it where it is," Cordero answered, disregarding the man's predicament and pocketing his notebook before squatting to examine the skull more closely.

"Timor is a land of skulls," the man began to protest. "What difference does one more make?"

"I told you what to do," Cordero said with more emphasis but not taking his eyes off the skull. "Now do it or I will arrest you for obstructing a police investigation!"

The truck driver scratched his chin and considered his options. "What if I reverse the truck back the way I came?" he pleaded.

Cordero thought for a moment. "Okay. I can live with that," he said not looking up. "But make sure you stay in precisely the same tracks you made coming down."

The man breathed a sigh of relief. "*Obrigadu maun*," he said thanking Cordero and headed for his truck before the policeman could change his mind.

Cordero gently turned the skull this way and that with his pen. It seemed weathered by age or, perhaps, exposure to the river: light brown in color with a few darker patches on the crown. One-third of its left side plus the lower jaw bone were missing. There were molars on the upper jaw and one canine tooth on either side of its center. Cordero had no way to determine a cause of death, or the age or sex of the deceased. He imagined that it might have been a person buried in a household plot—it was common in Timor to bury the dead among the living—and that the heavy rains of the last monsoon had washed the grave into the river. But if that was the case there should be more skeletal remains and perhaps remnants of a coffin and a grave marker.

Cordero stood and examined the riverbed around him. Looking closely from different angles working the sunlight over the drifts, he thought he could discern a stretch of darker, coarser sand protruding from a slight bend in the river where heavier materials washed down from the mountains would have collected. That gave him an idea and he took his cell from his pocket and rang the Police Training Centre to leave a message for its commander, his friend Julio Freitas. He would be there about 9am. He hoped Freitas would release six female cadets from their classes to undertake a practical policing exercise he was devising.

He checked his watch—8.15am—and wondered how long it would be before regular police officers came to relieve him and he could finally get coffee. He noticed two young boys, the arms of one around the shoulders of the other, staring at him on the riverbank. He uttered a roar and made to lunge toward them and they tore off to the roadway, shrieking excitedly. Cordero smiled, brushed himself down, and rang Dr. Howard Brooks.

2

Officer Estefana dos Carvalho of the Timor-Leste National Police was caught in the traffic chaos around Vera Cruz. She was not yet used to the congestion of a big city like Dili: in her far less populated native Suai, on the country's south coast, there were times she could drive through town and count on one hand the number of other vehicles she passed. At least it had been like that before the big development projects associated with the oil and gas fields in the sea further south had brought a lot more activity to Suai. But that was nothing like what she was experiencing this morning. Car and motorcycle horns blared out their owners' frustration in a cacophony. Drivers hung out of their trucks swearing at nothing in particular. Children walking to school stopped and gawked at the mayhem that was unfolding.

Traffic control, Estefana was thinking to herself as she inched her unmarked police car along the *Avenida Marginal* on Dili's seafront, was one of the more mundane jobs she had been given in Suai. But she now had the official title of Police Officer (INTERPOL Liaison) and she smiled, thinking of her changed good fortunes as she made what way she could from the room she rented in the crowded Dili suburb of Lecidere west toward the elegant white parliament building, and from there to the office where she worked. She also smiled thinking of her fiancé, Josinto Centavo Veddo, who had moved to Dili as an apprentice carpenter with the local coffin maker. Now they were at least living in the same town, if not the same house.

Up ahead she saw a police officer she knew, Julio Galego, and she popped her head out of the driver's side window of her car to shout hello in as loud a voice as she could manage.

"*Bondia, maun*," Estefana called out. "What's going on?"

"Hey *mana*," Julio replied, smiling when he recognised Estefana and giving her the friendly title of 'sister'. "A truck lost its front wheel on the corner with *Belamino Lopo*," he said, indicating one of the busiest intersections in this part of Dili as he walked toward Estefana's car and lent into the driver's window. "The thing came clean off. The truck was carrying a load of concrete pipes. Spilled all over the road. They'll need a crane to pick them up again." He laughed, enjoying his small part in bringing order into chaos. "But how're they going to get that through this mess? There's motorcycles and cars that've run into pipes everywhere." He looked up the street then back to Estefana, grinning "Can you believe that: a truck losing its wheel! They're up there now, the driver, a whole bunch of cops, a mechanic, angry truckers—all arguing about what happened and why. I heard the nuts weren't screwed on. And this is supposed to be the new Timor-Leste." They both stared again at the traffic up ahead. "Anyway, where are you going?" Julio asked.

"To work, of course. At the INTERPOL office," Estefana answered with more than a hint of pride in her voice. "Started a few weeks ago."

"I heard you impressed a big shot Timorese cop and an even bigger shot FBI agent on a child abduction case around Suai. That what got you to Dili?"

Estefana smiled. "Sort of," she said. "The American who works for INTERPOL asked for me as her interpreter." She stared straight ahead, thinking of the way she had been overlooked for serious police work as a twenty-two-year-old female officer in Suai. "But I help with her investigations too," she added. "And I'm going to be very late."

"Well, we can't have that when you're only a few weeks in the job," Julio said. "Drive off to the sidewalk there and up that driveway near the pole. Leads to a kind of alley that'll take you onto *Rua de Lecidere*. Your car's small enough to make it. Just follow the tyre tracks. I'll wave you through." And with that Julio was gesturing her on, but holding back the cars and motorcycles behind her.

"Thanks, *maun*," Estefana called back as she drove off the *Avenida*. After scattering chickens in the yard and making a few sharp turns around trees, sheds, and vegetable gardens she emerged on *Rua de Lecidere* as Julio had said. The traffic there was also at a standstill as a consequence of the concrete pipe catastrophe but not in the direction she was heading, and she was able to pull into the parking area of the building that housed the INTERPOL office in less than five minutes.

Estefana left her car in a space next to one marked "*Diretor*" and headed into the building and down a long, cool corridor to several offices with "INTERPOL" stamped on their doors. She knocked timidly on the first door, waited but heard no reply and entered. The room was empty, but off to its left was another where a female officer was tapping on a computer keyboard. Her name was Furaha Oodanta, and she was from Africa, but no-one had ever said exactly where. Whatever time Estefana had arrived at work in the past three weeks, Officer Oodanta was sitting at her desk using only two fingers on her computer keyboard. Each evening when Estefana left the office, Officer Oodanta would remain, tapping away. Estefana wondered if she ever left but the young woman said very little, engaged with her colleagues even less, and thus Estefana did not ask questions. It remained a mystery to Estefana who Officer Oodanta really was and what she was doing in Timor-Leste.

"*Bondia, mana*," Estefana said as she walked through to a third office.

"*Bondia*," Officer Oodanta replied, not taking her eyes of her keyboard.

As Estefana placed her bag on the desk and took her seat an adjoining door opened and the American FBI agent, Sara Carter, entered. Carter was dressed in blue slacks and a sheer black blouse that accentuated her slim, toned figure. She raised her sunglasses into shoulder-length brown hair, said hello to both women, asked how Estefana was this morning, and sat down at her own desk.

"I was held up in the traffic, *mana*," Estefana replied. "What a mess. Did you hear about the truck that lost its wheel and then its load of concrete pipes? All over the road!"

"Uh-huh. Driver of the taxi that brought me here told me all about it. Good thing I was coming from Motael," Carter said. "Was able to go down behind the parliament building and avoid the worst of it."

"How do you find Motael, *mana*?" Estefana asked, as she too was settling into the city. Motael was the old, Portuguese centre of Dili bordering the seafront. The US Embassy had found a small duplex apartment for Carter in one of the tree-lined back streets a month after she'd arrived in Timor-Leste. "It's been how long, four days?" Estefana added.

"Yeah. It's nice and it's quiet," she said. "Except for the nightly reggae coming from a house up the street. Musicians, I think. But even they're not too loud and I don't mind reggae. I'm upstairs. There's a European who apparently works for a United Nations agency living downstairs, but I never see him." She switched on her computer. "And I like the area," she added with more enthusiasm. "I can walk to the promenade without getting lost and I even went all the way to Bairro Central on Sunday. When I finish setting up the place you must come over and I'll cook dinner."

"I'd like that *mana*," Estefana said taking her cue to turn on her own computer although she could think of nothing to do with it. "Have you finished the report?"

After helping solve a child abduction case on the southern border with Indonesia, Carter had been assigned to INTERPOL's investigation of war crimes in Timor-Leste. This mostly meant collating past files, matching victim and witness interview statements with what other official documentation there was—if any—updating sites of known atrocities, and, most importantly, preparing reports that might lead INTERPOL to issue a Blue Notice, which was an international alert to locate a person of interest in a criminal investigation. That's what she'd been working on these past three weeks. Most of the people sought through a Blue Notice would be Indonesian or Timorese who had sided with

Indonesia during its occupation of Timor-Leste and then fled the country as independence neared. Estefana had been translating victim statements for Carter concerning an allegation of torture.

Eight women in a mountain village to the south of the district of Liquica, west of Dili, had said they were beaten and sexually abused by a member of the notorious pro-Indonesian militia *Besi Merah Putih* or *BMP*. The group was known to have carried out several massacres in the area. The women said they were targeted in the weeks leading up to the referendum on independence in 1999 in order to terrify local villagers into not voting. None of them had been interviewed about the incident until ten years after the event and it was only now, another five years later and with two of the women already having died, that their story had been looked into properly. Such was the backlog of cases and the scarcity of staff to investigate them.

Each of the women had named the same *BMP* militiaman as their torturer. He was believed to be living across the border in Indonesian West Timor. Carter's report would recommend that INTERPOL issue a Blue Notice for his detention and extradition to Timor-Leste for questioning. The chances of that happening were close to zero but at least there would be a notice issued and put on file as recognition of the victims' suffering.

"I'm almost finished but I just need to go over a few details with you again," Carter said, pressing a button that brought the office printer whirring to life. "I told you I've started learning Tetun, but I think the lessons have made me worse. Tetun really is a crazy language, you know that?"

"You think English is easy?" laughed Estefana who had been taught English throughout her school years by Filipina nuns. "Tetun's really a mixture of several languages," she continued. "As is English. For a start there's *Tetun Prasa, Tetun Terik, Bahasa,* and Portuguese. Then there are the words and phrases from small local languages like *Makasae, Fataluku* and *Tokodede.* The Tetun we call the national language has only been codified recently and most people on the street would take no notice of that when they speak it—let alone people in the rural districts."

"That really helps, thanks," said Carter, emphasizing the sarcasm. She walked over to the printer, and picked up the sheets of paper it had turned out. "We can go over this draft report before lunch, look at the bits I'm not sure about from the interview transcripts, and get it off this afternoon. What do you say?"

Estefana liked the fact that Carter asked her opinion rather than simply issue her instructions. It was one of the many things she liked about this American she regarded as a friend. "Good plan," she said and moved her chair closer to Carter's desk to enable the two of them to work on the report together.

"But first—"

"Coffee!" Estefana interjected, knowing the American's habits.

"That's right. I'm buying. It'll give me a chance to practice my Tetun. Furaha? Would you like a coffee?" Carter asked her colleague in the other office.

"No thank you," came a barely audible reply.

Carter handed the printed document to Estefana. "Here, you have a quick read of this while I go around the corner to the café." She took a bag from her desk and slung it over her shoulder. "Back in a tick."

"*Mana*?" Estefana asked as Carter was leaving.

"What's up?" the FBI agent said looking back.

"Isn't a tick a thing you make on a page? Or the sound a clock makes? Or a bug that gets into your skin? Or is it me that's confused rather than the English language?"

"Touché," replied Carter. She popped her head back inside the room. "And that's French."

3

Two police officers—one young and eager, the other older and disinterested—relieved Cordero at the riverbed just after 9am. He had ordered them to keep onlookers well away from where the skull had been found and then driven the few blocks to the Police Training Centre and called on Commander Julio Freitas. The two had first met five years ago and, later, had shared an apartment for six months in Portugal while studying investigative procedures and forensic science in preparation for the establishment of the Scientific Police for Criminal Investigation unit in Timor-Leste. But Julio had been appointed to head the police training centre and, as Cordero remarked good-naturedly upon entering his office, was growing fat behind his desk.

"It's true, Tino," Julio said, using the contraction of Cordero's first name. "But unlike you, I don't have to chase those young female cadets around: I'm their boss and they come to me."

"How are your children now, Julio? Have they finished their schooling?" asked Cordero, reminding Julio that he was married and a father.

"The girl is in the Jesuit school and one boy is studying at UNTL," Julio replied, indicating the public university in Dili. "The older boy is driving a taxi but what can you do?" he said raising his arms wide over his desk. "You can't talk sense into young people these days. You'll learn that when you have your own." He grinned at Cordero and lowered his voice. "Is that why you're after my girls? You thinking of starting a family?"

"Not quite," Cordero said. "A skull was found in the bed of the Comoro this morning. A skull but no bones. I think it may have come down in a load of soil shifted by the last big rainfall a few months back. But you never know. I need people to search through a stretch of the riverbed but I don't want clumsy males who'd rather be playing with guns and likely to miss things or mess them up. That's why I asked for female cadets. A lighter touch, if you like."

"Well I guess it's all good training—or at least we can pretend it is. You wanted six?"

"If you've six," answered Cordero.

"Oh I've plenty. The police force is an attractive option for girls now," he said and grinned. "There's a workshop this morning on police ethics. The cadets generally hate it but it's mandatory. We can call this a practical exercise in the ethics of handling the dead. I'm sure you'll get six volunteers."

Cordero found closer to twenty eager cadets and he chose his six based on nothing more than their smiles. They crammed into his SUV, two in front alongside Cordero, three sitting in back with another on their laps, and he drove to a rundown supermarket near a more expensive one in the modern Timor Plaza. He asked two of the cadets to go to the Plaza and buy coffee for everyone, including himself, and gave them a twenty-dollar bill—Timor-Leste having adopted American currency as its own. Then he went into the supermarket, bought six rakes, tied them to the top of his vehicle and drove to the riverbed, everyone spilling their coffee as he weaved quickly through the traffic along the way.

After he had indicated the patch of riverbed he wanted raked, and demonstrated how to do it carefully and how to mark any bones they found without disturbing the area more than was needed, Cordero climbed back up the riverbank to his vehicle. Just as he was opening his driver's door, Dr Howard Brooks pulled up in his Land Cruiser.

"*Bondia*, Tino," Brooks said, cut his motor and leant an arm out the driver's side window. "What's this about a skull?"

Dr Howard Brooks was an English pathologist who had washed up in Timor-Leste ten years earlier. Cordero did not know why exactly but he suspected it involved a marriage that had gone wrong with either a Portuguese or Brazilian woman. Brooks was now in his sixties, was perpetually casually dressed—today he was wearing baggy pants, a soiled T-shirt and tennis shoes—and his shock of grey hair never appeared to be combed. Usually Brooks worked as the chief medical officer (and pathologist as required) in the southern districts around Suai but he had agreed to fill in for Dili's pathologist for three months while the man went to New Zealand for further training.

"Well as I said on the phone, a sand digger came across it this morning. Probably from a grave washed down from upstream."

"Well if it is a grave that's washed down, why call me, dear boy?"

"There were no other bones found with it so I've organised six cadets to search a patch of the riverbed which looks as though it may have been the section of earth that the skull was washed down in. They've only been at it for five minutes. I just thought you should be here in case they turn up anything interesting."

"Okay," said Brooks stepping out of his vehicle. "There's nothing much else doing in Dili this morning. Just a quiet day in a tropical paradise. How's your sister doing?"

Cordero's sister Ana had recently undergone an emergency operation for a burst appendix that had resulted in peritonitis. Her husband was deceased, which in Timor's strict kinship society, made Cordero responsible for her and her children.

"She's home and slowly getting back to normal duties," Cordero said.

"Good surgeon that Montoya," Brooks said, referring to the Cuban doctor Carlos Montoya who had performed the operation. "I had dinner with him last week. Doesn't like his prospects in Cuba but blames the Americans, not the Castros." Brooks chuckled to himself. "He's a revolutionary but I suspect, truth be known, he prefers what the revolution promises to what it delivers. Anyhow he said he'd decided to stay on as part of Havana's medical aid mission for another year."

Cuba had provided doctors and nurses to Timor-Leste when it became independent and had taken several hundred Timorese to

Havana for medical training. But by now only a select few Cuban doctors and nurses remained in the country.

"He's quite a formidable character," Cordero said. "Can't say I warm to him but he did a good job on Ana."

"Get a few rums into him, dear boy, and he's a changed man. You should hear him sing 'The Internationale' in Spanish. Quite stirring, I must say." They both looked out over the river. "I see they are female cadets, Tino," Brooks observed raising his eyebrows. "The morning just got more interesting."

"I'm glad you think that, Howard," Cordero said and turned the ignition. "Let me know if you find anything interesting."

"Oh I will, dear boy, I will." Brooks took from his vehicle a camera, tape measure, notepad, and several small vials for collecting soil samples. As he headed down to the riverbed Cordero heard him singing:

"'*So come brothers and sisters, for the struggle carries on, The Internationale unites the world in song....*'"

4

The following morning a strong wind was blowing south off the sea and gusting through the fig and coconut palm trees along Dili's waterfront. Danique Jacobsen, the director of INTERPOL operations in Timor-Leste, was glad to get off the street and into the shelter of her building and the calm of her own small office. The night before she had returned from a conference on cyber-crime held in Baucau, the country's second city, three hours' drive along the coast east of Dili. Her absences always meant there was work to catch up on when she returned. Lots of it. That's why she was in earlier than usual. She had exchanged pleasantries with Officer Furaha Oodanta, who was sitting straight-backed and tapping on her keyboard when Jacobsen entered the office, and then settled down to go through the many emails and voicemails that had banked up the previous day and overnight.

But it was one early morning message on her answering machine from Dr Howard Brooks that caught her attention.

"Morning Danique, although it's actually dead of night here. Appropriate I guess for a morgue. *Dead* of night," the message began. "Howard Brooks here," was the next utterance although Jacobsen could tell who it was immediately from the accent. "I'm assuming you have been apprised of the skull discovered in the Comoro riverbed yesterday. Tino Cordero sent a team of police cadets down there to sift around. They did a good job. By late afternoon yesterday they'd unearthed five more skulls and assorted skeletal remains, one set of which seem to suggest a foetus. All co-mingled like a jig-saw puzzle." Jacobsen heard a long yawn before Brooks continued. "Anyway after we photographed and mapped the area, I had the remains sent over here to the hospital. Been trying to sort things out all night. After I catch a few winks I'll begin a proper autopsy. But I can tell you this already: as far as I can tell at this stage these people were murdered. They are not, as Tino first suggested, remains from the graves of people who died from natural causes. My guess is we're looking at a mass killing. And that suggests it may be a case your lot should be involved with." Another, longer yawn. "Can you send one over let's say around 4pm this afternoon? Good night, er, good morning." And with that Brooks had hung up.

Jacobsen hadn't heard about the skull and she called out to Officer Furaha Oodanta to see if she had.

"No *mana*," came the uncurious reply.

Jacobsen checked her watch. Carter would arrive soon and she would send her to the Guido Valaderes National Hospital, where Brooks' autopsy rooms were located. It was walking distance from the INTERPOL office. She would send along Carter's translator, Estefana, in case indications suggested a possible war crime requiring further investigation by INTERPOL. A few minutes later Carter and Estefana entered the office, each adjusting their clothing from the swirling wind outside, and engaged in an animated conversation peppered with laughter. The two cut short whatever was amusing them and exchanged greetings with Jacobsen and Officer Oodanta. The INTERPOL director called them into her room.

"I believe you know Dr Howard Brooks, the pathologist," Jacobsen began addressing Carter.

"Yes, we met during that abduction case in Suai. Why?"

"He left a message this morning. Said they'd uncovered the skeletal remains of six bodies in the Comoro riverbed yesterday." Jacobsen waited for a response. When none came she continued. "He's yet to do a full autopsy but he thinks they're murder victims. That could constitute a massacre and raises the possibility it was a war crime. I'd like you and Estefana to go to the hospital this afternoon and talk to Brooks."

"Did he say how they were killed, when, anything about who they might be?" Carter asked.

"No. It looks like they were washed down the river in the last big rains. He may know more by 4pm."

"Okay," said Carter. "By the way our report recommending a Blue Notice for that creep from the *BMP* is on your desk."

"Good work. I'll get to it before lunch," said Jacobsen. "There may be news in the papers or online about the recovery of the remains from the river. Estefana, you could have a look this morning. Also, Tino Cordero was involved apparently. Might be worth giving him a call, find out what he knows which is sure to be more reliable than whatever's reported in the newspapers. Maybe take him along with you to Brook's rooms."

"Okay, I'll do all of that," said Carter.

"Have you seen Tino lately?" Jacobsen asked.

"We've said 'Hi' in the corridor a few times when he's been in but we haven't really talked since we all celebrated our success in the Suai assignment. We've been busy."

"Well this could be a good day to catch up. He has a certain mischievous streak—it comes from acting half his age at times—but he's a good investigator when he wants." Carter and Estefana started back toward their desks. "Agent Carter, can I have a further word with you, please?" Jacobsen asked. Carter gave Estefana a quizzical glance, turned back, and stood behind a chair in front of Jacobsen's desk. "Are you not happy here, Sara?" Jacobsen asked when they were alone.

"I'm happy enough. Now," Carter replied. "Why do you ask?" she placed her hands on the back of the chair.

"I had a call from your embassy before I left for Baucau." Carter's mouth tightened but she said nothing. "They told me you want an early release from us."

Jacobsen waited.

Carter took a deep breath, looked down at the floor and back up to Jacobsen. "When I first arrived here, I was mightily pissed off. That much is true. But then I was thrown in at the deep end, met Estefana and Cordero, and helped solve that case down in Suai. During that investigation I knew there was no time or place for anger. You might even say the whole thing was therapeutic," she added. "But then you gave me a desk and the embassy gave me an apartment. It was like I was supposed to put down roots, you know?" The knuckles on her hands whitened as they gripped the back of the chair. "I'm not pissed off anymore but that doesn't change the fact that I didn't ask to be sent here. This is not my country, and these are not my people. I want to go home to work on the cases I'm responsible for *there* among the people I know and care most about."

Jacobsen nodded thoughtfully. "I can understand that," she said. "But you have to understand my position too. I'm responsible for INTERPOL operations in this country. Every Timorese is connected in some way to another who was killed or who died of malnutrition or mistreatment during twenty-four years on Indonesian occupation. The country is traumatised and its people are long overdue a reckoning. And now every Timorese lives in an underdeveloped country that is highly vulnerable to further calamities from drugs, guns, people smugglers, you name it. These people have suffered enough and their suffering must have an end. I've been thinking about how to respond to your embassy for the last two days. I sympathize with your situation, truly. But I'm driven by the larger objective to help bring about that end to the suffering in this country. INTERPOL lacks staff. Therefore, when your people said it was up to me to approve or refuse your early release, I decided I had no choice but to refuse. No doubt you'll get the paperwork in due course."

Carter held her stare for a moment. She brushed a hand through her hair. "Is that all you wanted to talk to me about?" she asked.

"Yes," said Jacobsen.

"Then I'll get on with this latest assignment," said Carter. She pushed herself off the back of the chair and left the room.

• • •

The wind had eased by the time they set off to the hospital that afternoon and they were able to walk in relative comfort. They passed children playing on the broken sidewalks, women laughing over shared gossip, and restaurants preparing evening meals of fried chicken and sate vegetables. Music blared from ghetto-blasters and young men revved motorcycles in an attempt to attract Estefana's attention, for like Carter, she was an attractive woman but closer to their age. As they made their way, Carter brought Cordero up to speed on her new assignment for INTERPOL, her apartment, and her attempts to learn Tetun. He realised that for reasons he didn't quite understand he'd been avoiding her and was surprised at how eager he was to see her. He boasted about his new leather shoes, which he had meticulously cleaned of river dust the night before, and complained about his SUV—anything really to keep up the conversation. When he became conscious of this make-talk he changed tact and asked Estefana about her transfer. She could hardly contain her delight as she mentioned her boyfriend and, of course, the new job. By then they were entering the area of the hospital set aside for the morgue. The corridor was cool, antiseptic in smell and clinical in appearance. It was also devoid of Dr Howard Brooks. Cordero found a pretty, young nurse in an adjoining corridor, exchanged pleasantries and asked where the pathologist might be.

"He took over the old building at the back," she said. "We had to clean it out late last night so he could get all his bones in." Her smile turned momentarily to a frown. "I was working until nearly midnight cleaning out the building for him. I'm really very tired."

Cordero commiserated with her overly-long before rejoining his impatient companions. Out back they found Brooks amid half a dozen trestle tables on which bones had been laid out in attempts to recreate whole skeletons. Bare light bulbs hung from the ceiling, all of them turned on to produce a bright, artificial glow. Brooks looked up as they entered, took off his glasses, rubbed his eyes, and grinned broadly.

"Ah Tino, dear chap. Come in, come in," he gestured. "And Agent Carter. How nice to see you again."

Cordero introduced Estefana and Brooks spoke to her in Portuguese—Timor-Leste's second national language along with Tetun. Estefana listened to Brooks with a strained look on her face and when he was finished lowered her eyes and said: "I am sorry Doctor but I don't speak Portuguese. Can you please repeat that in English?"

Brooks laughed and turned to Carter. "Don't you just love how delightfully absurd this country is, Agent Carter? Two national languages and yet many people who don't speak one or the other, or in many cases, either!" Then he turned to Estefana again and bowed slightly. "My dear, I said that while we had never been formally introduced I do recall seeing you several times at the police station in Suai and I heard that you did a wonderful job with these two officers on that child abduction case. It is a pleasure to finally be introduced."

Estefana blushed and took her gaze to the floor. Brooks washed his hands, dried them on his apron, and gestured them toward the rear of the room. They followed him through the trestle tables with their grim collection of half-assembled skeletal remains. At the back of the room Brooks turned and spread his arms out wide. With his unkept hair, drained face from lack of sleep, and filthy apron—from dirt, spilled food and the hazards of the job—he looked like he was auditioning for the part of Moses in an amateur theatrical.

"This," he said with an appropriate cadence in his voice, "is our haul." He turned to Cordero, lowered his voice and added: "I asked your pretty young girls to have another search around this morning Tino, but they found nothing more."

"Okay," said Cordero moving the subject along. "Six skeletons is it? What can you tell us?"

"Well," began Brooks, "you'll appreciate these are early days and I haven't had a chance to assemble them completely, let alone conduct a proper examination. The first skull that was found"—Brooks pointed to the object on the nearest table—"is an outlier. The skeleton was completely broken up and separated I'd say by the action of the water when it tumbled the thing down river. It was probably buried originally on the near edge of the other five skeletons—six if you count what I now know to be a foetus—because these other skeletons are more intact. Well, slightly more at any rate. They were probably protected to a degree by being more firmly encased in the load of sandy clay that brought these folk to town."

Brooks began to walk slowly through the trestle tables and the others followed him. "Here you have the second skull with the cervical and thoracic vertebrae still connected. My guess is that what you see on this table is the rest of the spinal cord, ribs, and larger bones of the arms and legs of this person." He paused, turned. "But as I said, that is a guess at this stage."

Brooks stopped at the next table. "The third skeleton is missing parts—the sacrum and coccyx for starters, a few ribs, and so on. This kind of brittleness in the skeletal structure could be due to the age of the bones, the violence of the river, or both. Again, too early to say with any confidence." He started walking through the tables again, but Estefana hung back intrigued by the display but also wary of what she was looking at. "The fourth and fifth skeletons are largely intact and the sixth is another outlier, probably originally buried furthest from water, and most probably the pregnant woman. And on these last tables are the bits and pieces I've yet to connect with the others." He turned to Carter. "As I said to your INTERPOL director, it's a jigsaw puzzle, really, you see."

"You said you thought this was the result of a massacre. Why?" asked Carter.

"In time, my dear. In time."

Brooks was enjoying his own performance. He walked them back to the first table. "You would know that in the real world of pathology, rather than the fantasy world of American television, the determination of age and even sex from bones is anything but a precise science. But examining each pelvis—not that all are yet connected to a skull, remember—I would say we have five probable females and one definite male. Plus the foetal bones." He shot a glance at Cordero. "And in a Catholic country like Timor-Leste, Tino, that would make seven victims not six. But my breakdown of who we have here may change on closer examination. In children, sex determination from the pelvic structure is quite difficult and in Timor-Leste, where people are small by design and often even smaller due to malnutrition, it is even more difficult. On the younger ones I think there is disruption in the enamel formation on the teeth which would indicate malnutrition."

"Children?" queried Carter. She took a particular interest in crimes against children, having been involved in the investigation of crimes against Native American children back home and having a half-sister—Rebecca, or Becky as she was known—who had been abducted at the age of eight never to be found again.

"Yes. The most accurate determiners of age are the teeth. Now our friend here" —Brooks pointed to the first skull—"has fully formed molars in reasonable condition. I would say late teens to late twenties. I'm not sure I'll be able to get more precise than that." He hesitated a second, peering closely at the skull as though seeing it for the first time. "No carbon dating or DNA analysis in Timor, you understand. On the second skull—the male— molars indicate an adult and the wear and tear and tobacco stains indicate a person of at least middle age. You can see that this third skull is noticeably smaller and the deciduous teeth have only just erupted. I would say between two and ten years old. On the fourth we have molars again but only just erupting, so again somewhere around ten years. Same for the fifth skull. The sixth shows molars with wear, tear and staining from chewing betel nut repeatedly. Forty plus."

"That could be a family then?" Cordero wandered aloud.

"Yes, possibly," agreed Brooks. "Now we get to the interesting part." Again he looked closely at the first skull. "This missing bone," he said and pointed to the missing third of its left side, "is largely the result of post-mortem trauma. You can see the lighter color of the bone around the missing section and the jagged appearance of the edges. This may be the result of the skull having been burned—I suspect it was, but need to do more tests—and for that reason made particularly vulnerable to damage as it washed downstream." He rose and paused for effect. "But even allowing for all that, I would say the initial damage was done by action that fractured the skull and caused death. Traces of such damage appear on the bone that remains." He walked them on to the second table. "And then I noticed this."

He took a pen from his breast pocket, bent down over the second skull, and pointed. "You can see here evidence of sharp force trauma. Look closely at this section of the vertebrae. You can just make out smooth fracture edges at an oblique angle and what look like cut marks from a sharp instrument. I'd also say that's consistent coloring between the fracture surface and the adjacent bone, indicating peri-mortem trauma." He stood up and moved quickly to the third skull. "Those features are even clearer here." He moved on to the fourth skull. "And again here. In fact in five of the skeletons there is evidence of the same peri-mortem sharp force trauma."

"Peri-mortem," pondered Cordero. "You're saying that these people were killed by a weapon cutting into their necks?"

"Weapon is a technical term. But in three of them I'd say definitely a sharp instrument. In another two possibly. And in the first, the original skull that was uncovered, blunt force I would venture was deliberate," said Brooks with a satisfied smile on his face.

"Deliberate why?" asked Cordero.

"Because the action I referred to consisted of two distinct blows to precisely the same spot. No one I know of has ever smashed their skull twice in precisely the same spot at the same time by accident, dear boy. No one falling down stairs or slipping down rock faces bounces in that fashion."

"Any idea of how long ago these people died?" asked Carter.

"My wild guess for most would be anywhere from ten to thirty years. Sorry but I can't be more precise than that. If I had better equipment here—" but he didn't finish the statement. "I may be able to narrow it down a bit in time but too much depends on the conditions of the ground in which they were buried."

"But it suggests we could have a massacre, possibly around the time of the referendum on independence?" Carter asked.

"Well, that's for you to determine and that's why I asked Jacobsen to send her people over. But there's more." Brooks moved them on down the line of tables again. "This first skull," he said, pointing, "is much more recent. If you look very closely you can still see traces of soft tissue. I'd day this is one for you, Tino—a person who was killed and dumped in a mass grave to make it look like a victim of a much earlier killing."

•••

It had just gone 5 o'clock when they left Brooks and walked back around to the front of the hospital. Cordero and Estefana checked their watches. "How about we grab dinner and go over what Brooks has found?" suggested Carter. She caught Cordero giving the toes of his new leather shoes a quick shine on the back of his trousers, like American boys used to do before sneakers became the fashion. Then she noticed the young nurse he had asked about Brooks' whereabouts wave in their direction from the entrance door of the hospital reception area.

"Um, not tonight," Cordero muttered. "I've arranged something. What if we meet in your office first thing in the morning?"

"Okay," said Carter. "Estefana? What about you?"

Estefana looked almost as embarrassed as Cordero. "I'm sorry, *mana*. My boyfriend's cousin is in town and we have arranged to see him."

Carter looked slightly deflated. "That's fine. You go and enjoy yourself. I'll take the chance to study more Tetun. See you both tomorrow."

And with that the three broke off in separate directions, Carter resigning herself to the leftovers in her refrigerator that she would reheat for dinner.

5

The next day was Wednesday and Carter was in the office early to brief Jacobsen on what they had learned from Brooks. She told the INTERPOL director that it was almost certain that the skulls were the result of a mass murder and added that it could also be an undocumented war crime and that possibility at least deserved investigation. Jacobsen agreed, collected her things and left for a meeting with the Dutch consul.

Carter had only just said good morning to Officer Oodanta and sat down at her desk when Cordero entered the office.

"*Bondia, mana,*" he said looking particularly bright eyed and alert. "*Diak ka lae?*"

"*Diak. Ita fali?*" Carter said, answering that she was good and asking about him, a coolness in her voice.

"Your Tetun is coming along," Cordero commented, pulling up a plastic chair. "Did you have a pleasant evening?"

"I studied Tetun for a while, then watched a DVD until the power went out. After that I made a coffee on the gas burner which I have and sat outside for a while. Pleasant enough."

"Power? Out? Must have been your area around Motael," Cordero said.

Just then Estefana greeted Officer Oodanta and walked in on Carter and Cordero.

"*Mana, maun!* What about that outage across Dili last night? Good thing Josinto and I had finished dinner," she said, gathering another plastic chair and sitting down. Carter glanced at Cordero, a question in her eyes.

"Must have been fast asleep," he said, his demeanor deflating.

27

"The lights went out at 8pm, Tino," Carter pointed out. Cordero shuffled a little more, coughed but offered no reply. "A bit young for you, isn't she?" Carter asked. "My father used to say it's the oldest rooster in the yard that'll cause the most trouble in the henhouse."

Cordero managed to look both offended and sheepish at the same time. "Timorese respect their elders," he said.

"It isn't respect I'm thinking about," said Carter. She rose from her desk and came around to face the other two. "What's your thinking about what Brooks showed us, Tino?"

"Well," he began, glad to follow Carter's lead and move the focus on to work. "I'd like more from Brooks but that'll take days. It looks like we have a murder which someone has attempted to conceal within a mass murder. Accordingly, the killer or killers must be connected to both crimes, but the killings are so far apart in time it's hard to see how."

"My thoughts exactly," Carter replied. "Any thoughts Estefana?"

"I agree with what *maun* said. It's hard to see a link but there must be one."

Just then Carter's cell rang. She turned to her desk and picked it up.

"Yes. Yeah. Thanks for calling back so quickly, Gerard.... You have? That's great... Doctor Henrique Merino...What? Oh, Mourinho... Just a second." She scribbled on a notepad. "Wait... inho. Got it. Do you happen to know if he speaks English?... Perfect. Okay. Where?...World Food Program, rear of Ministry of Agriculture in Comoro district. Okay. 10am. Yep, I'll be there. Thanks again. What?" She was silent for a moment while the person spoke at length. "It was a long shot, Gerard. It's only another two months. No hard feelings. Thanks again." She put the cell back on her desk. "That was my embassy. I called this morning asking if they knew of an expert hydrologist I could speak to. We need to know where those bodies came from." She looked at the notes she had just written, tore off the page and pocketed it. "Doctor Henrique Mourinho with the World Food Program. The embassy has made an appointment for me at 10am." She turned to Cordero. "Are you likely to be assigned to the case?"

"As soon as I walk down the corridor to my office and file a report, yes," he said. "This one seems a bit more complicated than your average murder the regular police would ordinarily deal with. And the other two guys down there are busy working cases. I'm kind of in-between so no problem."

"Right," said Carter. "Well, if we assume the killings are connected, we can work these cases together. Estefana, could you go back through our files here this morning and see if there are any records of a war crime—a killing or a disappearance—along the Comoro River involving at least five people, possibly a family?"

"The Comoro is a long river," Cordero muttered.

"Yes but until we can narrow it down, we need to check it all," Carter said and looked back at Estefana. "And of course the killing could have been done elsewhere from the burial. Keep in mind road access to the river and communities along each of those roads. Both sides." She looked again at Cordero. "Your friend in police records or whatever it's called? The one who keeps tabs on gangs and militia?"

"Pepe?" offered Cordero.

"That's him. It might be worth asking him if there are any records of militia activities along the river as well."

"Sure," said Cordero. "The best time to ask Pepe anything is around lunch time. If I offer to buy him food, he'll be more amenable to doing me a favour. And that gives me time to write my report and get assigned to the job."

"Okay, we have a plan. Let's meet back here this afternoon? Around 4pm and pool whatever we've uncovered?"

• • •

Doctor Henrique Mourinho proved to be a charming man in his mid-thirties—about five years older than Carter. He twisted from his computer screen when she was shown into the corner of the room he made do for his office and greeted her over a pile of reports, handbooks, maps, and notes that covered his desk.

He offered his hand and shook hers firmly but gently. He had a slender build, warm brown eyes, and curly dark hair that he hadn't tried to tame. He was wearing jeans and a light blue cotton shirt. Uncharacteristically, Carter felt herself slightly embarrassed by the fact that she was wearing over-sized linen trousers she had bought at a street market in Bairro Central the previous Sunday and what she now considered a dowdy blouse she hadn't washed in two days.

"Agent Carter," he said in a friendly tone. "May I suggest we go across the road for coffee?" He gestured around the room. "The office is a little crowded and I need a break."

They walked back down through the Ministry of Agriculture compound, across the hot and dusty Comoro River bridge and then weaved through the throng of traffic along *Avenida Presidente Nicolau Lobato* to the airconditioned coolness of the Dili Plaza complex. Along the way Mourinho was telling Carter that he had lived in Timor-Leste for almost 12 months on a Portuguese aid project with the World Food Program and that he had learned English at school in Lisbon but learned to speak it properly during an eighteen-month post-doctoral fellowship at Stanford University. But what she liked most about him was that he asked her questions: where she was from, what Missouri and then Arizona were like, why she had joined the FBI and what she was doing in Timor-Leste. His questions didn't sound as though they were prying, or asked out of courtesy, but seemed to reflect a genuine interest.

Mourinho paid for the coffee. He had an espresso; she a latte. They sat, and she told him about the skeletal remains uncovered in the riverbed of the Comoro and of her need to narrow down the location from whence they had come. She noticed he winced when she told him how they were most likely killed.

Mourinho stirred sugar into his espresso and took a few moments to collect his thoughts. "The Comoro is quite a long river," he said.

"So people keep telling me," Carter replied and sipped her coffee.

"Did they also tell you that the system of which it is a part includes two other sizable rivers, the Bemos and the Boera? The catchment area of the Comoro is close enough to two hundred miles long. At the upper reaches of the river, sixty percent of the water drops into an underground river system and then eventually re-emerges again. It is a big, complex drainage system." He glanced up to make sure she was following what he was explaining. "The power of the water in the monsoonal period can be immense," he continued. "Only a couple of years back, flooding along the river impacted on almost two and a half thousand people. Whole houses were swept down river. So the prospect of a major rainfall event washing a sizable section of soil down river is not surprising." Mourinho finished the rest of his espresso in one gulp. "Now most soil is composed of three predominant particles: sand, silt and clay. Different types of soil have different ratios of each. Throughout the Comoro catchment, sandy soil is predominant. If the section of soil your bones were found in is sandy—" he raised his hands as if to say, 'that tells us nothing'. "However," he continued and offered a reassuring smile. "Back in the office we could go over maps I have of the Comoro taken at different time periods. And of course if the Internet is working this morning we could also check satellite images. Agriculture is critical in Timor-Leste," he added. "I'm sure you know about the reliance on subsistence farming and the consequent extent of food insecurity throughout this country. Water is critical for agriculture. Since independence the government and a host of aid organisations have invested quite a lot in understanding drainage systems and that, thankfully for your purposes, has resulted in a lot of maps and aerial studies and images. What we would look for is a section or sections of land that have disappeared in the last, say, twelve months. Anything that had been washed down earlier would be out in the Wetar Strait by now."

On the way back to Mourinho's office, the conversation took a more casual direction. "Do you like Timor-Leste?" Mourinho asked.

"The country? What I've seen of it I like, yes," Carter answered. "But I'd rather be back in Arizona." She hesitated a moment. "Here I'm investigating cold cases and old bones," she added. "Back home I'd be investigating children who've gone missing and are in serious danger or killers on the loose and likely to strike again."

She turned toward him for reasons she couldn't quite grasp but perhaps for a glimmer of sympathy. He nodded and the beginnings of a smile appeared on his face. "I felt the same my first few months at Stanford," Mourinho said. "I missed my family, my friends, my then girlfriend, Carolina. I even missed Bacalhaul!" he said. "It's cod—you know, fish. Bacalhaul is the most important ingredient in Portuguese food. You can cook it many, many different ways." He glanced at her. "Excuse me for saying this but cheese burgers are no comparison." He laughed for a moment only. "Leaving Portugal opened up the world to me. I wouldn't be here otherwise. And I love this country." He looked around him, opening his arms. "I love the people most of all. Take where I live," he said and pointed vaguely. "Down the street are a handful of guys who have a reggae band. They're very friendly, very helpful and a lot of fun. I often go down and listen to them rehearse. They were very kind to me when I was settling in, you know, explaining things, showing me things, even taking me here and there until I became familiar with Dili."

He made to walk on. "May I ask where you live?" Carter asked after him.

"Motael. By the seafront," he said turning back toward her.

"You're not in the bottom apartment of a blue cement block duplex, by any chance are you?" she said.

"As a matter of fact I am."

• • •

Cordero found Alberto 'Pepe' Marcelino in his usual pose, head back and feet on desk behind a screen beside the office window. "*Hey maun, diak ka lae*?" he said greeting Cordero. "I hear you have a new girlfriend."

"What are you talking about Pepe?" Cordero asked, looking guilty.

"Come on *maun*. My cousin works with her at the hospital," Pepe said trying unsuccessfully to contain his mirth. "She rang me first thing this morning. This is Dili, Tino. Everyone knows everybody's business." Cordero put his hands in his pocket and took them out again. "Says she's quite a good-looking girl," Pepe said. He was grinning broadly. "Your friend not my cousin, that is."

"I'm not here to talk about your cousin, Pepe. Let's see if you know anything that can help my police business, okay?"

"Sure *maun*," said Pepe grinning. "What's your problem?"

"Did you hear about those skulls dug up in the Comoro the day before yesterday?" Cordero asked, and he sat down heavily in a chair opposite Pepe, making the man sit up straight to maintain eye contact.

"Well I heard they'd dug a lot of bones up, that's all," Pepe said, serious now.

"Six skeletons by the looks of it. Seven if you count a foetus one was carrying. According to pathology they were murdered."

"Pathology? You mean the Englishman? Brooks?" Pepe asked. "Colorful guy but he should know."

"I need to know if there are any records about gang or militia operations up along the Comoro river twenty, maybe thirty years ago."

"Tino, you're kidding me, right? Most of this country is a militia crime scene and twenty, thirty years ago? I'd be retired before I finished going through all those records."

Pepe started to lean back again in his chair and was bringing his feet back up toward the top of his desk.

"You eaten yet?" Cordero asked.

Alberto 'Pepe' Marcelino stopped his feet in mid-air and brought them back to the floor. His eyes seemed to grow bigger. At almost 150 pounds he was almost twice the size of the average Timorese male and his appetite was legendary.

"Well, now that you mention it…no. Why?"

"I hear there's a new restaurant around the corner," Cordero said. "Japanese. I hear it's good."

"They're Korean actually, but they pretend to be Japanese and, yeah, they do a nice lunch."

"I'll buy you lunch if you take a look for me," said Cordero. "Look, I'm only interested in any cases that remain unresolved. And where the victims are possibly from one family. One man, four or five women. That can't be too hard."

"Unresolved cases," Pepe chortled. "That narrows it down to a couple of hundred probably. You've got a good sense of humor, Tino." Cordero shifted to the edge of his chair. "But okay," continued Pepe to avoid an argument. "I'll get my boys to take a look. Give it an hour." Cordero started to rise. "Oh, and you can give me a bento box. Large. And maybe chicken yakitori on the side."

• • •

They reconvened in Carter's office mid-afternoon as arranged. Estefana opened by saying she had searched all the case files along and around the Comoro River area going back forty years. There were war crimes, yes, but nothing left undocumented. And there were no outstanding reports of families who were missing or small groups of people who had disappeared and remained unaccounted for.

Cordero went next. "First, I've been officially assigned to the case of the most recent murder. So we'll be working together on this. But as for gang or militia activity, my inquiries came up with nothing useful. Pepe—my contact in police records we were talking about this morning—said that the *Besi Merah Putih* militia was active in Liquica and elements may have strayed over the district border along the river opposite Aileu, but other than that he drew a blank."

"*BMP, mana*," Estefana said looking at Carter.

"Yeah," she replied and turned to Cordero to explain. "We just finished a report recommending INTERPOL issue a Blue Notice on one of its members over torture allegations in a village northeast of Railaco." She paused, looking at a map they had spread out on her desk. She put her finger on the village of Railcao. "But that's quite a way from the river."

"We've come up blank," concluded Cordero.

"Not quite," countered Carter. "Henrique thought—"

"Henrique?" Cordero interjected.

"Yes, Doctor Henrique Mourinho. The hydrologist," said Carter. "We went over aerial maps of the Comoro River going back twelve months. He found a section of riverbank that had disappeared after the last big rains. Here," she said, leaned over and pointed to a stretch of water which looked to be about fifty miles upstream of the junction with the Bemos River. "As you can see, this general area is framed by steep, heavily wooded ridges on both sides and sandy riverbanks. That means it is reasonably well concealed and unlikely to be worked by subsistence farmers. It's fairly isolated but there is a road or at least a track that is navigable by 4-wheel drive about ten miles from the river and there are a couple of small villages along it. Of course there could be tracks down to and along the river as well." She stood up and stretched. "I'd say that in the absence of anything more concrete we head up there tomorrow and make enquiries. What do you reckon?"

Cordero was thinking to himself that it might be useful to get out of Dili for a while if rumours were circulating about him and the young nurse. "Good idea," he said. "But we should be prepared to stay up there for several days, perhaps a week." He checked the map again. "It's a long drive in and out and it could take time before locals feel comfortable talking to outsiders. That's an isolated area probably little touched by the modern world. They'll be suspicious of outsiders. We may have to earn their trust and that'll take time as well."

"Estefana?" Carter asked.

"I think that is a good plan, *mana*. If there is a church, we should be able to find accommodation nearby. If there isn't a church, we may be able to stay with a local family. But we should take a tent and supplies just in case."

"Okay, it's agreed then. I'm seeing Hen—Doctor Mourinho later this evening. He said he would check survey maps to try and narrow down our ground zero further and go over it with me tonight." Cordero felt mildly jealous but said nothing. "INTERPOL has no spare vehicles, Tino. We'll have to go in yours," Carter continued.

"But my SUV—" he started to complain but knew it was useless when Carter had decided on a plan.

"How about you collect me from my apartment at 8am," she said, "and then we'll go pick up Estefana?"

6

"So, did he do the trick last night?" Cordero asked Carter who sat next to him in the SUV.

"Excuse me?" she said, surprised by the question.

"You know. Your meteorologist friend. Did he give you any more precise idea about where we should be heading?"

She turned to face him but couldn't decide whether he was trying to goad her or not. It was often like that with Cordero.

"Doctor Mourinho is a hydrologist not a meteorogist," she said, letting it go and looking back out on the road.

"He ruled out a lot of places in the general area so I guess you could say he narrowed it down quite a bit."

They were driving out of Dili, climbing the southern ridge behind the city on what locals called the "spaghetti road". It was possibly the busiest stretch of road in Timor-Leste, connecting the city with the central mountains, the larger inland towns of Aileu and Maubisse, and beyond them the southern coast. But it wound sharply this way and that—hence the nickname—and regularly collapsed in parts or washed away in others making it treacherous to drive and an ordeal to stomach as a passenger. Estefana was in the back. Her boyfriend Josinto Centavo Veddo had taken her to Carter's apartment on the back of his motorcycle to save them having to go into Lecidere where she lived and then back again through heavy traffic to the turn-off out of town. After she had extracted her things from the pannier, Josinto had kissed Estefana, waved to the others and taken off down the road to his job with the coffin maker. She had spent the last few minutes a little lost in thought about that kiss and what more lay in store when she and Josinto married.

"You said the area he identified is heavily wooded on both sides of the river. I don't get how a section of land like that could break away in a big storm," Cordero said.

"Well there are patches of ground that are, or at least were, treeless. Especially close to the river where the soil is sandy. Obviously it was a promontory like that gave way. My point is that the area is unlikely to be conducive to building permanent structures or even to people wandering around to potentially witness a massacre or mass burial."

Estefana drifted back into the conversation. "It could be *lulik, mana*," she said, referring to parts of the country regarded as sacred by local people because it was believed to be inhabited by ancestral spirits. If the area was *lulik*, it would also be forbidden for anyone to enter it without permission from the custodians in the nearest village.

"Could be, Estefana," Carter replied. She'd learned about *lulik* areas during their previous case in Suai where prohibited areas were used to smuggle stolen babies across the border with Indonesia. "Let's wait and see."

They approached a sharp curve heading up the ridge toward the town of Dare. A truck carrying bags of rice was belching black smoke as it lumbered up the incline in front of them and it slowed their progress to a walking pace. Within seconds they were surrounded by motorcycles, the riders cautious about taking the blind curve for fear of what was coming down the hill on the other side. A conversation struck up among the cyclists using horns instead of voices. Quite a few cyclists were recognizing friends or acquaintances—two bips by way of 'Hello'—, others were issuing cautions or instructions about who had priority—repeated bips until the cyclists lined up correctly—and others were simply offering thanks for courtesies provided—one bip. It amounted to a language all its own.

"Why are we taking this road anyway?" Carter shouted over the noise. "I told you Henrique told me last night that it was better to go west, along the coast toward Liquica and turn off south on the Ermera road. Better roads, less traffic."

Cordero shifted in his seat and sniffed. "That's what he says. The road down south toward Ermera can get difficult," he shouted back vaguely. "We're better approaching from the east side of the Comoro, heading to Aileu than over the river near Fatisi where's there's a road down to the river's edge. It's low water now and there'll be a causeway we can take to get across."

Around the curve the rice-laden truck moved aside to the edge of the road. A dozen motorcycles took off and Cordero pulled out and overtook when the road was clear. But up ahead there was another truck to slow them down, this time carrying cement. And another curve. Then another. The roadway itself was collapsing and they were bumping over small potholes or having to go around deeper ones all the time, avoiding other vehicles scrambling in both directions.

"Remind me again how many traffic accidents occur in Timor-Leste," Carter said.

"Only among people who do silly things," said Cordero as they passed a section of road that had washed away into one lane —the other lane lying in pieces several yards below. "And where there are landslides and wash-aways."

"You mean in places like this?" she said grabbing the door for support.

After thirty minutes they'd come only five miles out of Dili. Cordero stopped abruptly, took advantage of a break in the oncoming traffic and pulled off the road into a parking area on the right that would take a dozen vehicles. A sign read: 'Dare War Memorial Museum'. "This place was built by Australian ex-servicemen in honour of the Timorese who helped them when they waged guerrilla warfare against the Japanese in World War II," he told his companions. "There's a good view of Dili from up here but more importantly there's good coffee—the last we're likely to get for a couple of hours."

They stepped from the SUV stretching legs and backs. Cordero led them down steps to a small viewing platform that opened up below the car park. A small kiosk was operating at one end. The view was breathtaking. Close to a thousand feet below Dili sprawled out like a patchwork quilt on the edge of a shimmering blue sea. To the east, the Fatucama Peninsula wrapped a comforting arm around one end of the city. On its point stood Cristo Rei, the ninety-foot-high concrete statue of Jesus Christ erected by the Indonesians in 1996 to suggest they respected the culture of the people they were in the process of annihilating. To the west, across a sprawl of red iron roofed cement block houses, the snaking gleam of the Comoro River drained into the sea and a small plane was circling to touch down on the end of the airstrip. Here and there a modern building of glass and steel had been built, but none more than a few storeys in height. The shimmering white *Palacio do Governo* which housed the offices of the Prime Minister stood out clearly in the centre of the city, and through the distant haze beyond it could just be seen the ghostly form of Atauro Island sixteen miles to the north.

"*Ei pa!*" said Estefana before correcting herself for Carter's benefit. "Sorry *mana*. I have never been here before. This view is amazing."

"It certainly is," agreed Carter. "And I learned '*Ei pa*' in my Tetun class last week. The closest English equivalent would be 'Wow' I think."

"Wow?" said Estefana. "Okay, then wow!"

Cordero appeared with the coffee. First sips suggested it was as good as he had promised it would be and they sat at a small table to enjoy it.

"I didn't know the Japanese had occupied this island," said Carter. "Timor doesn't crop up in any history of the Asia-Pacific war I've ever read or seen."

"I'm not surprised," said Cordero. "It was a sideshow, really, with little strategic importance. And not many Westerners killed. No Americans." He looked up to see if that comment had caused offence. It hadn't. "But if you lived here it was a different matter. You see Portugal was neutral during the war," he continued leaning over his coffee cup. "Its colonies were as well, of course. The Dutch, who controlled the west of the island, were not neutral and invited the Australians in as the Japanese advanced through

Singapore and Indonesia. But the Australians went further than Dutch Timor and entered Portuguese Timor violating its neutrality. They did it to protect their flank—worried the Japanese wouldn't be able to resist over-running the whole island and using its airports to bomb northern Australia. The Australian presence brought the Japanese in. And because the Timorese chose to help the Australians rather than the Japanese, thousands of them ended up dead." He sipped from his coffee. "Forty thousand is the accepted number."

Carter offered no reply. Then she stood, took her coffee and began reading the story of the struggle which hung from the walls of the memorial in Tetun and English. Estefana took photos of Dili on her phone and sent them to her fiancé, Josinto. Cordero checked his own phone: there were two missed calls—one from a liaison officer in the Ministry of the Interior who'd been pestering him about appearing in a promotional video for the police and one from the young nurse. He ignored the first missed call and considered ringing back the nurse but thought the better of it and put his phone back in his pocket.

"We'd better get going," he said. "It's a long way to Aileu."

• • •

The town of Aileu, which also gave its name to the district, sat in a narrow flat plain 3,000 feet above sea level. As they approached the outskirts of the town, thick dark clouds were massing behind the mountains to the south and the breeze had begun to pick up. They passed simple concrete block houses set back from the road amid stands of eucalyptus and fields of banana trees, a *postu-bombeiru* or fire-station that looked deserted in a large lot covered in weeds and, toward the centre of town, a market where several dozen women guarded displays of vegetables from their gardens and men in grubby shorts and T-shirts squatted on the ground smoking cigarettes. A few ramshackle shops with racks of identical cheap clothing and assorted groceries were strung out on the other side of the market and there appeared to be three or four places providing meals, their owners leaning against doorframes awaiting custom. Cordero pulled up to a restaurant with seats under a pergola. "Let's eat here," he said and cut the engine and opened the driver's door before anyone could disagree.

An old woman busied herself wiping down their table with a grubby rag and shouting orders to a helper out back to bring drinks and prepare food. Before long, and without anyone actually ordering anything, a lunch appeared of fried chicken, rice, and three small, grilled fish along with a plate of green vegetables the taste and appearance of which left their variety uncertain. Cordero washed his meal down with a beer, the others with mineral water, neither of which was cold. Across the road was a school where small children could be heard yelping with excitement at a soccer game in progress as older children dressed in neat yellow and brown school uniforms emerged from the gates, their classes finished for the day. They walked in groups of twos and threes, many—both boys and girls—holding hands and singing and laughing as they walked home. A couple of girls even broke into a cartwheel competition while their friends cheered them on.

"You know," Carter began, "I've not yet seen a kid who looked unhappy in this country. Must be fun to be a child growing up here."

"They have very little to keep them happy other than each other, *mana*," offered Estefana.

"And maybe even less when they leave school," added Cordero.

"What do you mean?" asked Carter.

Cordero took another sip of his beer, wiped a hand across his mouth and gestured out to the passing children with his beer bottle. "These days every child in Timor-Leste gets to go to school. Free. Primary school, middle school, even high school if they wish and if there's one within walking distance, which can be ten miles away. And that's the way it should be, of course. But what are they going to do when they finish? You saw this place as we drove in. Did you see any opportunities for work here? There's farming. But a subsistence farmer doesn't need much education. He or she learns most of what they need to know by the age of twelve. These kids will graduate school. I don't think tilling the soil is what they'll be happy doing. They'll head to Dili in search of opportunity. That means this place becomes a ghost town and Dili a slum because it's never going to have enough jobs for everyone from the rural districts."

Carter looked at Estefana. Cordero read the doubt in her eyes.

"Maybe I'm being too cynical," he conceded. "And I know I shouldn't talk because I had the chance to be educated in Australia and came back when the world was pumping a lot of money into the country to ensure its stability and success. And I've got a well-paid job. Not everyone has. But that's my point. I worry if we can keep pace with rising expectations because soon all these kids will expect well-paid jobs too. That's all. I worry that we'll end up with a few haves and a whole lot of have-nots that destroys what's appealing about this place now."

"Which is?" asked Carter.

Cordero shrugged. "What you see in those kids, I suppose. Simple pleasures. The strength of community. Caring for and about each other. The feeling that we're all in this together," he said. "That's Timor-Leste to me."

A gust of wind ripped through the vine growing over the pergola where they were sitting, and they had to hold down their plastic tablecloth and steady their empty plates and loose cutlery. The cloud from the south had spread a grey-black bruise over the sky. Heavy drops of rain began to fall here, there and then everywhere.

"Let's go," Cordero said. He gave the old woman ten dollars for their lunch, and they ran through a heavy downpour to their vehicle. It was October and the rainy season seemed to have started early.

7

The road from Aileu to Fatisi became progressively worse. Much worse. Apart from the usual ruts and drop-aways where the surface had sunk, there were fallen branches and rocks to contend with and at times it was difficult to discern roadway from scrub. The rain didn't help. Cordero had to work the SUV hard as the vehicle slipped repeatedly on what became little more than a muddy quagmire. When they finally reached the upper stretches of the Comoro River, the causeway Cordero spoke about was visible but only just beneath the rushing water. Carter and Estefana had to wade carefully across it ahead of Cordero in the SUV to give him a better sense of the depth and strength of the flow. The water reached just below their knees soaking the jeans Carter and Estefana were wearing. On the other side of the river, as the road began to climb again, the SUV lost its grip several times and Cordero had to quickly correct each slide. Soon a quick succession of tapping sounds could be heard from under the bonnet. When, toward dusk, they approached the small village of Tepia about half way up a ridge on the western side of the river, the tapping was louder and more persistent but the performance of the vehicle seemed unaffected. The same could not be said for Cordero. His back was aching and his arms felt like they had been lifting cement bags all day. He pulled the SUV up beside a man walking toward the village, swinging a machete from side to side. The man seemed unconcerned about the rain that was soaking him.

"*Bonoiti maun,*" Cordero began, wishing the man a good evening. The man merely nodded. "We're looking for the village *xefe*. Do you know where we can find him?"

The man pointed with his machete. "*Uma mean, nebaa.*"

Cordero thanked him and drove slowly on. "We'll pay our respects to the village headman. It's customary in places like this. That fellow said the headman lives in the red house up ahead. We can ask about accommodation."

He drove into the yard off the road in front of a small cement block house with flaking red paint and a rusting iron roof. Smoke rose from a cooking fire out back. A man who looked to be no more than early middle age sat on a plastic chair in shorts and a dirty singlet, under a leafy canopy by the side of the house. His skin was the color of chocolate, his hair was matted, and a wispy beard rounded the bottom of his face. Cordero parked the vehicle, slid out of the driver's seat and stretched. Then he walked through the drizzle toward the man while Carter and Estefana stayed seated in the SUV. The man was repairing what Cordero recognized as a coffee pulper in the fading light. But it was not a metal pulper like the cheap Chinese variety more familiar to Cordero. It was a very old wooden pulper, the axle of which that ran from the fly wheel to just below the shute where the beans were fed through seemed to have split. A piglet scrounged the ground around the man's feet. Drops of rain fell through the canopy above his head but he ignored them.

"*Bonoiti senyor,*" Cordero said, using the more formal title as appropriate to a village headman. "I am Investigator Vincintino Cordero of the Timorese police and my two colleagues in the vehicle are also police officers." The man lent back and peered at the SUV but said nothing. "We're in this area on an investigation. With your permission we might be here for two or three days. Do you know if there's any accommodation available in the village?" The man said nothing. "It's just that it's raining," added Cordero, holding a hand out to catch the drops of rain for effect.

The man stopped what he was doing and reached inside his pocket for a cigarette. He cupped his hands and lit the cigarette with a match, inhaled deeply, and blew a stream of smoke into the vine above him. *He's taking his time to ensure I know who's in charge here*, thought Cordero. *And weighing me up.*

"Police," he said finally. "We don't often see police officers here." He gazed at the SUV. "And never in a vehicle as old as that."

"Well I'm actually a police *investigator*," Cordero said, emphasizing the status he was always keen to assert. "But we just need to talk to local people, find out a few things about a case we're working on. You know, look around. It's nothing dramatic," Cordero said trying to sound reasonable.

"You from Ermera, Railaco?" the man asked.

"No, Dili. We came via Aileu."

"Via Aileu," the man said surprised, looking up at Cordero. "That's a hard way to come. Few people do that unless they live around Fatisi and need to visit relatives here. And then they do it on foot or by pony not in a thing like that." Cordero appeared evasive, put his hands in his pocket and kicked at the ground with his shoe. The headman considered for a moment. "You don't mind roughing it?"

"Not at all," Cordero assured him.

The man took another drag on his cigarette and shooed away the piglet with his foot. Then he looked at the SUV again, at Carter and Estefana.

"What about the women?" he asked.

"They're pretty tough too," said Cordero. "You know what it's like these days with women."

For the first time the man allowed himself a smile. "There is a *tebedai* tomorrow night," he said, meaning a large, ceremonial dance. "For the new *uma lulik*," he added referring to the village sacred house. "People are coming from all around and beds are scarce." He pointed with his cigarette again. "There is a church up the road. You can't miss it. Next to it are two houses. In the larger one are a couple of nuns. They might have a room. They used to put up women like themselves from Ermera for a couple of months every now and then. Training them, you know. But not these days. They won't be using any spare room to put people up for a *tebedai*. They're strictly Jesus and Mary people. The other house is the priest's. It's little more than a shack. If the nuns can't provide you with a bed, come back. We have people staying but two more"—he gestured at the women in the SUV—"won't make much difference." He took a third drag on his cigarette and threw it away. "You can sleep outside in the vehicle."

Cordero thanked the headman and returned and reported to Carter and Estefana. Then he started the SUV, backed onto the road through the village, and drove up the hill. Houses and huts were scattered on either side of the road and Cordero had to avoid small children splashing in the puddles. As darkness fell, he could hear their mothers calling them back home and could imagine the appeals for a little more time to play. A few farmers were walking back from their garden plots, sodden and silent. There was a kiosk that hadn't closed, its owner, an elderly woman, leaning on the service window which was backlit by a kerosene lamp that produced a faint yellow light. Next door was a relatively new health clinic, its doors shut and locked for the night. Through the gloom, a portly man clip-clopped by on a chestnut Timorese pony, a bag of grain strapped across the beast's rump.

A little further along they passed a lean-to with assorted machinery parts barely visible through a rough-hewn wooden door. A young man sat on a motorcycle at the front under an awning, out of the rain talking to a girl. He wore dirty jeans and an even dirtier T-shirt. As they passed, he followed them with his eyes as he lit two cigarettes and passed one to the girl without looking at her.

Forty yards ahead was a large single-room school, dark and deserted—a damp Timorese flag hanging limp from a pole in the compound. Beyond that was the church—a small white building with a peaked red iron roof set back from the road up a small hillock. A hand-painted sign swung in the breeze through the misty rain. In the headlights of the SUV Carter could just make out '*Capela Santu Antonio*'. Next door to the chapel was a house with a dim yellow light shining through a window and a smaller residence dissolving into the darkness.

"This must be the nuns' house here," said Cordero pulling up at the first dwelling. "Estefana, perhaps it would be better if you go and ask about accommodation. I might only scare them knocking on the door in the dark."

Estefana jumped out of the vehicle and ran to the house with her jacket pulled up to cover her head from the drizzle.

Cordero and Carter sat in silence for a few minutes, both tired and sore from the trip. "Do you realize we've been on the road for nearly ten hours?" Cordero asked Carter, rubbing each shoulder with his opposite hand.

"Yeah," she said. "Henrique said it'd be about five or six tops had we gone the other way."

Cordero glanced at her, but she kept her eyes on Estefana, who was talking to a nun at the door of the house. Estefana pointed at the SUV and the nun peered out and then gestured that they should come in. Cordero made no further comment. Estefana came running back, a smile on her face, the jacket still covering her head. She approached the front passenger's window and Carter wound it down.

"The *madre* is Sister Felicia. She said they have a spare room with two beds we can take, *mana*," Estefana said, not hiding the fact that she felt pleased with herself. "And she will ask the other nun, Sister Agnes, to set up a bed for *maun* on the veranda. Also, they are having hot soup for dinner and she invited us to eat with them."

"Well that's the best invitation I've had all day," quipped Carter. She opened the passenger door then stopped. "You coming?" she said looking back to Cordero.

8

The next morning, on their way to the room in which breakfast was set, Carter and Estefana caught sight through a window of Cordero speaking to the nun who had greeted them the night before. The two were standing near a flourish of crimson bougainvillea at one end of the yellow-tiled veranda, a bed for Cordero having been improvised at the other, more sheltered end. The nun looked stern and insistent although neither Carter nor Estefana could hear what was being said. They could see Cordero shake his head, point to his vehicle, then his watch, nod, nod again and finally appear to surrender to whatever it was the nun was requesting. By the time he joined them they had almost finished their meal of *sasoro*—a bland porridge of overboiled rice—and were on to their second cup of strong coffee to wash it down. "*Bondia*," Cordero said as he sat and poured himself coffee from a pot on the table. "Did you sleep well?"

"Yes, *maun*," replied Estefana. "And you?"

"Mosquitoes kept me awake most of the night," he said draining his cup. "Must be all this rain."

"What was that all about?" asked Carter gesturing toward the window.

"What? Sister Felicia?" he asked. "The priest has been asked to give a dying villager the Last Rites. You know, the final prayers and blessing before death. Bit of an emergency, I gather. But his motorcycle is in with the mechanic. Needs parts from Dili. She was asking—well, insisting really—that I give him a lift. Place is five, six miles from here." Cordero shook the coffee pot and peered inside but it was empty. He looked around hoping for a refill but he was out of luck. "I couldn't say 'no'. After all, they are providing us a place to sleep, even if it is full of mosquitoes."

"How long you expect to be gone?" Carter asked.

"Most of the morning, I'd say," Cordero replied, stirring his spoon through the *sasoro* indifferently. "Then I need to get that knocking sound in the SUV checked out. We don't want to be stuck out here without a vehicle." And with that he began reluctantly to shovel the rice porridge into his mouth.

"Well I'd like to get to work and investigate that stretch of the riverbank Doctor Mourinho said had disappeared in the last big wet," Carter said.

Cordero stopped eating. "Thought as much," he said and stared outside the window for a moment where a thin mist had replaced the rain of the night before. It drifted across the landscape like a veil, suggesting it would soon burn off in the heat of the day. "Estefana mentioned it could be a *lulik* area," he said turning back toward them. "I'd check first with the headman we spoke to last night and, if it's *lulik*, ask his permission to look around there. No point getting the locals off-side." He finished the last of his breakfast and glanced at Estefana. "And while you're there, ask him if he knows of any massacres in the area or militia activity—that sort of thing. I'll question the priest about it as well, although I gather he's not a local and hasn't been here too long."

•••

Father Roque de Franca was actually Brazilian, a Jesuit. Cordero guessed him to be around sixty years of age, but lean and fit, with a healthy complexion and a full head of black hair. He was casually dressed and a cheerful expression broke easily on his face as he climbed into the passenger's seat of the SUV. The priest placed a small wooden box and a leather-bound Missal on his lap. "Tools of my trade," he said in English. "It would have been a nuisance to have to carry them there and back on what is likely to be a very humid day. Thank you for the lift."

"It's a pleasure, Father," Cordero said. "How did you know I speak English?"

"I overheard you talking to the other women. One is American, I suspect."

"Yes. Carter. She's with the FBI but seconded to INTERPOL in Dili," Cordero answered as he eased the SUV out of the church grounds.

"And you are a police officer as well, I understand," Father Roque said.

"Right again," said Cordero. "Well a police investigator actually. We deal in more serious crimes."

A microlet bounced passed them covered in a bright mural of smiling Indonesian girls but crammed with glum-looking passengers resigned to a long, uncomfortable trip to Ermera.

"And is that what brings you and INTERPOL to Tepia?" the priest asked, indicating Cordero should follow the microlet with a left hand turn onto the road away the village. "A more serious crime?"

"We found a number of skeletons in the bed of the Comoro River in Dili. They'd apparently been washed down river a while back in heavy rains. Initial forensic investigation suggests they may have been intentionally killed." Cordero drove slowly up the muddy road, avoiding puddles whose depth was hard to gauge. "This area's regarded as a possible origin site. We may be looking at a mass killing."

"Interesting," the priest said and indicated a rough track that they should take leading off through the forest to the right.

"You haven't been here long I was told," Cordero said.

"Just over two years," Father Roque replied. "Truth be known, I was causing a bit of trouble for my superior back home and it was thought a stint of missionary work outside Brazil would do us both good. There is a Jesuit mission in Railaco." He noticed Cordero had shot a questioning glance at him. "It was theological trouble, nothing more, I assure you." The priest lent forward, listening to the knocking from beneath the SUV's bonnet.

"You have tappet issues, I think," the priest said. "You should have that looked at."

"Yeah. I think a little adjusting'll do for now but I'll need a few tools and clean oil. You have your motorcycle in with the mechanic the nun said."

"I usually have my motorcycle in with him," the priest said and laughed. "It's very old. The canoe they gave me for visitations along the river is even older and I'm always patching holes."

"What's the mechanic like?"

"Moussi?" asked the priest. "Well, I'm not sure I'd call him a mechanic exactly. They say he worked on motors in Dili for a year or so then came back here to get a wife. There are basic things he can do with motors and he certainly can improvise with iron and steel. Tools and oils? Yes, he'd have what you need, I think. At least to adjust your tappets."

They drove on along the bush track and up a little rise through the pale blue-green of the eucalypt forest. The mist was lifting here and the morning was getting hotter and the air stickier as the priest had predicted.

"You say you've been here two years," Cordero began after a short while. "That's long enough to get to know the people fairly well."

Father Roque laughed at the suggestion. "The Portuguese were here for five hundred years and I doubt they knew Timorese well at all. Not really."

"Nevertheless, have you heard of any massacres in this area? Any militia activity, that sort of thing?" Cordero asked.

The priest considered a moment. "Not that I've heard of," he said shaking his head. "If you mean in Indonesian times or just after—there were very few troubles of that kind here. We're quite remote."

"Any stories about people going missing?" Cordero asked.

Again the priest shook his head. "Nothing I can help you with there either," he said.

Cordero glanced over at his passenger again, a cool stare to elicit more information. "Among the skeletal remains were those of a person who had apparently been killed more recently than the others. Perhaps only a year or less ago. Do you know of anyone who has gone missing in the last twelve months?"

The priest looked out the side window at the forest, one hand draped loosely over the wooden box and Missal in his lap, the other dangling out the window. He appeared unconcerned, Cordero concluded, by what others might have judged now to be a police questioning. "People come and go here all the time," he said without emotion. "Well they go mostly. The young. What life is there for them here? In the last twelve months maybe a dozen have left Tepia—many more if you include the surrounding villages. I don't keep track. It's the old who stay."

"Why does the Church maintain a parish here if the area is remote and the population is declining?"

"One thing the Church doesn't lack in this part of the world is priests and nuns," Father Roque said. "You have to find a job for them all. Besides," he added, "at times I think this is more a place of exile than a parish." He indicated a clearing up ahead and gestured for Cordero to stop the car. "The man I'm meant to see is here. Soon there'll be one less resident of Tepia."

• • •

After Cordero had left with the priest, Carter and Estefana headed down to the red house where the headman lived. Few adults were on the street but waves of children compensated for that as they headed in the opposite direction toward school. The children looked at the strangers. A few snickered as they passed; others greeted them with sing-song 'Bondias'. As Carter and Estefana approached the headman's house, a young boy came out of the yard singing softly to himself. He, too, had a school satchel on his back and wore the white shirt and brown shorts of a school uniform—presumably government issue because he was barefoot and sneakers or sandals the parents would have to have paid for themselves.

"Bondia, mana," he said.

"Bondia, alin," Estefana replied and asked the boy if his father was home.

"Sin, nebaa," he said and pointed to the arbor where the man had been sitting the night before. He was in the same plastic chair, in the same shorts and singlet, and apparently in the same struggle to fix the coffee pulper. Only the piglet was missing.

"*Bondia, senyor*," Estefana said addressing the man formally. She then introduced herself and Carter as police officers investigating a matter in the area and asked if he would answer a few questions.

"*Dia*," the man said and nodded his agreement. He put down the tool in his hands and kept an admiring eye on Carter, who stood to the side of Estefana.

"How long have you lived here, *senyor*?" Estefana began the questioning she and Carter had prepared on their walk to the man's house.

"The nuns gave you a bed?" the man asked, ignoring the question.

"Yes," she said.

"And the other one too—your friend who drives the vehicle?"

"Him too."

"How long are you staying?"

"That depends, *senyor*. With police work it's hard to say," Estefana replied. "What I need to know is how long you have been here," she added.

"All my life," he said.

"And how long have you been the headman of the village?"

"Since my father died. He was the headman before me."

"How long ago was that?" Estefana asked.

"My son, Ageo," he said and gestured after the boy who was heading up the road to school, "had just been born."

About twelve years Estefana guessed. She translated for Carter who prompted her to raise the subject of the skeletal remains.

"Recently we recovered human remains from the Comoro River in Dili," Estefana said. "Skeletal remains. They were old, maybe ten, twenty years. Maybe even more. From the information we have it seems they were washed down river in the last big monsoon from a burial place on the riverbank near Tepia." The man said nothing. "There were about six skeletons. Would you have any idea where these remains might have come from?"

The man held her stare for a moment then picked up the piece of wood he had been working on and continued to examine it. Carter could see the flywheel nearby and figured it was a kind of axle he was shaping. "Tepia is a long way from the river and it is up a rise," he said. "Our cemetery is behind the church where you stayed last night."

"As I said, there were six skeletons. Has anyone gone missing?" Estefana persisted.

She waited and took his silence as a no.

"We think they might have been victims of a massacre, perhaps in Indonesian times," Estefana continued. "We need to record these things."

The man fiddled with the pulper. "The Indonesians didn't come here much. There was a *binpolda*," he said, meaning the policeman the Indonesian military stationed in every village, "but he took a local woman for a wife. She hated him for it and cursed him every day. So of course he was usually drunk. A small group of soldiers was stationed in Railaco but we didn't see them much. They'd come every now and then to look around and see if the land was good for whatever they had in mind to grow or for settling people from the other side," he said pointing vaguely to the east. "They decided it was too poor to worry much about."

"What about militia activity?" Estefana asked.

The man stopped fiddling. He seemed to be recalling a memory. He smiled slightly. "A few wandered in here once," he said. "I think they got lost on the road to Railaco. It was just before that thing they called the vote to kick the Indonesians out. They told us not to take part. The people drove them out." He laughed. "I remember it like it was yesterday."

"Do you know the name of this militia?" Estefana asked. The man shook his head. "Could it have been the *Besi Merah Putih*?"

"I don't know what they called themselves."

"Did they threaten to injure anybody when they were here? Did they hurt anyone?"

"Threaten yes," he said. "They threatened anybody silly enough to take notice of them. I remember one had an axe. It had blood on it. He said it was the blood of a person who refused to listen." The headman thought for a moment. "But actually hurt anyone? Not that I know of. They weren't here long."

Estefana turned to Carter who handed her a map she was carrying.

"There's no point showing me your paper," the man said. "I can't read. My son is learning but it makes no sense to me."

"This is more like a picture," said Estefana. "It is not hard to understand." She squatted in front of the headman and laid the map out on the ground. "Here is Tepia," she said and pointed to a mark on the map. "And this," she ran her finger along the map, "is the Comoro River. We think that a section of the riverbank here," and she moved her finger back toward the village, "was washed away in a storm. And we think that the bodies may have been buried there."

The man pushed his pulping equipment aside. He seemed intrigued by the map and apparently oblivious to what Estefana was saying. "I know the area you're talking about," he said, "but I have never seen a thing like this," and he ran his finger along the line of the river. "You say this marks where the big river flows?"

"We think this area may be *lulik* and ask your permission to enter it," said Estefana pointing again to the area near Tepia. The man ignored what she was saying and continued to trace his finger across the map.

"*Senyor*," Estefana said. "We're asking your permission to enter this area."

"What?" he said and continued to stare at the map. "No one can go there."

"But *senyor*—"

"Where is the little stream that enters the river near Tepia?" the man asked.

Estefana lent over to check the map. "Here, I think," she said.

"From there along the course of the big river is *lulik manas*," he said meaning 'hot' or especially dangerous taboo country. "You cannot go there. Nobody can."

"*Senyor*—" Estefana began again but he cut her off and his face turned red with anger.

"You heard what I said. No one goes there!"

Estefana looked at Carter and back at the headman to try to reason with him. But he stood abruptly.

"Anyone who goes there will bring trouble to the village, maybe even death. You can't go. I forbid it!" he said, storming off inside his house.

• • •

At Father Roque's suggestion, Cordero stayed in the SUV while the priest took his wooden box and Missal and headed toward the hut. "It's not a good time for strangers to be calling," the priest had simply said.

Cordero resigned himself to a wait. After a few minutes, three old men arrived at the hut and stood outside. One held a spear and another carried a bundle wrapped in a woven cloth. The man set the bundle on the ground and unfurled what Cordero thought to be an old wooden statue of the Virgin Mary. The man with the spear squatted and lit a cigarette, the smoke drifted passed Cordero's open window. The men paid Cordero no heed and waited in silence by the entrance to the hut.

Cordero closed his eyes, tired from yesterday's drive and battling mosquitoes the night before. Presently he heard voices and opened his eyes to see Father Roque at the entrance to the hut. The priest handed his wooden box and Missal to one of the men, took his priestly stole from around his neck, wrapped and pocketed it. Little was said aside from the formal pleasantries. Father Roque took back his gear, touched the top of the statue, and made his way back to Cordero. The three men went inside the hut.

"It's the wife who wanted me to come," Father Roque said when seated beside Cordero. "Hedging her bets. Now the old man will get a customary sendoff for good measure through the spiritual power of the *lulik* objects."

"Wasn't that a statue of the Virgin?" asked Cordero. "You call that *lulik*?"

"Absolutely," said the priest. "That statue was brought by the first priests who came into this area. About two hundred years ago. They brought smallpox with them as well. After the village had been ravaged by the disease, what villagers were left sent the priests packing. They went in such a hurry that they left the statue here, right in the middle of the church. To these folks it was a sign. It that showed that their magic was stronger than the magic of the priests. As a result, they consider the statue to be infused with *lulik*. Instead of representing something symbolically, the statue itself has power—*their* power—to achieve *their* ends." Cordero started the engine and reversed back onto the track. "Perhaps they're right," Father Roque added.

"Strange to hear that from a Jesuit priest," Cordero said.

Father Roque chuckled. "Well I told you I was creating theological trouble back in Brazil." He looked sideways at Cordero. "The week before I was ordained my superior called me to his office. 'Roque,'" he said adopting a deeper voice. "'You are about to become a priest. But before you do tell me, is there anything that bothers you?' I thought for a moment and then said: 'Reverend Father, I'm no longer sure I believe in God.' And do you know what he said to that?" The priest shook his head. "'Let's not worry about that for the moment, Roque. After you are ordained we can talk of such nonsense but for now pray that your doubts will go away and prepare for your special day.'" The priest looked back out through the windshield. "Can you believe that?"

"Are you sure? Of God?" asked Cordero. "Now, I mean? It's been what, thirty years since you were ordained?"

"No," the priest said. "Or at least I'm not sure that the version the Church prefers has it right." He paused for a moment. "I became interested in liberation theology. Do you know what that is?" But before Cordero could answer the priest continued. "It's an attempt to make the gospel relevant in the here and now. Politically, economically, and socially. It was an idea, a movement really, that grew out of Latin America's experience of poverty and military repression in the 1960s and 70s—my time as a seminarian and a young priest. Liberation theologians argued the Church should work to build the kingdom of God on earth and not encourage people to wait until the next life. It was a perspective I was drawn to."

Cordero steered the vehicle carefully down the rugged track toward Tepia.

"After years of the Church siding with the rich and powerful it was an overdue corrective. But it invited awkward questions. For instance, if you can build the kingdom here what need do you have of heaven?" the priest said and left the answer hanging.

"Then why do you stay?" Cordero asked. "In the priesthood, I mean."

"You can't change the cards you're dealt," Father Roque said. "Only the game." He looked over at Cordero. "Are you a believer?" he asked.

"I was brought up Catholic, yes," he answered.

"That's not necessarily an answer," said the priest smiling. "Christianity, you see, represents a huge leap in human consciousness. We know it as the idea of redemption or salvation. But what are we being saved from? Answer: the assumption that we are forever condemned to live as those before us have lived. Jesus tells us that we are not condemned to repeat the past, that each of us has the power within us to create our own future. That's a powerful claim. More or less everything in Western civilisation since then is based on it, especially the idea of progress and its expression in liberal democracy and capitalism. Both have improved our living standards immeasurably. Both have seen us go to the moon and back. But at what cost? Over-population, resource depletion, environmental degradation." The priest was quiet for a moment, bouncing this way and that as Cordero avoided one obstacle only to be confronted by another. "When it all comes apart," Father Roque continued, "who is more likely to survive? Westerners in the air-conditioned office towers who have forgotten how to grow onions and tomatoes? Or folk like these who are connected to the land and understand its seasons?" He waved a hand at the scene beyond the windscreen. "Take this place. The local king, the *liurai*, died back in Indonesian times. The Indonesians wouldn't allow a replacement. The *lia-nain*—he's the keeper of the words, the storyteller, the traditional religious leader—became the de facto ruler of this village." He looked across at Cordero directly. "Primitive, superstitious, pagan rule you could say. But the sky hasn't fallen in yet."

"But is that a reason to doubt the existence of God?" asked Cordero.

"No," the priest replied. "But it's a reason to give these people credit for perhaps knowing more about life and death than we do. After all, what they believe they've believed for twenty, thirty thousand years. We count our beliefs back two thousand years, maybe five thousand if you take Judaism into account." The priest looked again at Cordero. "We are very much new comers on the scene," he said and smiled again. "But it sounds as though I'm delivering a sermon to you." He dangled his arm out the window again. "We shouldn't believe we have all the answers. That's an arrogance that could bring us all undone. That's the only point I'm trying to make."

9

"What do we do now, *mana*?" Estefana asked as she and Carter headed out of the headman's yard and back up the road to the church to meet up with Cordero.

"We go and have a look anyway," said Carter.

"Oh no, *mana*! We can't do that," protested her companion.

"We are police officers, Estefana," said Carter. "We have to find out where those skeletons came from and what caused the deaths of those people."

"But *mana*, to go into a *lulik* area when you have been forbidden is much worse than to go without seeking permission. Terrible things could happen! We could bring bad spirits back into the village!"

Carter offered no response and Estefana dug her hands into her pants pockets and lowered her head. They walked on in silence until a gaggle of children in school uniforms came racing down the road laughing loudly at the game they were playing. Behind them Carter and Estefana could just make out an awkward shape scrambling to keep up. The shape's head was too big for its body, and it carried a hump atop the left shoulder like a heavy sack. As it drew nearer, they could see it was a boy, perhaps no more than 12 years old but big for the age. The face was distorted, the eyes bulging in their sockets, and spittle dribbled from the corner of his mouth as he struggled to run and breathe.

The children dashed passed the two policewomen and as the disfigured boy approached them, he slipped and fell, spilling the contents of a cardboard box into the mud. Estefana was quick to go to him and help.

"Are you alright?" she asked stepping across to where the boy lay in the mud.

"*Sin mana. Obrigadu*," the boy said, thanking her. Slowly he twisted to face her, and his smile showed crooked teeth. "They race me every morning," he said pointing to the other children. The smile waned. "I never win."

"Brush yourself off while I collect these things you've spilled," Estefana said.

She took the cardboard box and bent down to pick up the scattered contents.

"No *mana*, no!" the boy screamed, and he pulled the box from Estefana's grip. "These are my special things. I only show them to my friends."

"Okay," said Estefana. She stepped back. The boy hurriedly gathered his few things. "You're not wearing a uniform," Estefana said to change the subject. "Do you not go to school also?"

"No *mana*," the boy replied closing the flaps of the box. "The teacher says I cause trouble."

Estefana smiled. "Well, you seem like a nice boy to me," she said.

The boy smiled broadly, showing the crooked teeth again.

"My name is Tomas," he said.

"Mine is Estefana."

"Now we are friends," he said and thrust the box forward. "Now I can show you my special things."

"Thank you, Tomas, but not now," Estefana said. "I have things I must do."

"But *mana*—"

"Not now, Tomas," Estefana repeated as she rejoined Carter.

"Perhaps later?" the boy asked.

"Perhaps," replied Estefana.

"Then I will wait for you, *mana*," the boy said and sat back down on the road, his raggedy clothes covered in mud, the box firmly in his lap, an expectant grin lighting up his ugly face.

• • •

Cordero was outside the nuns' house on his cell when Carter and Estefana arrived back at the church. "Well that doesn't give me much to go on but…. Uh-huh…. Yep…. Will do. Thanks Howard." He checked his cell. There had been a call from the young nurse in Dili while he was speaking on the other call. "Phew," he said to no one in particular, pocketed his cell and turned to his colleagues. "Did you get anything from the headman?"

"Mainly that the area I want to look over is *lulik*, as Estefana had suggested," Carter replied. "He knew nothing of massacres or missing families. He did say the village was visited by a few members of a pro-Indonesian militia but the villagers ran them off before they could do any damage. He said one was wielding an axe with blood on it the man had said was from a person who didn't follow orders but the headman thought that was just for show. On the other hand—" and she left the rest unsaid.

Cordero merely nodded. "That was Dr Brooks." He hesitated and looked off down the road. "I didn't think we'd get reception out here but I guess it's because there's a school and a health clinic in the village." He turned back to face Carter and picked up the pace of his news. "Brooks managed to piece together as much as he could of the skeletal remains. Remember the first skull that was found? And remember Brooks saying he thought it was a more recent death and possibly a murder? Well, he managed to re-assemble enough of the skeleton to confirm it was female. And he found that the left wrist had been broken and reset. In other words, properly treated, cast, by a professional sometime before death." He looked away again from Carter expecting her to draw the correct inference.

"If she came from around here it's likely she was treated in the health clinic or by a worker from the health clinic," Carter said and followed his gaze down the road.

"Exactly." He took the key to his vehicle from his pocket. "He also said he thinks that all of the skeletons were burned."

"Burned?" Carter said.

"Yeah. He found fracturing on parts of the backbones and ribs which he says is characteristic of bodies that are burned while the flesh is attached. On the skeleton of the person who died most recently, he also found what he thinks is evidence that bones have calcined."

"You mean become almost ceramic?" asked Carter. "That suggests that the bones burned at a fairly high temperature."

"But only the bones of the most recent skeleton," said Cordero.

"Well that strengthens the murder theory. Why would you burn the body of someone who'd died by accident?" Carter asked.

All three considered what this new information might mean but without coming up with anything that made sense. "They're holding a *tebedai* tonight—" Cordero said finally but Carter cut him off.

"A what?'

"A *tebedai*. A big ceremonial dance. It can go on for hours, even all night. It's to mark the opening of the new *uma lulik*, the village's sacred house. We won't get much more out of anyone today. They'll be too distracted getting ready. We can go along tonight and Estefana and I can ask the older people in the crowd if they know of a mass killing, mass grave, anything like that." He paused for a moment. "I need to work on that SUV to keep us on the road the next few days. While I'm doing that I want you"—he gestured to Estefana—"to go to the health clinic before it closes and ask around. Check their records. See if a female, aged late teens to late twenties, was treated for a broken left wrist. Get names, directions, any personal details, anecdotes, family, names of friends…standard procedure. Then meet me back at the mechanic's place if I don't come over to you first."

Cordero pocketed his cell, tossed the keys to the SUV into the air, caught them, and turned to leave.

"Aren't you forgetting me?" Carter asked.

"Ah…what do you know about tappets?" he said over his shoulder.

•••

Cordero could hear the rhythmic clanging of a hammer behind the wooden door that led into the mechanic's workshop as he eased the SUV up to the front awning. On one side of the awning he noticed the shell of a vehicle under a tarp, dull green weeds growing around deflated tyres. On the other side was a rusting steel drum nestled in the roots of a banyan tree. He'd dropped Estefana at the health clinic, along with Carter who said she'd prefer to stick with Estefana than play mechanic. He cut the vehicle's engine, applied the parking brake and slid out.

The sound grew louder as he shoved the wooden door aside as best he could. Immediately, smoke rushed out into the cooler air and he had to close his eyes tight to ease the burning sensation. When he opened them again he could see that the shed was little more than a flimsy façade fronting a dirt floor, old tarpaulins strung up on poles for a roof, and a poor attempt at bamboo walls. Scraps of iron and tools were strewn across the ground. Along one stretch of wall ran a row of jerry cans beneath benches with more tools atop them and smaller oil cans. In the far corner of the work space was the source of the clanging and the smoke.

A man squatted next to an open wooden fire hammering a piece of iron on a cement block. He was middle aged, in shorts, a grimy T-shirt and thongs, and his hair and thick moustache were gray from smoke and dust. Moussi, Cordero figured, the owner and closest thing Tepia had to a mechanic. A younger man stood to one side working two plungers alternately up and down inside metal castings. The castings were joined to a single pipe running along the floor to the fire. Cordero could see that it was an improvised bellows that fanned the flames whenever the older man placed the piece of iron back in the fire with a set of rusty tongs. The man continued to hammer the iron—it seemed to be taking the shape of a large machete blade—then placed it in a large tin basin containing water where it hissed and threw steam into the smoke-filled air.

Cordero admired the ingenuity and make-do character of the place. Then his eye caught the motorcycles just inside the door to his left. There were two. The furthest from the door's opening he guessed was the priest's because the fuel tank had been removed and placed on the ground beside the bike. The other was bright red and looked relatively new and intact. As Cordero was examining the motorcycles, the mechanic noticed him.

"*Maun, ita hakarak sa?*" the man said asking what Cordero wanted.

"You must be Moussi," said Cordero. "I need to do a little work on my vehicle. I was hoping you'd have tools I could use and clean engine oil."

"Out here engine oil is expensive," the man snapped back.

"I know that," said Cordero. "I have money to pay."

The man stood and walked slowly over to Cordero. "Where is the vehicle?"

"Outside," Cordero answered, nodding his head in that direction.

"What's wrong with it?" the man asked.

"Tappets," said Cordero. "I just need to adjust them. I've done it before."

The man walked to the door and peered outside. He said nothing. Then he walked to the bench on the side wall. "These are the only tools I have," he said waving a hand across the small collection. "Help yourself. The oil will be twelve dollars a litre."

"Twelve dollars!"

"I told you oil was expensive out here." And with that the man walked back to his fire. He grunted and gestured to his off-sider to go help Cordero. Then he took the blade he had fashioned from the basin of water, examined it, and, satisfied, shifted position to work on a wooden handle.

The young man sauntered over to Cordero who was examining the offerings on the bench.

"Hey *maun*," he said. It was the same youth Cordero had seen the night before, with the girl smoking cigarettes outside the workshop. He was wearing the same dirty blue jeans and T-shirt and he wore his cap backwards on his head. "My name's Rui. I work for Moussi. His assistant you might say. What are you looking for?"

"Hey Rui," replied Cordero without looking up. "I'm Tino. You got spanners and a large screwdriver?"

"Sure *maun*," said Rui. He shuffled through the collection of associated bits and pieces on the bench. "These do?"

"Yeah, thanks," said Cordero taking the tools.

"I'll help," said Rui.

They went outside to the SUV. Cordero put the tools down and lifted the bonnet.

"Where you from, Tino?" asked Rui peering inside the engine.

"Dili," answered Cordero, elbowing the boy aside.

"What brings you here, *maun*?"

"I'm a police investigator," said Cordero. He began to poke around the engine. "I'm here with two colleagues."

"What you investigating, *maun*?" asked Rui.

"Crime. What do you think police investigate?" said Cordero.

"What sort of crime, *maun*?"

"You ask a lot of questions," Cordero said. "Maybe you're in the wrong business."

"Nothing ever happens here, *maun*. Why wouldn't I ask questions? You coming here is the most interesting thing that's happened in a long time."

Cordero ignored the comment, intent on the job before him. "Hey, you know how to drain oil from an engine?" he asked.

"Sure *maun*."

"And you have clean engine oil?"

"Sure."

"Show me what you've got."

Rui returned to the workshop. Cordero could hear him shifting containers aside as he searched for the engine oil and then he came back and showed Cordero two bottles.

Cordero read what was left of the fraying labels. "This one," he said and set the other bottle aside. "Okay. You drain the oil. The engine is warm enough. By the time it starts to drain it won't be too hot for me to work on the tappets. There a jack inside?"

"Sure, *maun*."

Rui went into the workshop again and re-emerged carrying an old flimsy bumper jack. He placed the jack under the side edge of the chassis and began to lift the vehicle.

"That thing safe?" Cordero asked.

"Sure *maun*, if you know how to use it."

When the SUV had been gingerly lifted high enough to allow Rui space to crawl under, he stacked concrete blocks along one side of the chassis. Then he slid down, placed the can under the sump drain plug and unscrewed it. The thick black oil began to ooze out and soon formed a steady stream.

Cordero selected a spanner and went to work removing the engine cover. He then uncoupled the exhaust gas recirculation valve, removed the outlet breather hose and unscrewed the valve cover to expose the tappets.

"What crime you investigating, *maun*?" Rui asked again as he slid out from under the SUV.

"What crimes have you got around here?" asked Cordero. "How's that oil flowing?"

"Oil flowing good, *maun*," said the young man bending down to check the flow from the sump drain. "So, what crime?"

"Not sure yet," said Cordero as he put the valve cover to one side. "That's what we're trying to find out." He set to work to clean and adjust the tappets. "This isn't the best way to adjust tappets but a mechanic showed me how to do it this way in an emergency." He checked and slightly adjusted each valve in a non-sequential order. He then managed to remove the oil filter without the need of any tool, clean it as best he could and re-fitted it. "That should get us back to Dili," he said satisfied with his work.

"When you heading back?" Rui asked, scratching his head under his cap.

"When we get answers to the questions we came here to ask," Cordero said. "The oil should be drained by now. Re-seal the sump, will you?"

Rui crawled back under the SUV and sealed the sump while Cordero re-attached the engine parts. Then he took the bottle of fresh oil, unscrewed the oil cap and poured the contents in. Rui had come from under the vehicle. He raised the jack a little more, eased the concrete blocks from under the chassis and kicked the jack away. The SUV slumped down on all four tyres.

"The jack slips more when you lower it," Rui explained.

"You're pretty handy, aren't you?" Cordero said. "Very sure of yourself too."

Rui merely shrugged and grinned.

Cordero went to the driver's side, worked the ignition and let the engine run for a couple of minutes while he cleaned his hands on a rag. He tossed it into the steel drum beneath the banyan tree and turned the motor off. "I'm just going over to the health clinic for a few minutes," he told Rui. "Let it cool. I'll check the level when I get back and pay you then, okay?"

• • •

Cordero passed a figure huddled over a cardboard box as he approached the entrance to the clinic. It was a disfigured boy, who ignored Cordero and kept his eyes fixed firmly on the clinic's front door, one foot tapping incessantly where he sat. Inside Estefana was talking to a nurse and Carter was standing by her side: the apparent violent death of the most recent girl was not Carter's concern but it held curiosity value for her. A pregnant woman—a familiar sight in Timorese health clinics—slouched in a chair toward the back of the room with her eyes closed as if in sleep. She was the only apparent patient. The nurse seemed eager to have done with Estefana's questions and close up for the day.

"You were saying—" Estefana began but stopped when she saw Cordero come through the door. "This is Investigator Cordero," she said, turning toward him. The nurse checked the watch pinned to her uniform. "*Maun*, this is *mana* Sefa Soares, the head nurse here. I told her we were investigating remains found in Dili recently. She has been telling me about a girl who had her left wrist set here about a year ago. Her name is Clarita Araujo. This is her file."

"*Bondia, mana*," Cordero said taking the file. "Don't let me interrupt you. Please continue Officer dos Carvalho."

"*Mana*, perhaps you could tell *maun* what you were just telling me about Clarita."

Sefa Soares let out a long breath to show her irritation.

"She is twenty years old. Pretty girl. Bright too. Lived just the other side of—"

"Lived?" Cordero said, interrupting her.

"Well, lives I guess but I haven't seen her since we set her wrist."

"Okay, please go on," Cordero said. He examined the contents of the file.

"She had seizures, you see. Epileptic seizures. She suffered from epilepsy," the nurse said looking from Estefana to Cordero to see if they understood. "She was prone to what we call grand-mal seizures where a person loses consciousness, their body stiffens and they start to shake and can fall to the ground. It was during one of those seizures that she fell and broke her wrist."

"I see," said Cordero. "And this is the only girl or woman who has had a left wrist set in this clinic?"

Estefana was translating now for Carter's benefit. "Yes," said Sefa Soares. "I checked our records."

"Would anyone from this area go to another clinic to get a break like that re-set?" asked Cordero.

"I would say no. We are a very good clinic and the people trust us because they know us," the nurse insisted. "And besides, the nearest clinic is a long way from here and most people don't have transport."

"Was that the first time Clarita presented here?" Cordero asked.

"No. Before that there were occasional cuts and sprains to treat—the sort of thing you get if you shake yourself about against the furniture and end up on the floor."

"And the wrist—you say that was the last time you saw her?" Cordero asked to be certain.

"I think the seizures were becoming more frequent and more violent but I can get moved around to different locations and I never saw or heard of her again after the episode with the broken wrist."

"I don't see any X-rays of the break in this file," Cordero said holding up the file.

The nurse looked at him. "The nearest X-ray machine is

in Dili, *maun*," she said, "although one has been promised for Ermera. For the last five years."

"Does Clarita have a family here in Tepia?" Cordero asked ignoring the complaint.

"I don't think so," the nurse said. "I think they abandoned her when the seizures started,"

"Abandoned her? Why?"

"Many of the people here are very superstitious," she explained. "They view certain conditions as signs of spirit possession rather than as illnesses because they don't understand modern medicine."

"And this Clarita was thought to be possessed?" Cordero asked.

"By some, yes."

"Can you remember who brought her in when her wrist was broken?"

"How could I forget." The nurse shivered slightly. "It was *Avo-feto* Tereza Silveiro," she said, using the conventional title of grandmother for a very old woman. "But she is more commonly known as *Senyora Batibat*."

"*Batibat*?" Cordero repeated. His tone suggested surprise. The nurse merely nodded. "Why did she bring her in?" he asked. "What was her relationship to Clarita?"

"She let Clarita stay with her when no one else dared," the nurse said and looked again at the watch on her uniform.

"Where can we find this Tereza Silveiro?"

"She lives in a hut in the forest—just beyond the cemetery," the nurse said. "But it's getting dark. I wouldn't try her now."

"Why?"

"Night time," the nurse said. "She won't be there." Cordero looked at her as if to ask 'why' again. "*Batibat*," the nurse repeated.

Cordero closed Clarita's file. "May I keep this? We may need it to confirm the identity of the remains we found in Dili."

"You'll have to sign for it," the nurse insisted and she indicated a desk along a side wall. "They send people out to check our record keeping now."

The nurse walked to the desk and took a form from the top

drawer. Cordero lent over to sign it. "They were a pair those two," the nurse added as an afterthought.

Cordero straightened and looked at the nurse as she clicked her fingers for the pregnant woman to come forward.

"Why do you say that?" he asked.

"*Buan*," the nurse said clicking again to get the woman's attention. "They were both *buan*."

Cordero tucked the file under his arm and with Carter and Estefana walked out of the clinic. "What was that last bit?" Carter asked Estefana.

Estefana replied in a flat, soft voice: "She said Clarita and the woman she lived with were both *buan, mana*." They noticed Tomas waiting outside. Whether it was the sight of him that distracted her or something else Carter didn't know but Estefana hesitated.

"*Buan*?" Carter repeated.

"It means witch, *mana*."

10

"*L*ulik is what makes us Timorese, *mana*," Estefana was insisting, troubled by the headman's refusal to grant them permission to investigate the taboo land. They were sitting across from each other on the two single beds that crowded their room. Estefana's brow was creased, her hands pushed down on the bed, her arms rigid by her sides. Carter was leaning forward, forearms on knees, hands clasped, trying to follow what Estefana was saying by searching in her mind for similar ideas with which she was more familiar from her work with Native Americans.

"The source of life, right?" Carter asked.

"Yes. Where spiritual force comes from," Estefana said. "*Lulik* can be land, a rock, a tree, a sacred house, even an object. It contains the power of life."

"When a thing that's *lulik* is violated, bad things happen, to individuals even whole communities? Is that the idea?" Carter asked.

"It is not an idea, *mana*. It is real."

Carter sat up straight and Estefana could read the scepticism on her face.

"This world," Estefana began waving a hand loosely around the room, "must work together with the underworld for things to go right. In the underworld there is our creator, the spirits of our ancestors, and rules people must follow to live well. We must respect this other world even if we can't see it because it is real and connected to us. That's why we perform rituals to honour it. Like before planting—asking permission from the land spirits to use the land and their help to produce a good harvest." She took

73

a deep breath. "*Lulik* is alive, *mana*. It can be good to us if we respect it but bad to us if we don't."

Carter nodded. She now had a rough idea about what Estefana was saying. "But how is walking across that land along the river disrespecting it?"

"You heard the headman say that land was *lulik manas*—'hot' land. No one lives there because land spirits must be very active there. They are associated with death. Maybe something happened in the past to bring them there. *Lulik manas* means it's very dangerous for people to cross without permission that would appease the land spirits. It is what we call *rai bandu*—prohibited land. A person could become sick, go mad or even die if they go there. Worse would be to anger the land spirits so much that they come into the village to cause harm."

"But we need to know if anything *has* happened there," Carter counted. "We need to know if those skeletons originated from a place along the river there. It's our job."

"You know that there are many languages spoken in Timor-Leste, *mana*," Estefana replied and stood, her back to the window. "But everyone has a word that means the same as *lulik*. In Makasae it is '*phalun*', in Fataluku it is '*tie*'. *Lulik* is everywhere and has been forever. Our job is not a traditional job. The police force is a foreign idea that has come into this country only in recent years. *Lulik* is more powerful. It's not an idea. It's real." She folded her arms tightly and turned to stare out through the cracked window pane.

Carter was silent a moment. Despite the late hour a rooster was cock-a-doodling in a nearby yard. "But you were brought up Catholic, Estefana. Surely—"

"I'm a Catholic *Timorese*, *mana*," Estefana cut her off. She turned from the window to face Carter. "When you came to my house in Suai and spoke to my mother, what did she tell you about my father?"

Carter was surprised by the abrupt change in topic. "Well," she said, "what I remember most vividly is that she said he'd been imprisoned by the Indonesians for several years for his political activities and died not long after independence from—"

"Heart failure," said Estefana, finishing the statement for Carter. "That's what the doctor called it. But what caused the heart failure? It was *malisan*."

"*Malisan?*"

"It means a curse, *mana*. It's what can happen when you violate *lulik*." Estefana sat back down on the bed, her head bent. "The prison my father was sent to was on Atauro Island. My mother told you that. Several thousand Timorese were sent there. Several hundred died there. They died from malnutrition and mistreatment. My father was one of the men who had to bury them. The commandant wouldn't allow proper burials— people were just buried in mass graves. The land where the Indonesians ordered the graves to be dug was uninhabited. It was *lulik* land." She looked up at Carter, tears welling in her eyes. "Land soaks up horrors and sorrows, *mana*. There it became filled with the spirits of the dead, angry at their treatment. When my father came home he'd been cursed. That's what caused his heart failure. That's why he died." She wiped a hand across her eyes. "And before he died he was not the same. He was agitated all the time. My mother doesn't want to remember that but I remember. It was horrible." She stood again and returned to the window. "I don't want the same thing to happen to me. Not now or when I'm married or if I ever become a mother. That's why I'm afraid of going onto that *lulik* land."

Carter joined Estefana at the window and put her arm around her. The sun had gone down and it was dark now. Neither spoke. The rooster broke the silence again.

"What about me?" Carter asked.

"What about you, *mana*?" Estefana said turning to face her.

"Well I'm not Timorese. What if I go without you?"

"You are still at risk, *mana*," Estefana said. "You are a woman and it is worse for a woman to violate *lulik*."

"And Cordero? What about him?"

"*Maun* is Timorese," Estefana said. "But he grew up in Australia. He may not be as worried about violating *lulik* land as me but he is at risk, too, whether he knows it or not."

"Then it's settled," Carter said. "Cordero and I will investigate that stretch of land while you do other things associated with the investigation. Talking to local villagers, perhaps. That kind of thing."

"There is a risk to you, to *maun*, and to the village," Estefana repeated.

"Well that's a risk I'm going to have to take," said Carter.

She collected her things from the bed ready to leave the room.

"One other thing, *mana*," Estefana said. Carter stopped, turned toward her. "Can you not tell *maun* what I have told you? It may go against me as a police woman if he reports it."

"Okay I won't," replied Carter. "I'll make it my suggestion that he and I go out along the riverbank while you do something else." She reached out and put a hand on Estefana's forearm. "But you are going to have to think this through. The idea of the police may be new in Timor-Leste but it represents what the country is now—or at least what it wants to become. You have to find a way to reconcile your role as a police woman with any conflict that causes with your traditions and customs."

• • •

"If this Clarita is your victim, and she was killed, and she was regarded as a witch, you might have your motive," Carter said as they walked from the nuns' house to the *tebedai* ceremony

"Maybe," Cordero responded doubtfully. He had gone back to the mechanic's, checked his repair work on the SUV's tappets, paid the exorbitant price Moussi was charging for oil, and driven back to where they were staying. Carter and Estefana had strolled back, Tomas shadowing them at a distance after Estefana had said she was on duty and would spend time with him when she could, and not before. Cordero had then taken a nap before the younger nun, hollow-cheeked and shy Sister Agnes, had served them an evening meal of stale bread rolls and left-over soup which Estefana supplemented with canned tuna they had brought with them. It was simple fare but had been sufficient. "But if she was killed by a blow to the head," Cordero continued as they crossed the road toward the clearing in the trees on the other side, "that could mean anything—a farming tool, a piece of wood, a bottle, a rock—there are countless possibilities. And in a remote village like this almost anyone could have it in for a suspected witch." He gestured to where people were gathering up ahead. "Look at them all. Even if we have our motive, that doesn't narrow it down much. I need to talk to this Silveiro woman. Find out why Clarita had a reputation as a witch. Was it just because her epilepsy caused seizures or was there another reason? And if it was something else, who might she have angered that much as to cause her death? Or more likely, who might she have terrified that much they wanted to be rid of her?"

"Back at the clinic you seemed to flinch when the nurse used the other name for the old woman—*Senyora Batibat* was it? What was that about?" Carter asked.

Cordero broke his stride and faced Carter. "A *batibat* is an evil spirit that devours people at night in their sleep," he said. "Maybe that's why the nurse said we'd best look for her tomorrow—in daylight. A *batibat* disguises itself as a fat old woman who lives in the trees." He started off toward the *tebedai* again without waiting for a response.

As they reached the clearing, which was lit by bamboo torches, they could see that the crowd was several hundred strong. Several farmers had arrived on ponies, others on motorcycles, but most had simply walked no matter how far they lived from where the ceremony was to be held. A *tebedai* was an important occasion and not to be missed. Many of the women, no more than girls really, were suckling babies to their breasts. Other, older, women were chewing betel. Small children pressed tight against the legs of their parents unsure of what the commotion was all about; older ones looked on or giggled with nervous excitement as they ran back and forth into the gloom of the trees as if to prove their lack of fear in the dark. Over on one side of the crowd people were laughing. Across on the other was the raucous cry of a baby. Cigarette smoke hung over the scene in a thin blanket of motionless air.

Sprinkled among the many barefooted men in shorts and ragged T-shirts and women in worn jeans and cheap blouses, were other villagers in customary attire: men wearing the *tais mane* or male cloth—a single large woven garment wrapped around their waists; the women in *tais feto* or female cloth—a shapeless full-length dress that, unlike the men's version, bore rich colourful designs. Many wore scarves or bandanas wrapped around their heads, the more flamboyant donning elaborate feathered headpieces that reminded Carter of pow wows among the Navajos, Hopis and Apaches she'd visited on reservations near her posting at the FBI's regional agency in Arizona. This crowd, she noticed, was just as excited as the people of those tribes, just as loud, and just as eager to cram shoulder-to-shoulder into a tight semi-circle to witness the ceremony. It occurred to her how far she was from her home, how much she missed it, and how much she longed to be back. She thrust her hands into the back pockets of her jeans and tried her best to put all those thoughts out of her head for now.

The ceremony was to be held before a structure that resembled a giant cowbell. This was the *uma lulik,* or sacred house, Cordero was explaining above the din around them. It functioned, he said, as the social glue of the village, housing the sacred objects that encapsulated the people's identity—swords, spears, woven cloth—and would be used in the rituals for planting and harvesting. The building itself was constructed of what Cordero took to be rare teak beams, onto which wooden planks of a lesser quality timber had been tied by rope made from feather palm. The planks supported a single room no more than thirty feet by twenty in size and set on stilts. As high as the top of the room was from the ground—another twenty feet— was an equally high curved roof of heavy, thatched grass giving the building its cowbell appearance. "The whole structure you see has to be made from natural materials—no nails, no screws, no metal or glass—in order to connect the house with the forces of nature," Cordero was saying. "I know of similar sacred houses built quickly using nails and they've all blown down as though cursed." He drew her attention to where the roofing tapered at its highest point: a wooden carving of buffalo horns covered its length. The horns were painted black and symbolised male strength, he told her. They, in turn, were adorned with carvings of birds painted green to represent female fertility.

On each side of the raised room a small opening like a window had been cut. There was no door: entry was by ladder through the floor. "Inside that room," Cordero continued, gesturing only with his chin, "the local religious leaders and elders will gather to direct village affairs according to old myths and legends. They'll also apply sacred knowledge to important issues like conflicts over land or marriage disputes." People were buffeting them in the crush. Cordero asked a question of an elderly man puffing on a pipe to his right then turned back to Carter. "When the Indonesians were here they destroyed a lot of *uma luliks* to wipe out local customs," he said. "Now they're being rebuilt across the country. But I asked that man near me about this one. He said the Indonesians never destroyed the *uma lulik* in this village. It burned down about a year ago and this one's replacing it."

The crowd was pushing forward as the dancers and musicians began assembling for the *tebedai*. "Why don't you go up and get a closer look at the ceremony?" Cordero encouraged Carter. "People will make room for you as a courtesy to a foreigner. Estefana and I have a few minutes before the ceremony begins to ask around about the skeletons." He turned to Estefana and suggested she head off to their left while he went to the right.

After weaving through the crowd for ten minutes and questioning various people, Cordero encountered Father Roque. "Well Father, I didn't expect to see you here," he said by way of greeting.

"A Catholic priest, you mean?" Father Roque asked clearly amused.

"Well, yes."

"God is either everywhere or He is nowhere," the priest said. "And besides, this is certainly where His people are tonight, Inspector."

"I'm an investigator remember, not an inspector," Cordero corrected him. "I gather the nuns wouldn't see it that way. Attending a ceremony for an *uma lulik*, I mean."

"The good sisters have a more restrictive theology than I do," the priest said. He was silent a moment, watching what was going on at the front of the *uma lulik*. "Are you making progress in your enquiries?"

"Not a lot. No one here seems to know anything about a massacre, group killing or a missing family."

"I doubt they'd tell you if they did," said the priest. "Tepia is not Dili. The police, I'm afraid, count for little here. People tend to keep what they know to themselves."

The beat of a *tala*—a small disc-shaped cymbal—called to attention the dancers who were about to begin the traditional line dance known as the *tebedai*. "I must find the American," Cordero said. "You'll excuse me, Father."

"Of course, *Investigator*," the priest answered emphasizing Cordero's official position. "Enjoy the ceremony."

"Please, call me Tino," Cordero said as he left through the throng. "It's short for Vincintino—my name," he shouted back over his shoulder.

Cordero found Carter behind a small cluster of children to the side of the dancers. The crowd had fallen silent. Before it, in front of the *uma lulik*, ten women formed two lines of five. One woman at the back of each row tapped a *tala*: the others produced a fast 4/4 beat on a large drum called a *baba dook*, carried under their left arm. The women were of mixed ages but all were lean and fine-featured as Timorese women tend to be. They were dressed in *tais feto*, each with their own design of startling reds, yellows, purples and blue. Around their feet were ankle-bells that tinkled as they moved. On their heads they wore large plumages of ornate feathers that swayed back and forth across wide arcs created by moving their upper bodies in time to the drum beats. As they did this they shuffled in short steps through concentric circles that would end in the two lines abreast of each other before moving out, around, and back again.

The dance continued for ten minutes without a change to either the beat or the movements of the dancers and Cordero grew mildly impatient. He was, after all, a city-raised Timorese—most of his childhood in Darwin followed by university in Melbourne—and his tastes in entertainment reflected that. He searched the crowd for Estefana and noticed her standing behind a group of women on the other side of the throng of on-lookers. He caught her eye and raised his arms in a gestured question as to whether she had learned anything. She shook her head. Just at that moment the dancers stopped and their drumming was replaced by a loud, penetrating sound. A bare-chested figure in a *tais mane* adorned with bright tassels came from behind the *uma lulik* blowing a *karau dikur*—a traditional Timorese trumpet made from buffalo horn. The trumpeting continued as the man strutted through the centre of the dancers without taking a breath.

A second man appeared and the people gasped in astonishment. He also wore a *tais mane,* but with a bright red and white *salenda* or sash across his bare chest and a large *belak* or medallion hanging from his neck. On his head was an elaborate silver headpiece in the shape of buffalo horns, around his feet were anklets made of goat hair and each forearm bore a *keke* or ceremonial bracelet. The man's hair was thick but gray, as was his moustache, and the skin on his face looked like hide that had been left to dry too long in the sun. He was well-built, though Cordero guessed his age at about seventy years. "The *lia-nain*," Cordero whispered to Carter. "He's the head of the *uma lulik*."

As the *lia-nain* strode proudly forward, the man with the trumpet lowered it and slid silently to the side with the dancers. The *lia-nain* stopped, stood perfectly still, his head bowed, made a deep moaning sound and produced a *surik*—a thin, finely sharpened sword. He raised the sword above his head and waved it vigorously, kicking up dust at his feet as they pounded the earth in a tight circle. This he continued to do for ten minutes, until sweat was flying from his face and off his chest. Then abruptly he stopped, turned, and walked back behind the *uma lulik* as the repetitive drum beat started again and the women danced back to the center of the clearing.

"Well now we've heard from the big man of the village," Cordero whispered again. "In Tetun *lia-nain* means 'owner of words'. He's said to be familiar with the entire history of this village and everyone in it and he makes decisions based on his knowledge of customary rules. He's the highest religious authority in the village." Cordero rubbed a hand across his mouth and looked at Carter. "And since there is no *liurai* or traditional king in these parts, that makes him the most important person in town."

Carter was glancing beyond the dancers to a trickle of people who had followed the *lia-nain* behind the *uma lulik*. "I can see that by his fan club," she said pointing.

"They're paying their respects," said Cordero noticing the line of people she had indicated. "Offering him cigarettes or betel nut while he is in that rather imposing outfit he's wearing." He looked over at Estefana again. "I don't know about you but I've had enough of tradition for one night. What say we collect Estefana and head back for a night-cap? I made a point of packing the gin and tonic."

Carter followed him through the crowd and together with Estefana they headed back to the nuns' house. Cordero noticed the young mechanic's assistant, Rui, off to the side, talking to a girl and, further back in the trees, he thought he caught a glimpse of the disfigured boy who was outside the health clinic that afternoon. But he thought nothing of either. His mind was on a stiff drink and an early night after a largely inconclusive day.

•••

They sat on the veranda where the nuns had prepared a bed for Cordero. It was a pleasant night, a little cooler now, and crickets had started their chorus in the darkness. Only feint and occasional sounds came from the gathering outside the new *uma lulik* and the soft sweet scent of sandalwood had replaced the stale smell of sweat and cigarette smoke that had encased the crowd. Cordero sat on the side of his bed, Estefana and Carter side-by-side on the veranda itself, their backs against the wall of the house and their knees pulled up tight against their rumps. He poured them each a drink and the gin soon took affect and relaxed them all.

"No one you talked to knew of a massacre in the area, Estefana?" asked Cordero.

"*Lae, maun,*" she replied, her attention fixed on the drink he handed her. "I mean no," she corrected herself in English. "No one."

"We may have identified the more recent fatality today at least," he said. "Not that it helps your investigation," he added tilting his glass toward Carter.

"I'd still like to see that area Henrique identified as the possible site of the drift down river," Carter said and cast a quick glance at Estefana.

"Ah yes, Henrique," Cordero repeated, raising his eyebrows.

"It is *lulik, maun,*" Estefana said, "and the headman strictly forbade us going there."

"I see," he said. They were silent a moment. "I didn't want it to come to this, but we have to get to the bottom of things. So, we will go regardless."

Carter was surprised by the firmness in Cordero's voice, but she noticed Estefana stare out across the churchyard and take an uncharacteristic gulp of her gin.

"I think you and I should go," Carter said to Cordero. "We need to question the locals and I'll only slow Estefana down if she has to do that while translating everything for me. I suggest she stays, and we go."

Cordero nodded. "Suits me," he said. "I need to talk to Tereza Silveiro about this girl, Clarita, as well." He refilled their glasses. "But that can wait."

"I've worked so-called witch cases involving Native American communities," said Carter. She eased her head back against the wall, closed her eyes, and her tone became almost wistful. "In the high, dry country of junipers and piñon pine, eagles and coyotes." A smile broke out on her face. "Ever smelt piñon when it's burned, Cordero? It's fragrance is more uplifting than any incense in any church you could name. My father taught me that on a camping trip once when I was very young. He was right and I've never forgotten it." She took a deep breathe, lent forward, serious again, and sipped her gin. "When people go missing or turn up dead, witches or skinwalkers as they're called back there are often regarded as the culprits. Witchcraft represents the opposite of tribal cultural values. It's evil, terrifying. Usually, it's not hard to find rational explanations for behaviour attributed to witches but it's a lot harder to dissuade people from acting on their fears and superstitions. I take it the situation is much the same here?"

Before Cordero could answer heavy footsteps sounded just off the veranda. It was Father Roque, and he was panting from running. "I've been looking all over for you, Tino," he said.

"What's the matter, Father?" Cordero asked rising from the side of his bed.

"It's Sabu Bada," the priest said catching his breath.

"Who?"

"You know," said Father Roque collecting himself. "Tonight's main attraction. The *lia-nain*."

"Does he want to see me urgently, Father?"

"He can't," the priest said. "He's dead."

11

Cordero, Carter and Estefana hurried after Father Roque to the *uma lulik* and from there they wound their way thirty yards further into the trees at the back of the building. At the priest's suggestion they had borrowed a kerosene lamp from Sister Felicia and taken two flashlights from the SUV. "He was found by several boys playing in the trees here," the priest was telling them. "One of them tripped over the body in the dark."

A group of about two dozen people stood around the body of Sabu Bada, crying, wailing in grief, or standing silent in shock and horror. "*Polisia, hakbedok*," Cordero ordered and all but one of the onlookers slowly did as they were told and stood aside. The exception was Eusebio Leite—the headman Cordero had spoken to when he first drove into Tepia. He was standing closest to the body and didn't move.

"We will take care of this in our own way," Eusebio said as Cordero squatted down beside the dead *lia-nain* and raised the lamp just above his shoulder to cast its light over the body.

"You will do as I ask or my officer here will place you under arrest," Cordero said in a flat, determined tone. Eusebio hovered for a moment above the police investigator who ignored him as he inspected the body. Grumbling unintelligibly in the direction of Cordero, Eusebio moved back into the darkness with the other villagers.

The body was lying on its back, the *surik* Sabu Bada had wielded in his performance at the *tebedai* sticking out of his chest where it had pierced his heart. Both hands were clenched around the sword. His eyes were open, drained of all life. The *tais mane* was tied around his waist but he had changed out of the rest of his traditional costume for what had been a white shirt now soaked in blood. Cordero quickly examined a canvas bag next to the body. It appeared not to have been opened and inside bore Sabu Bada's sash, anklets, bracelets and buffalo horn headpiece.

"Are the boys who found the body here?" Cordero asked of no one in particular. A boy of about ten years of age was pushed forward by a short, slight woman in the crowd. "What's your name?" Cordero asked in a calm voice as he turned to face the boy who was trying hard not to be noticed.

The boy hesitated a moment. The woman prodded him again. "Lago," he said.

"It's alright, Lago," Cordero said. "You've done nothing wrong. I just need your help to know what happened here." The boy stood rigid. "You found this man here, right?"

"Yes."

"When you found him, was there anyone else around here? Anyone you saw?"

"Yes."

"Who, Lago? Who else did you see?"

The boy hesitated, the woman poked a finger into his back. "Manuelito and Vento."

Cordero thought for a moment. "Your friends, right?"

"Yes."

"Did you see anyone else?"

"No."

"When you found the body—"

"I was running. There was no light. I *tripped* over him," Lago corrected him.

"Okay, sorry, you tripped. When you got up, did you touch anything here?"

"No," Lago said. "I was frightened."

"You didn't touch the bag?"

"No."

"Was there anything apart from this bag near the body that you might have touched, picked up, you know?"

"No. I told you, I was scared."

"And your friends, Manuelito and Vento—they touched and saw nothing?"

"We were all scared—not just me," Lago insisted. Cordero waited for an answer to his question. "They didn't touch him or the bag or see anyone else either," Lago said.

"How long ago did you find the body?"

The boy looked up at the woman behind him. "He came back screaming not long ago," the woman said. She seemed to be his mother.

"I wasn't screaming," Lago protested to the woman. "I was calling you."

"I heard the commotion and came to investigate for myself," offered Father Roque who was standing nearby. "It couldn't have been more than ten minutes after the dancing and drumming had stopped. Then I started looking for you, another five, ten minutes, no longer."

Carter had been scanning the area and now squatted next to Cordero, waving the beam of her flashlight around the body and the bag. "The scene has been completed corrupted. Footprints, cigarette butts, cigar stubs—they could belong to anybody," she said.

Cordero nodded. "Estefana," he said. "You have your cell?"

"Yes *maun*."

"Give it to me, please," Cordero took the cell and photographed the body from various angles.

The small crowd was getting restless—starting to move about and talking to each other—and the children among them were complaining that they were tired and wanted to go home. "Ask those standing here if they saw or heard anything," Cordero told Estefana. "And get their names in case we want to talk to them again. Leave the headman to me. I'll talk to him in a moment."

He began to examine the body more closely. Sabu Bada's knuckles showed no signs of a fight, his face was unmarked and his shirt had not been ripped or torn apart from where the sword had cut through it. The index fingers and thumbs of his hands were directly behind the small guard at the blade end of the hilt. If Sabu Bada had been stabbed and grabbed reflexively at the weapon as he was dying, his hands could have ended up in that position but more likely the index fingers and thumbs would be at the other end of the hilt, closest to the pommel and tassle, in an instinctive attempt to pull the sword out of his body.

Cordero took several photographs of the hands. "Help me unclench his grip," he said to Carter and placed Estefana's cell next to him on the ground. "I'm interested in something," he added.

Carefully they prised Sabu Bada's hands off the hilt. "See that?" Cordero said. "There's very little blood on the palms of his hands," and he picked up the cell and took more photographs without explaining the significance of the find.

"Prints?" Carter asked.

"Even if there are prints on the sword there'd be no way to test for them unless we were in Dili," Cordero answered. "And there'd be no records to compare them against anyhow."

"Bring the lamp closer," Carter said. She leaned in close to the dead man's head and neck. "See that?" she said pointing to a slight nick near the man's Adam's apple. She examined the face up toward the left eye. "And look here," she said and pointed. Across the eyebrow, eyelid, and onto the eyeball was a barely visible streak of grey powder. "That's fallen across the eye post-mortem or a blink would have smudged the line on the eyeball."

Cordero photographed the eye and the side of Sabu Bada's face and placed the cell back down on the ground beside him. He reached into his pocket for a penknife. "Do you have a tissue?" he asked her.

"No," Carter replied.

"I thought American women always carried tissues," Cordero said.

"Not this one. I have a bandana."

"Is it white?" asked Cordero as he removed a shaving of the powder with the tip of his knife.

"It has white patches in the design."

"That'll do," he said taking it from her and wiping the tip of the knife on one of the white patches. He folded the bandana carefully and put it in his pocket. Then he closed the eyes of Sabu Bada, regathered Estefana's cell, and stood. "I don't think we'll find anything more and they'll want to move the body quickly," he said gesturing to the people encircling the scene. Carter stood as well but said nothing. "Now, where's our friend the headman?" Cordero asked.

• • •

Eusebio Leite was brooding about Cordero taking charge. After all, Eusebio was the headman of Tepia and Cordero a stranger. The fact that Cordero was also a police investigator made no difference. Eusebio had taken a cigarette from his pants' pocket when Cordero approached and he took his time to light it and take his first drag before acknowledging Cordero.

"Do you know anything about what happened here?" Cordero asked.

"No. Why should I?"

"How long have you been here?"

"Not long. I came because people were yelling and screaming," said Eusebio.

Cordero studied the headman. "Tell me about Sabu Bada," he said.

"He was the *lia-nain*," Eusebio answered.

"I know that," replied Cordero. "Tell me what I don't know."

Eusebio took another drag on his cigarette. "Like?"

"Where did he live? Who did he live with?"

"He lived alone," said Eusebio, looking across at the body. "His wife died five or six years ago and his three boys had all moved to Dili and have never come back." Cordero noticed people had started drifting away and he looked over at Estefana. She was speaking to the last stragglers. Carter was carefully examining the dead man's bag of ceremonial attire. "He lives—he lived," Eusebio corrected, "out toward the end of this ridge."

"He would have walked this way home?" Cordero asked.

"Yes. Can't you see the track?" Eusebio said and indicated it with his cigarette.

"Did he always walk?" Cordero asked ignoring the slight. "Doesn't he own a motorcycle or a pony?"

"He has—had—a motorcycle but he often walked and when he was doing anything that involved the *uma lulik* he liked to keep it authentic. Always on foot."

"And people would have known this?"

Eusebio turned up the hand that held the cigarette as if to say, 'Who knows?'

"Did Sabu Bada have any enemies?"

"No," Eusebio answered. He took a long drag on his cigarette and tossed the butt into the brush behind him.

"Know anyone who didn't like him?"

"He was well respected," Eusebio said growing tired of the questioning.

"That's not what I asked," Cordero said.

"I don't know anyone who didn't like Sabu," said Eusebio.

"Did you speak with him tonight?"

"No. He was focused on the *tebedia*."

"But you saw enough of him," Cordero said. "Was there anything unusual in his manner?"

Eusebio looked uncertainly at Cordero. "What do you mean?"

"Did he seem agitated, worried, angry about anything?"

"Not that I noticed, no," the headman said.

"And you didn't see or hear anything, anyone, who might have been involved in his death?" Cordero asked.

"I told you—no."

"The body will have to be—" Cordero began.

"I will take care of the body," insisted the headman. He noticed the reservation in Cordero's eyes. "I will have men carry him into the *uma lulik*. I will post a guard to stay with the body all night. And I will call a meeting of the elders first thing tomorrow morning. We will arrange a coffin. Because he's wife is dead, and I don't know how to contact his sons, we will organise people for the *lutu*," he said referring to the customary night of mourning in which the man's good deeds would be recited to release his spirit on its journey to the next world.

Cordero couldn't think of anything else to do with the body of the *lia-nain* in a village without a morgue, hospital or secure lockup and he nodded his agreement. "If Sabu Bada lived alone I'm going to want someone to come with me tomorrow and stay and keep watch on the house," he added. "For a day or two."

"You think this is a village of thieves and looters?" Eusebio asked, his impatience showing.

"No. But I don't want things disturbed until we've had a chance to find out what happened," Cordero replied. "It's a precaution, that's all."

The headman rubbed the back of his neck. "My son Ageo can go. He doesn't like school anyway."

That could be a little too convenient, Cordero thought. "No. I want someone older," he said. "What about one of those teenagers over there?" and he pointed to a group Estefana was talking to, not giving Eusebio time to think about it.

The headman grunted. "I'll see what I can do," he said.

"Tell one of them to wait outside the church tomorrow morning," Cordero instructed him. "Early but not too early— about nine if he can read the time on his cell." He turned to rejoin Carter. "I may need to talk to you again," he said as he left.

Father Roque walked over to Carter as well, and then Estefana joined them.

"I talked to over a dozen people, *maun*," Estefana reported. "They all have theories but nobody actually saw anything."

"Among these people theories, suspicions, conspiracies are common but facts are often hard to come by," Father Roque said.

Cordero handed the cell back to Estefana and collected the lamp. "We've done all we can for now," he said. "Father I'd like to talk to you about this Sabu Bada. I'd also like information about Eusebio and the elders. Would you care to join us for a well-earned nightcap?"

• • •

"Sabu was a fairly commanding figure in Tepia," Father Roque was saying as Cordero handed him a gin and tonic. "I wasn't all that close to him personally—he wasn't a practising Catholic and we were competitors in a sense. This is a very traditional village. Quite a few elders go by their traditional names during ceremonies rather than what they call their 'Portuguese church names'. But Sabu had no other name as far as I know." The priest paused. "He was tough and rigid but decent enough in his own way and people took a lot of notice of him."

"Decent how?" asked Cordero as he passed a glass to Carter and another to Estefana and sat back down on his bed.

"Well for a start he supplied the nuns with coffee free of charge," the priest said and sipped his drink. He was sitting on a chair they'd brought for him while Carter and Estefana had resumed their spots on the floor against the wall. "I suspect that may have been a case of keeping your enemies close but he was never openly hostile toward them—or toward me. And of course he built the new *uma lulik* virtually out of his own resources."

"I was wondering how it was built so quickly," Cordero said. He turned to Carter. "Remember me telling you the old *uma lulik* burned down about a year ago? Many villages are so poor they're still waiting to have their *uma lulik* rebuilt after the Indonesians burned them down ten, fifteen years ago." He turned again to Father Roque. "How did he manage that?"

"From his coffee crop I imagine," the priest said. "I didn't ask questions. The *uma lulik* wasn't my concern. But he wasn't what we call *espalhafatoso* in Portuguese." He clicked his fingers once, twice. "What's the word in English for showing off your wealth?"

"Ostentatious? Flashy?" offered Carter.

"Flashy. I think that's the word," the priest agreed. "Anyhow he wasn't like that at all."

"What caused the old *uma lulik* to burn down?"

"No one knows," Father Roque said. "It just went up in flames one night. No reason has ever been found although the talk around the village was of sorcery and witches. Of course."

"You don't know of anyone who would want Sabu Bada dead?" asked Cordero.

"Certainly not," said Father Roque. He finished his drink. The night sky was a black canvass covered with the diamond flicker of stars. A group of Timorese horseshoe bats flew west back to their roost in caves carved out of rock by Japanese soldiers during the Second World War. The bats were now endangered and the sighting of this small colony was rare. It was late and if any villagers had seen the bats they would connect their appearance to Sabu's death and consider the two things linked.

"What can you tell me about the headman, Eusebio?" Cordero asked.

"Bisoi—that's his traditional name, but only the very old people would call him by that. Capable enough," said Father Roque considering the question. "Likeable too, I'd say, once you get to know him."

"Did he get on well with Sabu?" asked Cordero. "I mean they were both competitors in a sense too I imagine—one an elected headman and the other an hereditary *lia-nain* who exercised a lot of influence in the village."

"It's true they could have clashed but I am not aware they did," said the priest. "The headman has little to do in a small village like this one. In any event they both exercised their authority in conjunction with the other elders."

"And none of them had issues with Sabu?"

"None I ever heard about."

Carter finished her gin. Estefana was struggling to drink the last of hers and stifled a yawn.

"I'll have a talk to the elders tomorrow morning," Cordero said. "Then go out and have a look around Sabu Bada's place. While I'm doing that, Estefana, could you talk to people who stayed overnight for the *tebedai* and are heading back home? It's a long shot that they'll tell us anything useful but we can try. Start early and talk to people on the road heading out—did they see anything, do they know anything? If you get a chance, check the tracks leading out of the village to the north and west." He turned to Carter. "As you suggested earlier she'll do better on her own. After the elders, I'll come back for you and you can come with me to Sabu's place."

"Let's not forget I have an investigation to conduct as well," Carter said standing and stretching. "If this guy's place is in the direction of the area along the river I want to look at, put that on the itinerary as well."

12

Early next morning the sky was the color of sapphire and the air already warm and close when Cordero left the nuns' house and walked back to the *uma lulik*. Nobody else in the house had yet appeared but he was eager to check on the body of Sabu Bada and he knew the elders would have gathered already to make arrangements for the man's burial. As he entered the clearing where the *tebedai* had been held the night before, four men blocked his path. Two slapped machetes against their legs. None looked friendly.

"Where are you going, *maun*?" a heavy-set one who looked to be the oldest asked.

"I'm a police investigator," Cordero said, "and I want to speak to the elders."

"They're in a meeting," the man said holding Cordero's stare. "No one disturbs them. This is a sacred thing. It's none of your business."

Cordero noticed that two of the men had slipped behind him. He was encircled And didn't like his options.

"How long is this meeting?" he asked.

"As long as it takes," the man replied.

"That doesn't help much," Cordero said, keeping his tone neutral.

"The *lutu* will begin at sunset," the man said. "The elders may take a break before then."

Cordero figured that to assert his authority could at best only end up undermining it completely. "Okay. I'll come back then," he said and forced the two men behind him to stand aside as he strode out of the clearing.

As he crossed the road to the nuns' house, his cell rang. It was Brooks.

"You're up early, Howard," he said by way of greeting.

"Always am, Tino," Brooks replied. "Any progress?"

"Not a lot. And now another body has turned up."

"Is that so?" said Brooks. "Interesting. I do hope you're not sending it my way, dear boy. I have rather enough on my plate as it is. Which is why I am ringing. I've been able to do a bit of testing. With the equipment at the hospital here. Bones and tissue samples. Forensic science in Timor is only fifty years behind the times. All we lack is proper fingerprint analysis, carbon dating and DNA testing." He took a breath. "Oh, and rubber gloves—the ones we have are made in China and keep splitting apart at the tips when you pull them on."

Cordero noticed a boy sitting on the steps of the church, smoking a cigarette. As he waited for Brooks to get to the point, he walked up and stood in front of the boy. The boy ignored him and puffed away. Brooks stopped complaining. "Uh-huh," Cordero said into his cell. "Right….Uh-huh. Yep….Okay Howard. I don't see how that helps at the moment but I'll factor it in. Thanks." He pocketed his cell and stared down at the boy through the cigarette smoke. "I'm Vincintino Cordero, the police investigator," he said. "Did the headman send you?"

"Yeah," the boy grumbled.

"You shouldn't smoke on the steps of the church."

The boy looked up for the first time, took a drag on the cigarette. "Eusebio said you'd pay me," he said.

Cordero took the cigarette from the boy's mouth. He ground it with his shoe until the tobacco, paper and soil were indistinguishable. "You'll come with me to the house of Sabu Bada after I've put my things together," he said.

"Who?" asked the boy.

"Sabu Bada— the *lia-nain*."

"Oh, him. Eusebio mentioned him."

"I see you have no provisions. I'll get them for you. I want you to stay there until I send word for you to come back. Two, maybe three days and possibly nights. You're to touch nothing of Sabu's, you understand? Nothing. And you're to let no-one else touch anything. If anyone comes while you are there, you're to report that to me. You have a cell?" the boy nodded. "I'll give you my number. And I'll pay you five dollars if you do as I say."

"Only five dollars?" the boy complained and looked down in the dirt at what was left of his cigarette.

"Where else around here are you going to make five dollars for three days work?" Cordero asked. "Wait here until I get back."

Cordero found Carter and Estefana picking at their breakfast. Carter was dressed in jeans and a pale red shirt; Estefana was in her police uniform.

"Rice porridge again, I'm afraid," said Carter by way of greeting. "I think the nuns might be trying to send us a message."

"I'll settle for coffee," Cordero said.

"Where have you been?" Carter asked.

"I went to talk to the elders at the *uma lulik* but they were having a meeting and I thought it best not to disturb them," he lied. "I'll talk to them later today." He filled his cup with coffee. It was lukewarm and he drank it quickly. "Estefana—" he began.

"I was about to leave to catch people heading out of the village, *maun*," she said and scooped up the last of the porridge.

"Good," he said and poured himself the dregs of coffee from the pot. "Are you ready to leave?" he asked Carter.

"Teeth, hair, then I'll get the map, water and whatever leftovers I can find for us to eat," she said. "Five minutes."

"We're taking a boy out to keep watch on Sabu's hut," Cordero informed her as she rose from the table. "He's waiting outside the church. I need to throw a few supplies together for him from the stuff we brought with us—cans of tuna, two-minute noodles." He finished the coffee. "I'll meet you at the SUV."

They took a different track to the place where Sabu Bada had lived from the one on which he had been killed: it was longer, but according to Father Roque, more suitable for vehicles. Carter tried to practice her Tetun on the boy.

"Ita nia naran sa?" she said, asking him his name.

"Halibo," the boy answered.

"Tinan hira?"

"Sanulu resin neen," came the reply.

"Let me see now—"

"He said he's sixteen," Cordero chimed in.

"Don't do that," she scolded him. "I'm trying to practice." But she couldn't think of how to frame another question and soon the boy went back to sulking in the back seat. Carter consulted her map while Cordero tried to keep the SUV steady on the ruttered track. It jolted this way and that, at times violently. Several times Carter and Cordero bumped heavily against each other. Her shirt offered a thin barrier to her body. "Perhaps you should tighten your seatbelt," Cordero felt he had to suggest. "It gets rough out here." After a moment their colliding together stopped. She'd taken his advice—and he felt strangely regretful.

"Where we end up seems to border the top of this *lulik* area," Carter said, the map crumpled on her lap. Cordero said nothing. "After we check out this guy's place what say we take a look along the river?"

"Fine by me," said Cordero, shifting gears again.

• • •

Estefana had been talking to people on the road out of Tepia for over an hour. At first there had been a steady stream returning to their subsistence gardens and she wasn't able to catch them all as they passed by her. But the stream had become a trickle. Everyone she spoke to had heard of the death of the *lia-nain* and thought it shocking, but nobody had any idea who might have done it or why. Now the blue had been burned out of the sky leaving only a hot, dazzling glare. Her police shirt clung to her skin with sweat. Off on the side of the road, unshaded but uncomplaining, sat her disfigured companion like a faithful old dog with nowhere else to go.

"Would you like water, *mana*?" asked Tomas when Estefana finished questioning another couple. "I know where to get it."

Estefana checked her water bottle. It was empty and she was thirsty.

"That would be nice, Tomas. Get water for both of us?"

His expression brightened, he jumped up, and hobbled away, moving like a crab under the hump on his back and with the cardboard box tucked securely under his arm. About ten minutes and the fruitless questioning of two more farmers later, Tomas returned with the water which he held in a small lidless cooking pot.

"Here *mana*," he said thrusting the pot forward. "You first."

Estefana examined the water. There were flecks of dust floating in it. Even so, her thirst made her less choosy than she might otherwise have been. She took a sip, considered, and drank a mouthful before handing the pot back to Tomas for him to drink as well.

"Thank you, Tomas," she said, wiping her mouth. "Where did you get the water—and the pot this fast?"

Tomas didn't drink. "The pot is mine, *mana*. *Amu*," he said referring to Father Roque, "let's me put things behind his house where he keeps his motorcycle. There is a tank for water there as well. It comes off the roof of his house, you see, *mana*." He smiled broadly. "He lets me sleep there as well." The boy put his cardboard box on the ground, flopped down next to it, and placed the pot of water between his legs.

The road was clear except for an old woman walking away from the village with a bag of rice balanced on her head and two motorcycles heading down in the opposite direction.

"Do you not have a home, Tomas?" Estefana asked sitting down beside him on the ground.

The smile left the boy's face. He looked embarrassed. "No *mana*."

"Where is your family?" Estefana pressed him.

"My mother died when I was born, *mana*." The expression turned quickly from sadness to anger. "And my father left when I was older."

"Left? Do you mean he died too?"

"No *mana*. He went away from Tepia," Tomas said. The boy had sad brown eyes like those of a cow or a buffalo but there was accusation in them now. "And he left me here." He turned away from Estefana. "He used to beat me and say I was cursed."

"That's terrible, Tomas," Estefana said. "And you are not cursed. You should never think that." She noticed the hump rise as the boy took a deep breath. "You have no sisters, brothers—"

"No *mana*," Tomas said, his face turned away from Estefana.

"Aunties, uncles, grandparents?"

"No *mana*." He turned back to look up into her face. "They've all gone. Everybody leaves."

"Then how do you live?"

"Like I said, *amu* lets me sleep next to his motorcycle. He says I guard it for him," he seemed to fill with pride at the notion that he had an important job to do. "He's my friend." Tomas laughed a little then stopped. "At times the nuns give me food and other times people let me eat the scraps they put out. I sleep in the forest too. It's not hard." He seemed to notice the pot between his legs for the first time. "Would you like water, *mana*?" he asked pointing.

"No thank you Tomas. You have a drink. You must be thirsty too."

Tomas ignored the suggestion, picked up his cardboard box and held it out. "Would you like to see my special things now, *mana*?" he asked hopefully.

Estefana checked her watch. It might still be possible to question people on the track north out of the village.

"I can't just now, Tomas," she said and he cast his eyes to the ground. "I have a lot of police work to do, sorry." She thought she heard him sniffle. "But tomorrow is Sunday. I will have time in the morning. How about I come to the place where Father Roque keeps his motorcycle and we can sit down and look at your special things then?"

"*Amu's* motorcyle is not there now, *mana*. It is being fixed."

"But you'll be there Tomas," said Estefana. "It's settled. Tomorrow morning it is."

•••

The ridge started to flatten out as they approached the property of Sabu Bada and they pulled up at a compound on a cleared space a full half acre or more in size. At one end was the hut where Sabu had lived. It was a traditional *uma* made of wood, bamboo and thatch on a foundation of rocks built around two large poles that extended through to the roof. On one side of the hut a betel vine crept up the wall. Off to the left were two outbuildings of bamboo slats with tin roofs—the tin being a practical concession to modernity of sorts. On the right, unsheltered from the sun, were half a dozen large tables covered in a mesh fabric. Cordero turned the vehicle off and told Halibo to stay put while he and Carter took a look around. Halibo seemed disinterested and said nothing. A strong odour of raw coffee seeped into the SUV on a breeze that raised dust from the bare dirt of the clearing.

Carter was the first to exit the vehicle and she walked slowly toward the hut, hands tucked fast in the back pockets of her jeans. To the side of the hut was a tomb covered in red and blue tiles with no Catholic markings but a pole with totems of feathers and bones at its head. "I'd say there lies Mrs. Sabu," Cordero said as he caught up with Carter and they entered the hut together. There had been no lock on the door. The inside was divided into two separate spaces by the large poles. In one space, hanging from what would have been regarded as the female pole—in recognition of Sabu's late wife—were woven bags. Carter peered in to one of the bags, wrinkled her nose and moved on. Cordero looked too, recoiled, and looked again. "They look to me like the dried placentas of the occupants," he said, "hung here to protect them from bad spirits. A customary practice." Little light penetrated either space but where it did dust drifted through the rays. Both spaces were sparsely furnished: a cheap table surrounded by four green plastic chairs in one, a bed not much bigger than a single in another, together with a cabinet, a collection of metal boxes, and little more. Clothes were draped from a line that had been strung opposite the bed and there was a kerosene lamp on a small stand and another next to the back wall. Most of the huts in Tepia lacked electricity and Sabu Bada's was no exception. In fact, he seemed to have lived a life little changed from that of his forebears a century earlier.

The metal boxes contained nothing of interest: tools, old sandals, a few fraying ceremonial paraphernalia. Similarly the cabinet offered little that shed light on the man's personality, interests, or connections. There was an old, framed sepia photograph on the wall of a proud and confident man in traditional dress—Sabu's father, the previous *lia-nain*, Cordero assumed—and another of three small boys—his sons? There were no documents, letters or papers because he couldn't read, only a smattering of small coins on the top of the cabinet, and a pipe and tobacco pouch beside the bed which represented the only indulgence Sabu Bada seemed to have allowed himself.

Outside in the yard, chickens had heard the SUV pull up and were clucking anxiously around in the expectation of food. Cordero and Carter ignored them and walked on to the tables covered in mesh. "Drying tables," he said as they passed by them. "For the coffee beans after the cherries have been pulped and the beans fermented." They continued over to the first out-building. It contained a motorcycle inside another unlocked door—the key in the ignition—and further back, machetes, pruning knives, four hand-driven metal pulping machines, stacks of large plastic buckets that would have been used to wash the coffee cherries after they had been picked, and various lengths of hose. "Did you notice the fans of the windmill above the tree line as we topped the ridge on the way in?" Cordero asked, picking up one of the hoses. "I'd say he pumped water up from the river and stored it in a tank. It's important to use clean water, and lots of it, when treating the coffee."

"You seem to know a lot about coffee," Carter said.

"Well I've processed a little coffee in my time," he responded and put the hose back with the others. "And I like to drink it." They headed back into the yard. Carter stopped, crouched and picked up a soiled baseball cap. It was a child's cap with a Bart Simpson image on the front. She handed it to Cordero who twirled it around absently as he walked on.

The second outbuilding was a shed used to store the coffee beans while their drying was completed. Large burlap bags were stored in one corner and wooden pallets that would ensure airflow under them were slanted against the walls. "The only thing of interest here is how much equipment he had," Cordero said. "After all, he was one man living here on his own." He rubbed a hand through his hair. "Let's have a look beyond the clearing."

They noticed a small vegetable garden at the back of the hut— the usual maize, sweet potato, tomatoes and onions—and nearby a lean-to that served as a kitchen. "Long way to come from the house for your supper," Carter quipped.

"Wood fires can affect the taste of the coffee," Cordero said. "I guess he wasn't taking any chances. You might have noticed there were no cigarette butts in the clearing either. Even cigarette smoke can affect the coffee." He stared down the steep slope toward the river. Below were rows and rows of coffee trees, their glossy green leaves shining in the sun. "Phew," he said and whistled. "Look at all those coffee trees. He must've had help."

They made their way down the ridge for a sixty yards or more. The coffee trees had all been pruned to encourage the lateral growth of the branches for easier picking. Most of the trees they could see were only six feet high, and were covered in plump green cherries. Here and there grew tall mahogany and eucalypt trees, and toward the river itself, oriental plane trees. A pair of bright green Iris Lorikeets swooped above their heads and off into the foliage, expertly dodging the branches as they went. Cordero couldn't help being excited by the sight of them. "Wow, look at that," he said to no one in particular. "Aren't they beautiful!" Carter looked off after the birds and, a little surprised, back at him. She turned away quickly when he caught her eye. He turned quickly and focused again on the task at hand. "Do you have that map on you?" he asked. Carter took it from her back pocket and they held it out between them. Cordero looked back up the ridge toward the compound and down to the river. Then he let his end of the map go and stared for a long time in the direction from which they had come. Again he looked back up the ridge and down.

"What?" asked Carter.

"I'd say we're on the *lulik* ground here," he said and picked up his end of the map again. "Look at the map. Sabu's hut is about here," he said placing a finger on the spot, "and the *lulik* land boundary runs along here." Again he looked this way and that. "And I say most of Sabu's coffee crop is growing on land that no-one, least of all a *lia-nain*, is meant to even walk on."

13

They'd gone back to the SUV for water bottles and snacks in case they were gone a long while and grew hungry. Cordero began to recite his cell number to Halibo but the boy stopped him. "No service, *maun*," he said. "What am I supposed to do out here?"

Cordero could see the point. "Okay, if anyone comes, pretend you have service and tell them you are ringing the police investigator. Find out who they are, or get a good description and give me the details when I arrange for you to come back to Tepia."

"I don't mean that, *maun*," Halibo said. "I mean what am I supposed to *do* out here? I can't call anyone. I can't text. I can't—"

"You can do what I've told you to do and what you're being paid to do—keep an eye on the place and don't touch anything," said Cordero. "Oh, and grab one of those hens."

"What?"

"You heard me. Grab one of those hens and bring it here."

Halibo dawdled over toward the chickens. "Hurry up!" Cordero shouted after him. The chickens thought they were to be fed and gathered around Halibo's legs. He reached down to grab one but it squawked and kicked and eluded his grip. He reached out for another, grabbed hold of it by one wing, and cradled it in his arms as he headed back to Cordero and handed it over.

Cordero wrung the chicken's neck and motioned to Carter, who was startled by what he had done, to head with him back down the slope toward the river. The chicken's carcass he carried by the legs. When they crossed into what they assumed was *lulik* land Cordero stopped. He hesitated a moment, took the penknife

105

from his pocket, roughly cut open the chicken's belly, and drained the blood in a rough circle over the ground. "Can never be too careful," he said. He pocketed the knife, placed the carcass in the center of the blood and moved on before she could respond. They followed a rough track of sorts that inclined sharply through the coffee trees but after a hundred yards they were on the riverbank and the land flattened out, covered by stands of black bamboo and creeper vines thinning out to spindly causarina trees, shrubs, and grasses. Carter took out her map to get her bearings. The main channel of the river was twenty yards wide at this point and edged either side by another fifteen yards of dry sand and gravel. The water was fast-flowing, yellowish-grey in color and she guessed about four or five feet at its deepest point. They could see scouring where soil, vegetation, and rocks had been removed. New growth covered parts of the disturbed area but had yet to take firm hold suggesting the damage had occurred relatively recently. Nothing unusual along a river but encouraging, nonetheless.

Carter took a long drink from her water bottle and studied the map again. The stream that the headman had said was the boundary beyond which everyone was forbidden to go appeared to be down river just out of sight toward Tepia. Cordero looked at the map. "Let's head toward this bend in the river here," he said, a finger tapping at the map. "Looks like a possible area for major erosion in a big flow." He handed the map back to Carter and they set off through the brush again, avoiding prickly stalks and stems as best they could and lifting their legs high to clear the more stubborn undergrowth and avoid tripping on the rocks underneath. They made slow progress and were tiring quickly in the bright sunshine although they were only beginning to search the area that most interested Carter.

"You don't seem too concerned about being on *lulik* land," Carter said to get her mind off the exertion.

"Well I'm not a traditional," he said. "And even traditional Timorese can traverse *lulik* areas if the situation warrants it. And this warrants it. But as I said, you can never be too careful. You saw the chicken. It's customary to make an offering when you enter *lulik* land. It might make up for us not having permission to be here."

Carter didn't comment. They pushed on a little further, Cordero following close behind her. "What about you?" he asked.

"Customs and traditions you mean?" Carter said.

"Uh-huh."

"Well you know most of my work back home is among Navajo, Hopis and Apaches," she said without turning. "You become sensitive to beliefs a lot different to your own after a while." She was puffing and stopped, hands on knees as she bent for breath. "Often had to ignore superstitions, interrupt religious ceremonies and break taboos in the course of investigations." She straightened and pushed on again. "I've done all three by mistake as well," she added. "It's just part of the job."

"And that never bothered you?"

"I'm a police officer, Cordero," she said as though that was sufficient explanation.

They came to an area of riverside with less brush to negotiate and they could walk with more ease. But the heat and humidity were taking their toll. Carter was sweating heavily. She drained her water bottle and walked out to the main flow of the river to refill it. The water was cool and fresh and she splashed a little on her face, under the hair at the back of her neck, and across the top of her breasts.

They continued along the riverbank feeling their energy drain away with every step. Both were a lather of sweat, their clothes soaked through. Carter stopped. "Shit it's hot," she said and undid all the buttons on her shirt to let more air in, exposing a brief quarter-cup bra above a flat-toned stomach.

"That bend's just up ahead," Cordero said doing his best not to stare. "Let's follow it around and take a break on the other side."

But as they rounded the bend, they noticed tree roots exposed by massive soil destabilisation along the bank. Up ahead was a rock overhang jutting out above the river and underneath it, the stoney outline of what might once have been a promontory. The closer they drew near, the more apparent it became.

"Looks like a cave," said Carter.

"Looks more like a giant skull without a jaw," Cordero offered. "The bottom seems to have been all but washed away."

As they closed in on the overhang they began to examine the area carefully. "If there had been a kind of cave here," Carter said, stopping and looking around under the rock, "it would have been quite a large, enclosed space, perhaps ten yards by eight that were covered by this rock and another four by five of relatively flat exposed promontory beyond that." Cordero nodded his agreement and Carter continued to inspect the area. What soil remained was a mixture of clay and sand, easy enough to dig into and easy enough to wash away in a big storm. She looked up at the rock above her head. "The rock seems to have been blackened—by fire I think, but I can't reach it," she said. There were no other markings on the overhang and only a few large rocks scattered beneath it but well-spaced.

"You reckon this could have been a ceremonial site?" she asked.

"Possible," answered Cordero.

A few weeds and native grasses had begun to colonize the area but nothing to suggest they had been growing there very long. The place drew Carter in. Something had happened here, she knew it, something that wreaked of menace.

Without saying anything Cordero started walking back up the slope, looking for a stick, a fallen branch, anything that might help him dig beneath the overhang. He slipped repeatedly on the incline and the third time slid back down the slope. He swore, regained his footing, brushed off his trousers and climbed a little higher until he came across a fallen causarina tree. He broke off a piece four foot long and three inches thick. He cleaned off the dead needles, broke off the straggly offshoots and tested its strength.

"Let's have a poke around with this," he said returning to where Carter stood beneath the overhang.

He began to dig and scrap as best he could in a systematic pattern. Carter took the water bottle from her bag and took another drink, feeling quite giddy. She half fell, half sat on the ground and Cordero dropped his digging stick just in time to catch her by her arm and waist. "You okay? Sit for a while and eat something," he said. "I'll keep digging around."

The closer to the river the more soil had been washed away. If the skeletons that had been found in Dili did come from this spot, he thought it unlikely any evidence would remain in this particular section. But he knew he'd have to be thorough to satisfy Carter who was watching him closely and he slowly worked back from the outside edge of what he imagined as the cave to the wall of the overhang.

Part of the ground he was scraping back revealed the same black coating she had noticed on the roof of the overhang. He knelt to examine it better, rubbed a trace between his fingers and smelt the result. He held out his hand for Carter. "Charcoal," he said. "No doubt about it. But what would cause a fire around here?"

"Could have been caused by just about anyone doing just about anything," said Carter. "Or it might have had a natural cause." Cordero went back to his scraping, and prodding without comment.

After twenty minutes he was about to give up when he uncovered what looked like a bone on the edge of the overhang in its shadow. "Well what do we have here?" he muttered. He dropped the stick and took his penknife from his pocket. He scraped carefully around the object until he had it uncovered. It was a femur. He showed Carter, who examined the bone, rose and stood over him while he took the stick and dug again. He'd soon uncovered a tibia, a patella, a pelvis, vertebrae, mandible—everything but a skull.

Carter sat back on her haunches and blew out a deep breath. "Well what do you know?" she said.

• • •

When they returned to Tepia, Estefana had gone to change out of her uniform and wash in the rudimentary facilities in the nuns' house. The nuns themselves were busy preparing dinner. Carter stepped out of the SUV and stretched: Cordero did likewise. "I think I'll slip over to the *uma lulik* and talk to the elders," he said. "Let's review what we know over dinner." Carter nodded and headed inside.

As he reached the clearing, he saw a small group had gathered for the official mourning that would send Sabu Bada to the spirit world. They were mostly old women, but they had dragged reluctant children along to sit with them while they recounted Sabu's good deeds in this life. The women slowly climbed the steps into the *uma lulik* where the body lay. The four men who had confronted him earlier that morning were even now lurking around the building to ensure nothing disturbed what was going on inside. Cordero noticed two men he took to be elders, squatting on their heels off to the side, smoking under an areca palm. As he approached them the sun was setting, and the heat of the day was abating as a slight breeze rippled the palm fonds.

"What is your name, *senyor*?" Cordero asked the first of the pair after he had identified himself and edged him aside from the other man.

"Balbo Fuentes."

"Were you at the *tebedai*?"

"Of course. I am an elder in this village," Balbo replied in a hoarse whisper. He took a drag on his cigarette and let the smoke drift from his nostrils.

"Did you see or hear anything unusual at the *tebedai*?"

"No," he said staring across the clearing.

"Did you see or hear anything connected with Sabu or his death?"

"No," Balbo said and coughed a phlegmy cough.

"How long had you known Sabu?"

"Maybe since the days the foreigners were here," Balbo said and stomped his cigarette into the ground.

"The Portuguese or the Indonesians?" Cordero asked.

"No. The Japoneza," he said, referring to World War II.

Close enough to seventy years, Cordero figured. "How long had he been the *lia-nain* of Tepia?"

"Maybe since the time of the other foreigners," Balbo said and coughed again.

"Which other foreigners? The Portuguese who came back after the Japanese had left or the Indonesians?" Cordero asked.

"The *bapa*," replied Balbo meaning the last of these—the Indonesians. He patted his pockets, found his cigarettes, took another from its pack, cupped his hands and lit it.

"How did he become the *lia-nain*?"

Balbo inhaled deeply and coughed smoke. "His father was the *lia-nain* before him." Balbo cleared his throat, spat. "He died."

"Did Sabu have any enemies?"

"Everyone has enemies," Balbo said and looked Cordero directly in the eyes for the first time. Cordero noticed the cataract almost covering Balbo's own left eye. "Maybe even you."

"Anyone want to see him dead?"

Balbo looked off into the distance. "No."

"Had he argued with anyone lately?"

"No."

"Did you speak to him the night he was killed?"

"No."

Balbo Fuentes was a man of few words and he uttered them cautiously. He was clearly saying nothing more than he needed to get this outsider off his back. Cordero was getting nowhere and so he changed his line of questioning.

"Sabu grew coffee," Cordero said but it was a question disguised as a statement.

"Everyone grows coffee in Tepia," Balbo replied. He flicked the ash from his cigarette and took another drag.

"But he grew a lot of coffee."

"Maybe his land is richer for growing coffee."

"And maybe he had more land than others," Cordero said. "Or access to more."

Balbo shrugged.

"You can tell me nothing about how he died or who wanted him dead?"

"Nothing."

"Then what can you tell me about the *lulik* land below Sabu's hut?"

Balbo stared at Cordero again and the eye without the cataract fixed him in a strange, defiant stare. A stream of smoke rose crookedly from the cigarette in his hand as it trembled slightly. "Only that it is *lulik* and people are forbidden to go there."

Cordero reckoned the second elder—Juno da Silva—to be much the same age as Balbo. His expression was sterner, his eyes even more guarded. Cordero asked the same questions only to get the same replies but in a more hostile tone. "We will deal with this in our own way," Juno said as he stood to end the interrogation.

"I represent the law around here," Cordero said.

"Your law maybe. Not ours," Juno replied and walked off with Balbo toward the *uma lulik*.

Cordero pushed his hands into his pockets and kicked at the dirt, lost in thought.

"I said you have no business here," he heard a gruff voice saying. He looked up to see two of the men who were guarding the *uma lulik* and it was the older one who had warned him off earlier addressing him.

"I was just—" began Cordero but then he noticed Carter coming toward him and didn't finish the sentence. He stiffened himself. "I'm a police investigator—" he said changing tact in a more determined voice.

"You said that before and I said you're not welcome here," the man growled back. "Leave!"

"I'll go when I please," said Cordero.

"Here you don't," the man said growing in anger. Carter had joined them and sensed the tension although she couldn't understand what was being said. She looked from Cordero to the other two men and her attention stayed with them.

"Go! Now! And take this *kadela* with you!" the man yelled, referring to Carter as a bitch.

"What did you say?" Cordero asked, getting closer and sizing up the man.

"I said you're not welcome here and neither is this *malae feto-*

luron!" the man said upping the ante by calling Carter a foreign whore.

"It's a good thing my friend doesn't speak Tetun but you'll apologize to her anyhow," said Cordero who, from the corner of his eye, noticed the second man toss his cigarette to the ground, crush it with his foot, and edge around behind him as he did. The older man leered at Cordero but said nothing.

"Now!" demanded Cordero.

The man threw a roundhouse punch that Cordero easily slipped and he countered with a hard right to the body which forced air out of the man's lungs like a ruptured balloon. He folded in pain. From his waistband the second man drew a pruning knife and he raised it to slash Cordero from the side but Carter was too fast. She pivoted on her left foot and kicked the man behind his knees with her right. He collapsed onto his haunches and let out a yelp. She straddled him, grabbed the hand that held the pruner and jerked back the wrist until it gave way and the knife dropped. She kept the man in a wristlock while Cordero helped his companion stand upright.

"Well…where's the apology?" Cordero asked.

The man looked from Cordero to Carter and held a hand against his ribcage. "*Deskulpa senyora,*" he said and limped off, the other man following minus his pruning knife which Carter picked up.

"What was that about?" asked Carter, handing Cordero the knife when the two men had gone.

"Respect," said Cordero.

"You just going to let them go?" she asked.

"They got the worst of it." He looked at Carter. "Good thing you were here though," he said. "Thanks. But what brought you?"

She straightened her clothes and turned to walk away. "The nuns prepared an early dinner because they have special devotional duties tonight," she said. "But they wouldn't let the rest of us eat until you're there. And we're hungry."

• • •

"Sabu Bada was growing coffee on *lulik* land. A lot of coffee," Cordero was saying as his mouth watered at the fried chicken, eggs, and rice Sister Agnes had placed on the table. "Strange behavior for the village's principal religious figure," he added. The nun appeared again with a small plate of chilli peppers.

"And yet he doesn't appear to have had expensive tastes," said Carter as she loaded her plate and attacked it like she hadn't eaten for days.

"No, but he did build the new *uma lulik*," Cordero pointed out. "That would have cost. And the man I saw performing at the *tebedai* seemed to take his role seriously." He piled chicken and rice on his own plate and took some chilli peppers to spice it further. "Perhaps his position was under threat after the old *uma lulik* burned down. You know, without that as a focus for the village and his leading role in it. The exodus of young people to Ermera or Dili wouldn't have helped. Further undermined his influence. Even his own sons had gone." They could hear the nuns banging pots in the area that passed as a kitchen. "He might have channeled what he made into the construction of the new *uma lulik* to strengthen his position from all the changes going on."

"But none of that gives us a motive for his murder," Carter said.

"If he was murdered," Cordero said and began attacking the food on his plate.

"What do you mean *if*?" she asked.

"Remember there wasn't much blood on the palms of his hands," Cordero said, lowering his fork and pointing a finger of his right hand toward the palm of his left. "If he had been stabbed and then grabbed at the hilt of the *surik* I would expect to have seen more blood on his palms because it would have been gushing out of his chest. But if he had been holding the thing, and maybe fallen on it, the blood would have tended to flow around his fists as they tightened in death rather than seep inside them."

He went back to eating. "I hope you not suggesting he was walking home and tripped and fell on his sword," Carter said.

"Not at all," answered Cordero. "You wouldn't carry a sword like that if you were walking home. But perhaps he was warding off someone else. Perhaps there was a fight. And then—"

"Maybe he was killed because of jealousy about his coffee output," suggested Carter. "Or he was being blackmailed for growing coffee on *lulik* land."

"Perhaps," said Cordero. "But jealousy and blackmail are more Western motives than Timorese ones."

Carter gestured to Estefana if she would like the last piece of chicken. She didn't and Carter took it herself. Estefana soon finished eating and aligned her knife and fork neatly beside her plate.

Sister Agnes appeared with a salad of tomatoes and onion. She placed it in the center of the table and left without speaking. Carter forked a little on to her plate and devoured it quickly to cleanse her palate.

"Nobody you spoke to knew anything?" Cordero asked, looking across at Estefana.

"No *maun*. They all said they were watching the *tebedai*. And while they knew about the *lia-nain*, none I spoke to knew him well personally."

"As you say," Cordero gestured with his fork toward Carter, "we have no clear motive." He finished his rice and chicken and took salad onto his plate. "But at least we know where the skulls came from."

"Yes but nothing else about them," complained Carter. "Who they were? Why they were killed? And by whom?"

"It is terrible to think that they were buried like that on *lulik* land," Estefana said. She shook slightly.

"Maybe they were buried there because it is *lulik*—it's just possible a militiaman who killed them might have known, you know, maybe the one with the bloody axe the headman mentioned." Cordero scratched at his chin again. "Or maybe it's because they were buried there that it is *lulik*," he suggested. "That way no one is going to go poking around." He drank from a glass of water in front of him. "I'm not sure we've anything like a clear picture yet."

"We haven't talked about Clarita," Carter said pushing her plate into the center of the table and throwing an arm over the back of her chair.

"I need to talk to Tereza Silveiro about her," Cordero said.

"You mean the mysterious *Senyora Batibat*?" asked Carter.

"Yeah," replied Cordero. "But that can wait. We have to deal with Sabu's death first. It could hold the key to the skulls." He stood up from the table. "And I suspect the elders are up to no good," he added.

"Why?" asked Carter.

"Just a feeling," he said. "I'd like to know how Sabu harvested and processed all that coffee."

"This burning of the bodies—" Carter began.

"I've been thinking about that. It's what they do to witches," Cordero said. "To be rid of them and their magic completely."

Estefana shivered again. Carter kept Cordero's gaze. "You think the skulls—"

"I'm just saying it's a known practice," said Cordero. "Whoever's in dispute with the so-called witches kills them and burns their bodies. Of course militiamen could have done that too, you know, to intensify the fear surrounding the bodies. But then if that's the message you want to send why bury the dead in such a remote spot?"

Carter considered that for a moment. "But the girl seems to have been burned in a different way," she said.

"Yes," he said. "With an accelerant rather than twigs and leaves. That's what Brooks said he was thinking when he rang this morning. He'd had bone and tissue from the more recent skeleton examined. He can't be sure which because accelerants degrade rapidly in soil and water, but that's his best bet."

"Petroleum distillates, gasoline, diesel, turpentine, flammable solvents," Carter listed them off. "They're all highly volatile. But who would have any of those lying around in a place like this?"

Cordero stood up from the table and collected the plates they'd been eating on. "Moussi. The mechanic," he said. "Now, who's up for a nightcap?"

"Not for me. I'm tired," said Carter. "I'm off to bed."

"Estefana?" asked Cordero.

"*Deskulpa maun*," she apologised. "I think I'll turn in also."

"Well I can't ask the nuns," said Cordero, looking dejected. "Looks like I'm off to bed as well."

14

They could hear Father Roque ringing the old bell that hung from its crude wooden gallows outside the church. The nuns were scurrying to get ready for Mass. Roosters and dogs had come to life and were announcing the fact throughout the village. The early morning mist had almost burned off and it looked set to be another scorching day.

"Back to rice porridge again, I'm afraid," said Carter as Cordero came into the dining room. She dripped a spoonful back into her bowl to demonstrate how unappetizing she regarded the porridge.

"I'll settle for coffee," he said and sat. "Where's Estefana?"

"She's got a hardier stomach for porridge than I have. She raced hers down and went off to see that kid she's befriended. Apparently sleeps in the lean-to out back of the priest's house."

He poured his coffee. "You might have suffered a little heat stroke yesterday," Cordero said. "Are you feeling okay this morning?"

"I'm fine, thanks," she said trying to conceal a smile and averting his gaze. "I managed to speak to Henri last night. We had coverage here for a while."

"Henri?" he asked.

"Doctor Mourinho. You know, the hydrologist," Carter said.

"Oh yes. Your hydrologist, of course. And?"

"Well, I told him we think we found the area of riverbank that was washed away with the skulls," Carter said. Cordero sipped his coffee, added a little sugar and stirred his cup. He made no comment. Carter took a mouthful of porridge,

118

grimaced as she forced it down. The bells had stopped. Outside the window the last of the village parishioners were hurrying up the path toward the church. "He wants to celebrate when we get back," She added.

"I'm not sure I—" Cordero began.

"Not with you, with me," Carter said.

"Oh, right."

"Have you spoken to your nurse friend since we arrived?" she asked.

"Um, no," Cordero answered. "No I haven't. Haven't had a chance, you know." He kept stirring his coffee as though his mind was elsewhere.

"You don't love them then leave them do you, Cordero?" she teased him.

"*Maun! Mai maun!*" Estefana shouted as she burst into the room, interrupting them. "*Hau hanoin buat ruma halo ta'uk akontese ba mane-oan. Mai!*"

Cordero put his spoon back down on the table. "*Mane-oan?*" he asked.

"*Sin. Tomas,*" Estefana noticed Carter trying to unfathom the Tetun. "It's Tomas, *mana,*" she said to her. "He's not there. He's gone! I think he may be in trouble!"

Carter pushed her plate of porridge aside, not quite sure yet what to make of Estefana's agitation. Cordero stood and drained the remainder of his coffee. "Calm down," he said. "He's probably just wandered off. Maybe to Mass."

"No *maun,*" Estefana insisted. "He's been wanting to show me what he calls his special things for days. They're scattered all over the shed. He wouldn't go anywhere without them. And we made arrangements to meet this morning. I think something has happened to him. I'm sure of it."

Estefana was out the door again as quickly as she had entered. Cordero and Carter quickly packed up the breakfast things and followed her to the lean-to where Father Roque allowed Tomas to sleep. Estefana had run on ahead and was crouched down hurriedly gathering up the contents of Tomas's cardboard box.

"These are all he owns," Estefana said looking up at the others, her voice quivering slightly.

The improvised cot Tomas slept in had been overturned against the far wall and a grubby blanket and a pillow had been tossed onto the earthen floor where oil stains betrayed the usual parking spot for the motorcycle. An empty bottle and an old pot lay on their sides near the cot along with Tomas's worn sandals and a dirty T-shirt.

"Well he didn't just up and leave," Carter said. "It certainly looks like there's been a struggle."

"Where does the boy go?" Cordero asked Estefana.

"Go?" she repeated. "I told you we were supposed to meet here this morning. I don't know where he goes. Ever since I met him he's stayed close by me."

"Okay," said Cordero. "You two stay here and I'll see if he's in the church."

Cordero hurried over to the church, blessed himself from the water font as he slid through the door, and carefully eyed the people scattered around inside. There were several dozen men, women, and children standing, sitting, and kneeling but no sign of Tomas. He tip-toed as unobtrusively as he could down the side of the church. At the altar end he caught Father Roque's attention. The priest momentarily stopped reading a scriptural passage to the congregation. Cordero smiled and gestured that he was fine. The priest looked back down at his Bible and continued to read the passage aloud. There was no Tomas to be seen.

Cordero returned to the lean-to. Carter was standing in silence, thinking, while Estefana was rummaging through Tomas's meagre possessions. Both turned to Cordero as he entered. He shook his head. "By the looks of the bed and the sandals I'd say whatever happened, happened during the night," Carter said.

"We need to talk to the priest and the nuns," Cordero said. "They may know where he is. But they won't be finished in there for another thirty minutes or more. Why don't you two head down to the village and see what you can find? I'll go over to the cemetery"—he caught Estefana's eye and realised the implication—"you know, the forest there, and take a look around in case he's wandered off in that direction."

They split up. "Why would anyone want to harm Tomas, *mana*?" Estefana asked as she and Carter headed down the road. "He's a nice boy. Gentle."

"We don't know that anyone has harmed him, Estefana," Carter said, trying to sound reassuring. "He might have had a nightmare or been scared by a noise outside. You know, thrown things around and simply walked off."

"But he wanted so much to show me his special things," Estefana added. "And he never went anywhere without the box he kept them in."

They saw only a few people in the village—most were at Mass in the church or working their garden plots—but those they did see were spread out.

"Let's approach them separately to save time," Carter suggested. "Check my Tetun. *Ita haree* Tomas? Have I got that right? Have you seen Tomas?"

"Yes. But add *labarik-mane bonko*—the boy hunchback—just in case they don't know his name," Estefana said.

"*Labarik-mane bonko*. Got it. If anyone's seen him, I'll call you over because I don't know enough Tetun to understand any more than 'yes' or 'no.'"

But none of those they spoke to had seen Tomas or knew where he might be. They searched deserted yards to no avail and around the health clinic and the mechanic's workplace. As they finished the old woman appeared to open the window of her small kiosk. Estefana approached her.

"*Bondia, tia*," she said, giving the woman the respectful title of auntie. A baby was crying in a far-off hut.

"*Dia*," the woman said.

"We are looking for Tomas, the one with the hump on his back. Have you seen him this morning?"

"Why are you looking for that one?" the woman asked.

"We just need to talk to him. Have you seen him?"

"That one knows nothing. He's *bulak*," the woman said, meaning insane.

"Well we'd just like to talk to him. Have you seen him?" Estefana repeated. The baby's crying had become a wail.

The woman picked up a cigarette from under the counter. She lit it, inhaled deeply in a wheezy breath and blew a stream of pale blue smoke.

"No," she said.

"Do you know where he might be?" Estefana asked.

The woman took another draw on her cigarette and spat onto the ground to the side of the kiosk. "No," she said in her own good time.

Estefana looked at Carter, her anguish written large across her face. "We'd better head back," Carter suggested. "The Mass'll be over soon."

"*Obrigada tia*," Estefana said without conviction but the woman was taking no notice. Instead she looked off to where the racket from the baby was coming from and swore under her breath.

They trudged back up the road to the churchyard and found Cordero standing at the entrance of the lean-to, hands on hips. "Any news?" he asked.

Estefana said nothing by way of an answer. "No," confirmed Carter. "You?"

"Same."

Just then people began spilling out of the church, the children rushing out first eager to begin playing together. Soon the nuns appeared as well, smiled and waved to a few of the parishioners, and headed back to their house.

"*Bondia* sisters," Cordero said as they drew near. "Do you have a moment?"

"*Bondia senyor*," the nuns replied in unison and stopped.

"We are looking for Tomas. Have you seen him this morning?"

"Tomas?" said Sister Felicia and she turned to face her companion.

"No *senyor*," said Sister Agnes. "Occasionally I take him left-over food after breakfast but we generally don't see him until then. And we haven't eaten yet."

"He's not in the priest's shed," said Cordero. "Do you know where he might be? Where he might go on a Sunday morning?"

The two nuns looked at each other again. "I'm sorry *senyor*," the older said. "We don't pay attention to his movements."

"We have to find him, *madre*," Estefana broke in. "He could be in danger. Is there anything you can tell us? Think *madre*!"

"They can't help us," said Cordero placing his hand on Estefana's arm. He thanked the nuns and they strode off to their house. He waited for Father Roque to finish exchanging pleasantries with his parishioners. "*Bondia* Father," Cordero said urging the priest over.

"*Bondia* Tino. Ladies," the priest said. He wore a bright green chasuble for the celebration of Mass with his white albe visible underneath. "Why for a moment I thought I had a new parishioner, Tino," he added grinning.

"I was looking for Tomas, Father," Cordero said. "Have you seen him this morning?'

"Tomas? No. Why?"

"Estefana was meant to meet with him this morning. He's not in the shed. And it looks like there's been a disturbance in there. Maybe a struggle."

The priest led the others back to the shed and ducked his head inside. "That's not like Tomas," he said. "He always keeps things tidy."

"And his special things were scattered all over the floor," added Estefana. "I gathered them up again in the box."

"Odd," said Father Roque. "Very odd indeed."

"Do you have any idea what might have happened to him? Where he might have gone?" Cordero asked.

The priest was silent for a moment, studying the upturned cot, the strewn bedding, and discarded sandals. "No," he said tightening his grip on the Missal he carried in his hands. "But I'll help you look."

"We've already been down to the village and Cordero has searched the tree line up yonder," said Carter pointing toward the cemetery.

"There's a market. Just out of town," the priest said gesturing with his chin. "And there's the river, of course, in the other direction. Let me change quickly and I'll come with you."

"Why don't you and Agent Carter take the market, Father," Cordero said. "The people there will know you and may be more willing to talk. Officer Estefana and I will head down to the river."

15

"We haven't been properly introduced," the priest said as he and Carter set off for the market on the far side of the village. He had changed into jeans and a casual shirt and grabbed a ragged old straw hat against the sun. "My name is Roque de Franca. Call me Roque."

"I'm Sara Carter," she said. "But people call me Carter."

"And you're from America. FBI I understand." They were walking with a sense of urgency but not too briskly that they couldn't converse.

"Well that's what it says on the cap," she replied and doffed it. "Yes. FBI. Seconded to INTERPOL here for a few months. You?"

"I'm from Brazil," he said. "Outside Sao Paulo."

"You're a long way from home," she said.

"You as well," Father Roque said without venturing more information.

"You speak English well," Carter commented.

"I studied moral philosophy for several years at Georgetown University in Washington."

"Georgetown," she said and stopped. She took off her cap to wipe the sweat from her forehead. "I'm impressed."

"Don't be. I never graduated," he said and laughed. "I was too busy being what you call an activist. Civil rights, anti-poverty programs, campaigns against the death penalty, and against many of your country's less-commendable foreign adventures." He took off his own straw hat, waved it to cool his face, put it back firmly on his head. "I thought moral philosophy was best learned in practice and so I spent more time in the streets demonstrating than in the library reading."

"Well, there's not many streets and no library here," she said, repositioned her cap, and walked on. "What brought you to this place? To Timor, I mean?"

"I carried on with my activism when I returned to Brazil," he said as an old woman passed them returning from the market with fresh produce in a string bag. She bowed before the priest, took his hand in hers, kissed it and pressed it to her forehead. "*Bondia avoo feto*," he said referring to her as grandmother. "*Obrigadu*." The woman mumbled and walked on. "Including inside the Church," he continued as though nothing had interrupted him. "This time my targets were clericalism, the all-male priesthood, the wealth and privilege the Church enjoyed. I was becoming a problem. I was sent here for five years before I became a threat."

Carter took her gaze to the ground. "We have things in common then."

"We do?" he asked and his voice lifted. "In what way?"

"I was becoming a problem for my superiors back home as well. They wanted to be rid of me for a while too. Regarded my policing techniques as too robust."

He glanced at her. "Better not get on your wrong side then," he said. "How long have you been in Timor?"

"A few weeks."

Neither spoke for a few moments. "Timorese are an interesting people," the priest said finally. "Who would have thought that so few people could win their independence from a huge country like Indonesia?" He adjusted his hat. "You know Indonesians outnumber Timorese two hundred to one. And winning that struggle has convinced them they can do anything. Like build a modern democratic nation. Here. Out of this," he said and spread his arms. "Well, a lot of them are convinced of that at least. Others, like those in Tepia, don't care about anything on the other side of these mountains. Or the other side of the river. They're very parochial and very much tied to the old ways."

"But the Church is not parochial and it's been in every village I've visited. Surely that unites people," she suggested. "And brings them into the modern world to a degree."

"Oh yes," he conceded. "There are churches everywhere. This is the most Catholic country in the world in terms of the proportion of the population who are baptised. But that means they're signed up. It doesn't mean they belong."

Another woman approached on her way back to the village. Two small girls skipped along beside her, their clothes grubby but hair neatly braided. The woman stepped to the side of the priest and pushed the children gently in front of him. They each smiled, took his hand in turn and touched it to their foreheads. Father Roque patted their heads playfully and thanked the woman. She walked on and the children resumed their skipping.

"Out here, as a priest, you can be tempted to feel like Jesus must have felt in Galilee," the priest said, grinning at the thought.

"Be careful about that," said Carter. "It didn't end well for him."

The priest nodded. "That's certainly true," he said. "Are you Catholic?"

She hesitated for a moment not sure whether to open up a little or to keep things on the professional level she routinely tried to maintain. But he was a priest after all and seemed amiable enough. "I was brought up Catholic, yes," she said. "But I started to doubt the existence of God in my early teens. My step mother forced me to go the Mass every Sunday for a few more years." She stopped walking and turned to him. "One day," she said, "I was sitting there in church leaning down to be inconspicuous—I'd fallen off my pushbike, scraped my knees, and couldn't kneel— and the priest was at the altar turning the bread and wine into… you know, consecrating them. 'This is my body' he was saying when I felt a tickle on my finger." She lifted her right hand and extended the index finger. "When I looked it was a tiny spider. I turned my finger this way and that, watching the spider keep its balance, when all at once it launched itself out toward the back of the pew in front of me. Midair. Its legs were turning like paddlewheels but in the glare of the sun through a side window

I noticed it was producing a web out of its rump and on the strength of the end of that web it was propelling itself forward, straight out, through thin air." She lowered her hand. "The priest finished consecrating the bread and wine, the people asserted their belief that he'd turned both into the body and blood of Jesus Christ." She looked him directly in the eyes. "But I was the only one who saw the miracle that day." She started to walk on. "I never went to Mass again."

Father Roque took a moment to catch up with her. "In the seminary we learnt rejoinders to comments like that," he said smiling. "When all the others fail, you were meant to say, 'You just need to pray more, then you'll see the light.'" He laughed. "To me that's all bullshit."

"I wouldn't have expected that from a priest," said Carter.

"Priests are people too. We come in all shapes, sizes and beliefs."

"But you do believe in God?" she said, mild surprise in her tone.

"I believe in the God I see in people," he said. "Especially, the lepers and the lame."

"You could have become a social worker or a revolutionary," she taunted him.

The priest scoffed at that. "In my experience most social workers are part of the problem. And I never found a genuine concern for people in Marx or Lenin or Mao. Their commitment to people was always in the abstract." He stopped and scratched the back of his neck. "If you'll pardon me for saying this, I never saw much of it in your country's political leaders either. Except perhaps in the one who never got to be president."

She had stopped as well to consider what he'd said. "Al Gore?" she offered.

"No," he laughed again. "Bobby Kennedy. Oh he was a bastard at first but I think that he was wrenched from his moorings by his brother's assassination and by the time he himself was killed he'd become perhaps the most truly radical leader your country ever produced."

"Well he was also quite the Brahmin, you know," Carter countered.

"I was meant to be quite the Brahmin myself," he said smiling and they both walked on. "My father owned a big cattle ranch," he explained. "A very big ranch. And he was a very rich man. I was his only son and heir."

"And yet you're out here living in little more than a shack. I don't get it," she said.

"I never liked the way he treated people who worked for him," he said. "I was in love with a girl. Mariella was her name. I was sixteen. She was seventeen." He shook his head slightly. "Her family were workers on my father's ranch. One day Mariella's father was gored by a bull. Badly. But because he was just a mere worker he wasn't considered worthy of proper medical care. He died." He raised his arms out from his sides. "Mariella was angry, of course, and she challenged my father. His right-hand man had her arrested and sent to prison. For impertinence. Can you believe that? I protested to my father and you know what he said? 'Take another one'—meaning another girl from among the workers' families. I left soon after and never went back. But I never found Mariella either. I don't know if she is alive or dead." Carter said nothing. "Eventually I forgave my father. He was a product of his circumstances. It's when people break those bonds, like that second Kennedy, that they become free to change history."

• • •

They parked the SUV at a spot where what was left of the road ran out entirely and they walked down a stoney track to the riverbank. The main stream flowed turquoise in the morning sun while in a small pool of trapped water on the near side toward the bank two wallowing buffalos had stirred everything around them into a muddy brown puddle. Estefana scanned down river but could see no sign of Tomas or anyone else. Cordero, looking up stream, caught a flash of red metal lying in the grass. "This way," he said and they made their way through the tall grass.

It was the fender of a motorcycle. Beside it lay a pile of clothes—two pairs of blue jeans, two brightly colored T-shirts, panties and a bra. Cordero kicked the jeans aside with the toe of his boot. Two pairs of sandals lay underneath. It was then they heard excited howls and yelps coming from the edge of the main stream and looked across to see two heads bobbing up and down in the water. Cordero walked over and waved his arms to get their attention. One head turned, a hand appeared and pointed in Cordero's direction, and the second head turned as well. Cordero, cupped his hands, called: "*Polisia*," and waved them in. The two heads turned to face each other but the bodies remained submerged. "*Polisia*," Cordero called again. "Don't make me come in after you!"

A skinny body rose from the water. It was a girl and she threw an arm across her naked breasts, held another over her groin and skipped out of the water as quickly as she could. She ran passed Cordero to the clothes, turned her back in embarrassment, and slipped her wet body into jeans and T-shirt. The other person dipped below the water then shot upwards flicking spray from his hair. He stood erect, naked also but unabashed and walked slowly to the bank. As he approached Cordero and Estefana he spread his arms in a show of bravado and casually asked: "Hey, *maun*. What's up?" Cordero recognised Rui—the boy who worked for the mechanic—but ignored the question. The sun glistened off Rui's taut brown body and he was enjoying the performance. "You look too pretty to be a police officer," he toyed with Estefana but she turned away. He walked over to the girl and slowly put on his jeans and T-shirt.

"What's your name?" Cordero asked the girl.

"Concetta," she said avoiding eye contact.

"Concetta who?"

"Concetta Luana," she answered.

"How old are you Concetta?"

"Fifteen," Concetta said in a nervous whisper. Cordero looked from Concetta to Rui, who only grinned.

"You two come here often?" Cordero asked the boy.

"Sure, *maun*. It gets hot, you know?" Rui said.

Cordero turned his gaze to the river. "We're looking for Tomas. Either of you seen him this morning?"

"Who?" asked Rui.

"Tomas. The boy with the hump. You know him," said Cordero.

"Oh, him. Yeah I know him but no, we haven't seen him. Why?"

"That right Concetta?" asked Cordero.

"Yes, *maun*," the girl said. "Are we in trouble?"

"Do either of you know where Tomas might be?" Cordero asked.

Rui and Concetta looked at each other and shook their heads. Cordero edged closer to Estefana and, keeping his eyes on the river, whispered in her ear. "This is Officer Estefana dos Carvalho," he said turning to face the couple. "She'd like to ask you a few questions Concetta." The girl looked nervously at Rui before Estefana walked between the two and gently ushered her out of earshot.

Rui took a cigarette from his jeans, lit it with a yellow plastic lighter and blew smoke out the side of his mouth. "How's your investigation going, *maun*?" Rui said trying to turn Cordero's questioning into a conversation between equals.

"What investigation would that be?" Cordero asked.

"You know, *maun*," Rui said puffing on his cigarette. "You told me about a crime when I helped you fix your vehicle. Remember? But you didn't say what the crime was. Seems like murder. But you weren't talking about no Sabu guy in the workshop. His killing came later. Maybe you got two murders now, *maun*, the hump back and Sabu," Rui added smiling with the cigarette between his lips. "That it?"

Cordero ignored the question. "You like girls, Rui?" he asked.

"Sure *maun*. Don't you?" Rui said. "Concetta there," he said taking the cigarette out of his mouth and pointing after the girl with it. "She's just a friend, you know. I keep a proper girlfriend in Ermera." He lent in close and lowered his voice. "Another one in Dili too, *maun*. I go there now and then. Keep her keen, you know?"

"Do you know a girl by the name of Clarita Araujo?"

"Clarita?" He took another puff on his cigarette. "Yeah I know her. Everyone knows everyone in Tepia. But I haven't seen her in a while. I think she went to Dili. Why you ask? She been murdered too?"

"Why would you ask that?"

"I don't know, *maun*. Just asking."

"How well do you know her?"

"I used to see her around, you know. I don't know her real well. She's *eskizitu*," he said, meaning odd, strange.

"How do you mean?"

"Don't know, *maun*. She hung around a lot with that old *buan*, *Senyora Batibat*. Talked a lot of shit. She thinks she's a witch too."

"When was the last time you saw her?"

"More than a year now, *maun*. Why you asking all these questions?" He finished his cigarette and threw the butt on the ground.

"Because I'm a police investigator," Cordero said. "One more thing, Rui. Did I see you at the *tebedai* the other night?"

"Sure, *maun*. Everyone was there. Not good in a place like this to ignore those things."

"I didn't see you at Mass this morning," Cordero noted.

"That's just Jesus shit, *maun*. The *uma lulik* is strong stuff."

"What do you mean?"

"Elders, *maun*. They're very powerful in Tepia. They expect everyone to respect the old ways. You be in trouble if you don't."

"Do you know anything about the death of the *lia-nain*?"

"No *maun*. I was talking to girls that night, you know," he said. "Walked off before that dance thing finished." He grinned. "Had my own dancing to do," he added and winked.

When Estefana returned Cordero gestured to her to walk with him along the riverbank, away from Rui and Concetta. When they couldn't be overheard he turned and said: "He's very sure of himself that one. What did you learn, anything?"

"Concetta insisted she was his girlfriend," Estefana said. "But she is very young and impressionable."

"What about Clarita?"

"She said she'd only been hanging out with Rui for a few months and she hadn't seen Clarita for a lot longer than that. She didn't know if he knew her or not."

Cordero pointed up the track to the SUV. "I don't think there's any more for us here. If they'd seen Tomas I think they would have said. No reason not to."

"There's one more thing, *maun*," Estefana said. "Concetta said she remembered Clarita as an attractive girl. And Rui likes attractive girls, she said. That's why she's his girlfriend, she said. She insists she is much prettier than Clarita and all the other girls in the village who get pregnant and grow old really fast. Made me think that girls might be this boy's main interest."

16

They'd reached the outskirts of the market but it offered little relief from the sun. Four elderly women dressed in drab full-length *tais* sat together in the half shade of a eucalypt tree, scarves covering their heads, competing to sell the few onions, tomatoes, clumps of garlic, and small fiery chillies they'd picked from their gardens. The produce was fresh and it gave a scent to the air. A few yards further on, a man in shorts and a singlet offered them clumps of mahogany and coffee-colored tobacco and, when they declined, he held out dried tobacco leaves from a canvass bag. A woman with a weathered face, her gums red from chewing betel nut, sat behind four cabbages. She paid them no mind as they passed. Racks of second-hand Indonesian-made T-shirts, dresses, jeans, and baseball caps lined the other side of the road along with men and women selling roasted and ground coffee the rich sharp smell of which overpowered everything else around them. A short man in a drooping grey moustache held up a white hen, its legs tied, and smiled toothlessly at Carter. Behind him other hens squawked at their confinement. Two stray dogs growled over scraps of food before one yelped and ran into the trees. There were only whispers among those selling and little conversation between those looking to buy.

"There aren't many people here today," said Father Roque. "It's out of respect for the *lia-nain*." He pointed to a crude corral off to the side of the road. "Even the cock fight has been cancelled until he's buried."

"When will that be?" Carter asked, declining a brown hen

the man with the moustache tried to interest her in after she'd rejected the white one.

"Tomorrow, I think," said the priest. "They won't want to delay for too long."

"Will you do the funeral?"

"For Sabu? Hardly. He was the *lia-nain*. The religious leader of the village. I'm just the imposter." He chuckled. "He was very traditional. They'll send him to his ancestor spirits in the underworld without any interference from me."

As they walked through the market Father Roque had been asking people if they had seen Tomas or knew where he might be. He'd only gotten blank stares or negative answers.

"Let's talk to those children," he suggested indicating a group playing around trees at the far end of the market. "We might have more luck."

Six young boys had been chasing each other around an open patch of land, laughing, falling, and tagging each other. They stopped and stared expectantly when it was clear that Father Roque was coming toward them. "*Bondia, amu,*" they all sang to the priest.

"*Bondia oan,*" he replied his hand outstretched to the nearest boy. "*Bondia oan,*" he said to another, referring to each as his own child. He took off his hat and waved it at them playfully. "Are you having fun at the market today?" he asked, crouching to their height.

"*Sin amu,*" was the chorus of agreement.

"This is my friend *mana* Carter," he said gesturing toward her with his hat. "She is from America."

"I know America, *mana,*" the older of the boys said excitedly. "I saw it in a book in school."

Father Roque was translating for Carter and she smiled. The other boys caught her reaction and instinctively sought to heighten it. "I saw it too," shouted a second boy.

"Me too," insisted a third. "It's blue and pink," he said referring to the coloring of the country's individual states on a map.

"And green and yellow!" insisted a fourth boy.

"I'm sure you all saw it," Father Roque said interrupting them. "And it was all those colors, maybe more. But now I need you to help us. It's very important that you do." He placed his hat on his knee. "We are looking for Tomas. You know Tomas?

"The monster?" the older boy cried and all the children laughed.

"Tomas is not a monster," Father Roque said.

"He walks like this," said another boy who began an exaggerated hobble around the others. Again they all laughed, pushing the showman among them this way and that.

"And he looks like this," said another stretching his eye sockets with his fingers to attract attention.

"Tomas was born with a deformity," the priest said holding up a hand to stop the hysterics. "That's all. It happens. It's not his fault. Just like it's not your fault"—he reached out and tickled one of the boys who squirmed and squealed—"that you're ticklish. I don't want to hear you making fun of him like that. And God doesn't want to hear you calling him names either. He loves Tomas as much as he loves each and every one of you. Okay?" He let that sink in and the children pretended to be chastened. "Now, have any of you seen Tomas or know where he is?" The children stayed tight-lipped. "Well?"

"No," said one.

"Not me," said another.

The others merely shrugged.

"Does he ever go off by himself, you know, to a secret place perhaps?" They looked at each other and shrugged. "Was anyone angry with Tomas? Or wanting to hurt him for any reason?" the priest said changing tact.

He looked at each of them in turn. A small boy, standing behind the taller children, raised his hand gingerly and popped his head out to be seen. Father Roque knew him. His name was Ziggy da Silva and his nose was running. "Ah Ziggy," the priest said. "Please, come around here and tell me what you know."

The boy shuffled to the front of the group. "My grandfather was angry," he said without prompting but the other boys were watching him. He stopped and sniffled.

"Angry about what, Ziggy?" asked the priest.

"Tomas," the boy mumbled.

"Why was your grandfather angry with Tomas?" Father Roque asked. The boy looked at the other children and said nothing. He wiped his nose with the back of his hand and appeared frightened. "It's alright, Ziggy," the priest said. "Don't worry about the others. Look at me." Ziggy did as he was told. "Why was your grandfather angry? You can tell me."

The boy looked like he would burst into tears and his nose was running again. "I don't know," he said and sniffled several times in quick succession.

"That's alright," Father Roque said. "Did you hear him say something about Tomas?"

The boy nodded and wiped his eyes.

"What, Ziggy? What did your grandfather say about Tomas?"

"He said something must be done about him," the boy answered. "Something like that."

"And he was angry when he said it? Not 'something must be done' in a nice way but in an angry way. Is that right?"

The boy nodded again.

"Do you know why he said that?"

"No."

"Who was your grandfather talking to when he said this?" Father Roque asked but the boy was silent. "Your grandmother? Your mother?"

"A man," the boy said and sniffled again.

"Yes, okay. But who Ziggy? Who was the man?"

"Balbo Fuentes. He came to our house. I saw him."

"When was this Ziggy?"

"When?"

"Yes, when?" the priest persisted.

The boy closed his eyes tight and scrunched up his cheeks in a huge effort to recall. "Last night," he burst out finally his eyes wide with excitement. "They woke me up they were talking so loud. I got up and looked through the curtain." He paused and his demeanour changed. "Am I in trouble, *amu*?"

"No Ziggy," Father Roque reassured him. "You did nothing wrong. Was your grandfather at home this morning?"

"No."

"Was he in his garden?" the priest asked.

"No."

"Is he home now?"

"No," the boy said. "I haven't seen him since last night."

"Do you know where he's gone?"

"No," Ziggy insisted.

The priest turned and looked up at Carter. Then he stood and patted the boy on the head. "Okay Ziggy. You have helped me and my friend a lot. You are a brave boy. Thank you. Thank you all," he said to the group of children. "Now off you go and play," and brushing them away with his hat they ran off with Ziggy sniggering and yelling excitedly with the others.

He turned back to Carter and replaced his hat securely on his head. "It's the elders. I think they've taken him. And I think I know where they've gone. We need to get the others. If I'm right Tomas is in great danger and there's no time to waste."

17

They drove back along the ridge toward the hut and the coffee plantation of Sabu Bada. Father Roque was giving directions from the passenger seat. Carter and Estefana were holding on as best they could in back against the sways and jolts of the vehicle. The priest kept checking his watch. It was well passed 10 o'clock and, if he was right, the elders would have had Tomas for maybe four or five hours. The only chance they had to save the boy was if his abductors were on foot, slowed down by his awkwardness and struggling. Perhaps they could get ahead of them in the SUV.

Cordero pulled up in the yard that fronted Sabu's hut. Again the chickens heard the vehicle and came clucking and running, more desperate for food than before. "There's a track down to the river through the coffee trees over there," Father Roque said uncoupling his seat belt and pointing.

"I know it," said Carter but it was Estefana who was first out of the vehicle and heading toward the track.

"I'll catch you," Cordero said. "Just want to check that boy's keeping an eye on things. Be a minute." He hurried to the hut and called: "Halibo!"

Father Roque was running behind Carter who had just caught up with Estefana. "This way," he said and pointed down the track. As they descended through the coffee trees they could hear Cordero call the boy's name again and Carter, looking back over her shoulder, thought she saw movement at the door of the hut.

It was Halibo, blinking, an unlit cigarette dangling carelessly from his lips. "What's up, *maun*?" he asked before recognizing Cordero. He yawned and the cigarette slipped out of his mouth to the ground. "Oh, it's you," he added and bent to pick up what he had dropped.

"Has anyone been out here?" Cordero asked.

"Out here?"

"Yes, out here!" said Cordero.

"No *maun*. No one." He lit the cigarette and let the smoke drift out of his nose and mouth. "Hey, when do I get paid?" he asked, scratching his stomach.

"When the job's done," Cordero said. "Now wake up and keep an eye out. Shout if anyone comes this way."

With that Cordero headed after the others, half jumping, half slipping down the track where it dropped at an angle off the side of the ridge. Within minutes he was on Carter's heels. Puffing, he slowed his descent. "Anything?" she asked.

"No. But he's been sleeping and fairly soundly I'd say."

Father Roque had overheard the comment and turned to them. "I don't think they'd come that way," he said. "There's a direct route along the river. It's slower because of the undergrowth and the creeks you must cross but I think they would want to stay clear of Sabu's land, given what they probably have in mind." He hadn't said what that was since they left Tepia but the anxiety in his tone spoke for itself.

Estefana had reached the riverbank ahead of the others and she looked back at the priest for guidance. "Left," Father Roque shouted and she was on her way before he could finish, "and around that bend up ahead." Estefana was lithe, athletic, determined and made ground quickly. But around the bend she came to a halt. Ahead four men hovered above a figure kneeling on the ground. It was Tomas and she could hear him crying, and pleading for his life.

• • •

Rui had tried to coax the girl into sex again on the riverbank after Cordero and Estefana had left but she hadn't been in the mood. "They might come back," she'd said and pushed his hands away. He told her they'd gone and wouldn't be back, but she said

'No' a second time. He thought about forcing the issue but decided against it. She tucked her panties and bra into her jeans' pocket, threw a leg over the back of his motorcycle, and he doubled her up through the village and out along the side track through the trees that led to where she lived with her parents and seven siblings.

"What did that policewoman ask you anyway?" he asked as he pulled up one hundred yards from her home, placed his left foot on the ground to steady the motorcycle, and cut the engine.

Neither wore helmets. The girl climbed off the back of the bike, brushed down her clothes and fiddled with her hair. "She wanted to know my name, where I lived, what kind of work I do. You know, that kind of thing," she said looking at her face in the handlebar left mirror.

"That all?" Rui said, taking a cigarette from his pocket.

"Why you asking me these things, Rui?" the girl said, annoyed now. "Isn't it enough you got me questioned by the police. Now I get questioned by you."

"*Doben*," which meant beloved, he cooed. "I didn't get you questioned by those police officers. They just turned up. But I care for you. I don't want you in any trouble, that's all."

"Trouble? What trouble?" she asked, looking more concerned than angry now. "Shit Rui. What do you mean?"

"They're investigating a crime," he said as though privy to information other people didn't possess. "And they're from Dili. They won't want to hang around in a place like this. They'll blame anyone just to get back to the city as soon as they can. I don't want it to be you they blame."

"But I haven't done anything Rui," the girl protested. She hesitated and looked him in the eye. "Have you?"

"Shit no!" he said. "We just need to be careful, that's all."

He lit his cigarette, inhaled deeply, and offered it to her. She took it absently, stared out into the trees and puffed without inhaling. "What else did she ask you?" Rui said.

The girl looked at him again and handed back the cigarette. "She asked me if you knew that girl Clarita Araujo." She adjusted her sandals.

"And?"

"I said I didn't know Clarita very well and hadn't seen her for a long time," she said and looked off into the distance. "And I told her I'd only been your girlfriend for a couple of months." Rui followed her gaze for a moment considering that and ignoring her. He dragged on his cigarette. "I am your girlfriend aren't I, Rui?" she asked.

He looked back at the girl and brushed her check gently with the back of his hand. "Of course you are *doben*. Of course you are."

"And there's no other girlfriend, Rui, is there?" she pressed him.

"Eh? What?" He focused on her. "No *doben*. Only you."

"Promise?"

"Yes, I promise." The girl broke into a silly grin. He took another drag on his cigarette. "She didn't ask you anything else?"

"No!" The girl said and she finished tidying herself up to go home.

"And you didn't tell her anything else?"

"What else could I tell her?" she said thrusting her hands on her hips, irritated by his questioning.

"Of course," he said, tossing the cigarette away and kick-starting the motorcycle.

"When will I see you again, Rui?" the girl said reaching out to him above the noise of the engine.

"Soon Concetta. Soon," he said ignoring her advances and turning his motorcycle around in the other direction. "Go now, I saw your mother in the yard."

• • •

The men standing around Tomas didn't move as Cordero and the others closed the distance between them. Cordero noticed the two elders he'd spoken to the day before—Juno da Silva and Balbo Fuentes. Father Roque said he recognised the other two as Braga Bucar and Fonseca Lage. The men were in shorts and old T-shirts and each carried a machete. Each also had a cross painted across his forehead—Catholic symbolism adopted by traditionalists as added protection when they ventured onto *lulik* land. They were on the near side of the overhang. Tomas's hands were tied behind his back and his arms were fastened to his body with a length of rope. As they drew nearer, Tomas noticed Estefana and, through his tears, his big cow eyes looked up at her as his last hope of staying alive.

"*Mana*, help me please," he cried. "Please, *mana*! I didn't mean to do it!"

"*Polisia*," Cordero said. "What are you doing?"

Three of the men looked at him without alarm. "We're removing *laran-aat ida* from the village," Juno said, referring to Tomas as the wicked one. Juno kept his eyes firmly on the boy and his hand closed tight around the machete so that the white of his knuckles showed.

"You know we are police officers," Cordero said.

"That means nothing here," Juno said. He was breathing heavily through his nose.

"It means we represent the authority of the state," said Cordero.

"There is no state in Tepia," Juno said.

"We—" Cordero began but Juno cut him off.

"You call a flag flying over a school where the teacher hardly ever turns up a state?" the elder said looking at Cordero for the first time. "Or maybe you're thinking of the clinic that employs two local women. Just two! No more. Your state means nothing here."

"The state is the law," insisted Cordero.

"We are the law in Tepia," Juno spat.

"I can make a call now and have a dozen armed police officers in Tepia tomorrow," Cordero said.

"Then make your call!" barked Juno. "It will be over by then."

Estefana had moved closer to Tomas, her hand outstretched a little in a vain attempt to reassure him. "*Mana, mana*," he moaned. Carter had positioned herself behind Juno, ready to take him quickly and grab the machete from his hand when Cordero signalled her to strike. Father Roque was standing to Cordero's side, urging the other men to lower their machetes.

"Why do you call Tomas wicked?" Cordero said, buying time while he thought through the options.

"Why? Look at him!" Juno said. "He's not human. He's cursed. His mother died when he was born. Our *uma lulik* burned down. I say it was because of him! And now Sabu is dead. He's possessed. That's why he looks like he does."

"Tomas has a physical deformity," countered Cordero. "Nothing more. Lots of kids in Timor have birth defects. You know that. It's no one's fault. He's deformity is what he *has* not what he *is*. If we had better health care his back would have been fixed when he was a baby." As Cordero edged closer to Juno he noticed Carter adjust her stance slightly primed to strike. She kept an eye on Cordero for a signal but he shook his head slightly against what he guessed she was thinking. Neither he, Carter or Estefana had a pistol, a baton, anything with which to defend themselves. A pre-emptive move that left even one elder standing with a machete could end with them all cut to pieces. "And women die all the time in childbirth in Timor-Leste," Cordero continued. "You know that as well as I do."

"Fewer would die if you men allowed them to go to the health clinic," Father Roque added drawing Juno's attention away from Cordero. "Now stop this senseless thing. You know it's wrong."

"Maybe wrong to you," said Juno. "But you and your Church have never understood how things work here. You think you know. You have your rituals but ours are older and more powerful than any of yours and *they* make us what we are, not you."

Cordero noticed that Braga had grown a little doubtful since the priest spoke. He was comfortable in the old ways, as was his wife, but she kept a picture of the Virgin Mary she'd asked Father Roque to bless. Braga cared little about Tomas but he didn't want to risk an argument with his wife by harming Father Roque in any way.

"Why do you blame Tomas for Sabu Bada's death?" Cordero asked the men. "He didn't do it. Sabu was a strong man. He could easily have overcome a boy like this."

"Someone has to pay for the *lia-nain's* death," insisted Balbo. "It will restore the balance. Only then can things be set right. It's tradition, as Juno says."

"What things need to be set right?" asked Cordero. But Juno had already raised his machete and was ready to strike at the boy.

Estefana lunged forward and threw herself over Tomas. "You must kill me first!" she shouted. Juno's arm stayed raised above his head. "You talk of tradition," she said. "Does the power of your tradition come from that?" and she pointed to a bottle Fonseca Lage was carrying. It was *tua-tein*—palm brandy—and the bottle was almost empty.

Fonseca raised the bottle and stared at it. Braga and Balbo also looked at the bottle. All three shifted slightly with embarrassment. Juno lowered his arm a little, enough to suggest he might be having second thoughts, although his face showed anger rather than doubt.

"It's what the spirits demand," he shouted, his voice his main weapon now. "They say—"

"The *lia-nain* is dead," Cordero interrupted him. "I thought he was the one who interpreted messages from the spirits." Carter ignored the machetes and slipped between the elders toward Estefana, breaking the wall the men had formed around Tomas. "How do you men know that what Juno says the spirits demand is actually what they do demand?" Cordero asked. "Maybe he hears what he wants to hear."

Balbo's fingers opened and closed on his machete. Fonseca began slapping the blade of his against the side of his leg as though trying to decide what to do. Soon Braga was copying him. Neither they nor Balbo spared any thought for Tomas—who was whimpering on the ground. His life, his death meant nothing to them. The only thing that mattered was what was required. As for Estefana—who lay across the boy still—and now the foreign woman beside her, these were complications they hadn't expected. If they had to be killed, they could be killed. If that was required. But was it?

Balbo looked around, his concentration on Tomas broken. He noticed a pair of eagles circling the ridge to his left and gliding down to the riverbank beyond the overhang. Was it a sign, he thought? The spirits of these two female police officers, perhaps?

A gust of wind blew a fine spray of water from the river across them. What did this sudden wash of rain mean, on such a hot, cloudless day? Things were becoming confusing.

All three elders looked uncertainly at Juno. He brought his machete to his side, his hand loosening on the handle. He looked from one to the other. "Maybe we should let it go," Fonseca muttered. Juno fixed him with a scowl.

"I think he's right, Juno," added Balbo, and Juno heard but ignored him.

"Haven't you got a burial to organise?" Cordero asked and Juno turned to him with a face now drained of the grim determination it showed before. "And time is running out." In the silence they could hear the rush of the river and feel the cooler air sweeping across the bank. One by one the three other elders turned on their heels and trudged in single file back along the track. Juno held Cordero's stare a long moment then looked around as though it was only slowly dawning on him that he was alone. "Go home," Cordero said. "It's over." And Juno, shoulders slumped, followed after the others.

18

As they drove back to Tepia, Tomas sat in back between Estefana who stroked his arm and Carter who was holding his hand. Father Roque was up front next to Cordero. Carter was still waiting for one of them to explain what had been said on the riverbank. "What did they have to say for themselves?" she asked at last, unable to contain her impatience.

Cordero ran a hand across his face. "They said someone had to pay for the *lia-nain's* death so that things could be restored. It was as vague as that but connected to the idea that everything has an opposite. It amounts to revenge killing where the killing balances the original death even though who it's done to doesn't seem to matter." He shifted to a lower gear to take the vehicle slowly through rough ground. "The boy was chosen because he looks different and he's a loner. He doesn't have anyone to stand up for him."

"He does now," Carter said.

Cordero knew it was Estefana she meant.

"Even though you couldn't understand what was going on I could see you taking in the location. Are you thinking what I'm thinking?" he asked.

"About the overhang? Yeah. They were a bit too close for comfort. something has drawn them to that spot and I don't think it was coincidence," Carter said.

"Me neither." He accelerated now the track was in better shape. "I'll talk to them after the *lia-nain's* burial tomorrow or the next day but I don't expect them to be forthcoming. You may have picked up on their contempt for the police," he said, grinning at her in the rearview mirror.

"I could imagine those guys wielding their machetes in a way consistent with the injuries Brooks identified on those skulls that washed up in Dili. But if they were involved in those deaths what could be the motive?" she asked.

"If it's connected to tradition or superstition—which at times amount to the same thing—it could be anything. The crops fail, the chickens don't lay, it rains too much, it rains too little," Cordero answered. "Take your pick."

"Or someone turns up dead," suggested Father Roque who had been listening to the conversation in silence.

"Yes, that too," agreed Cordero. "In a place like this anything that can't be explained invites scapegoating. And when you have likely candidates for scapegoats, like Tomas for instance, but no police presence, you get trouble."

It was another thirty minutes before they arrived at the church. Father Roque saw parishioners waiting to talk to him and he excused himself and headed off to see what they wanted. Estefana took Tomas into the nuns' house to help clean him up and settle him down. Cordero noticed Carter staring out across the churchyard as he collected his things and exited the vehicle.

"You okay?" he asked but she didn't answer. He waited a moment, stepped in beside her and tried to follow her gaze.

"Tomas held my hand the whole way back," she said. "Tight. Wouldn't let go. And he hardly knows me." Cordero noticed a tear well in her eye. She wiped it quickly. "Reminded me of a boy I once rescued from a sex ring in Arizona. Only ten he was. Clung to my arm for hours as we drove back from the reservation." She looked at him, her face creasing in distress. "Reminded me of my half-sister Becky and how I should be looking for her right now and holding her hand." She looked away. He stood there unsure of what to do. "I'm alright," she said but immediately corrected herself. "No I'm not!" He put his arm gently around her and she moved closer to him. Her breathing became erratic, tears flowed freely but after a few seconds she moved out of his grasp, wiped her face, and tried a smile. "But we're here to do a job, right?"

"Right," he said and smiled back. He moved to stroke her back but thought better of it and pulled his arm away. He puffed out a breath. "We need to know more. A lot more. I think I'll pay a visit to an old Tepia resident who has little connection to *their* sense of tradition," he said gesturing toward the *uma lulik*.

Carter looked at him. "*Senyora Batibat?*"

"Well, there are a few hours of daylight left," he said and she caught the mischief in his eyes.

"You have all the fun," she said and suppressed a half laugh. "I'd like to come along but I think Estefana's a little shaken and I should stay with her and the boy."

He nodded and they parted, both wanting to say more but neither knowing quite what.

• • •

"I admire what you did out there today," Carter said to Estefana. "For Tomas, I mean. That was very brave of you to protect him like you did."

They were sitting next to each other on the veranda, their backs against the wall. Father Roque had instructed Sister Felicia to allow Tomas to clean himself up at the nuns' washbasin, to find new clothes he could wear, to feed him, and finally to allow him to stay in the bed beside Estefana tonight in case the horror of his ordeal caused him a restless night. Carter had agreed to move to the bed on the veranda after Cordero, graciously if reluctantly, offered to sleep in the SUV.

"I was scared, *mana*," Estefana replied, rubbing her hands together nervously. "I was very scared."

They could hear Tomas humming to himself from inside the house. "Me too," said Carter. "Actually I was terrified." Estefana looked at her and chuckled to release tension. She stopped rubbing her hands and clasped them together on her lap. "What do you think bravery is?" Carter asked. "It's when you overcome your fears and do what's right regardless. And you did exactly that."

Estefana was silent for a moment. "Do you think they would have killed Tomas?" she asked.

"I do," said Carter without hesitation. "And I think they would have killed you too."

"It's a good thing *maun* was there," said Estefana referring to Cordero.

"Yes. He handled it well. But I think things might have turned out differently if you hadn't put yourself at risk to shield Tomas. That caught them by surprise. And it complicated things for them. All at once their plan to kill Tomas and be done with it involved killing at least one other person and a police officer at that." Estefana tapped her feet, her arms rigid on the floor of the veranda. "And you went onto that *lulik* land despite your concerns. That took a lot of courage."

"I didn't have a choice when I knew Tomas might be killed," Estefana said.

"You *did* have a choice, Estefana," insisted Carter. "You could have stayed back, thought of an excuse to give Cordero and stayed. But you didn't do that, you chose to go. And that's what makes what you did all the more courageous."

Estefana tapped her feet once more. "I don't feel courageous," she said. She turned abruptly to Carter. "And I might even now be cursed for going onto that land."

"Then I'm sure you have the courage to face that as well," said Carter.

Estefana held Carter's stare but said nothing. After a moment she looked away and said: "Were you ever in danger like that, *mana*?"

Carter thought of the time, as a cop in Missouri, a biker high on ice had fired a shotgun point blank into her cruiser. She had only escaped by ducking below the dashboard just before he fired and a fellow officer shot the man. Or the time she ran a line of fire to help a wounded fellow FBI agent to safety during a shoot-out at a right-wing terrorist compound west of Flagstaff. Or the time a guy spiked her drink at a bar in Phoenix, said he'd help her home when she felt ill and tried to assault her when they got there. She'd managed to ward him off with a kitchen knife and dial 9-1-1 before she collapsed.

"Not like that," she said. "No."

Estefana fell silent again until they heard Tomas emerging from the washroom. "There are fresh clothes for you by the door, Tomas," Estefana called without turning. "And the nuns have put food out for you to eat. I'll be in to see you soon." Tomas acknowledged her instructions. "Josinto says I shouldn't take risks," she said almost apologetically to Carter.

"Your boyfriend?"

"No *mana*," Estefana said with just a hint of exasperation in her voice. "He is my fiancé."

"Sorry," said Carter amused at the seriousness of the distinction. "My mistake. Your *fiancé*."

"Yes. Josinto Centavo Veddo." Estefana was quiet a moment. "I'm—" and then she hesitated and wiped a hand under her nose. "I'm thinking of leaving the police force when we get married."

Carter looked at her directly, frowning, and then glanced away. "Has Josinto told you to leave?" she asked.

"No. He wouldn't do that. He says he loves me as I am. But I worry about what would happen to him—to us—if something, you know, happened to me."

Carter paid that concern the respect it was due by not jumping in to comment. "You told me Josinto is a coffin maker, right?" she asked eventually.

"A coffin maker's *apprentice*."

"Okay. A coffin maker's apprentice. What would you do if he cut his hand off or lost his arm in an accident with an electrical saw?"

"I don't think he has an electrical saw, *mana*. The coffin maker is very busy but not very wealthy and an electric saw would cost a lot."

"Okay then, a coffin fell on him, broke his spine and crippled him?"

"I don't think that would happen, *mana*. Josinto is good at what he does and he is always careful—"

"But if an accident did happen," Carter interrupted trying to conceal her impatience, "what would you do?"

Estefana looked out over the churchyard and stopped tapping her feet. "I would take good care of him, of course. I would take on extra shifts or even get a second job to make sure he didn't have to work if he wasn't able to."

"Why?" asked Carter.

"Because I love him, *mana!*"

"Exactly," said Carter. "And he would do the same for you, I'm sure. That's why you are marrying each other." She looked across at Estefana again. "You're a damned good police officer, Estefana, and it's what you enjoy doing. So do it. He'll understand. If you give up being a police officer you'll end up a very unhappy, grumpy wife. And you don't want that. Neither would Josinto."

Estefana smiled and turned to Carter. "I wish I was as strong as you, *mana*," she said.

Carter looked away from her. "I'm not that strong, Estefana. I just pretend to be."

"Oh no, *mana*. You are very strong and—"

Carter turned back. "And what? Hard?" Estefana didn't answer. "I'm not *that* hard. Not really. I'll show you," and she tickled Estefana on the ribcage. Estefana clamped her arms against her sides and laughed out loud, begging her to stop. "Now do it to me," Carter said. Estefana hesitated then did as she'd been told and each tried to get the better of the other until Sister Felicia appeared at the doorway. The old nun sniffed loudly and deliberately. "The boy is ready now," she said and disappeared back inside. Estefana and Carter looked at each other and couldn't help but smile like school girls.

• • •

Cordero took a detour on his way to the home of Tereza Silveiro, known in the village as *Senyora Batibat*, and stopped where the headman lived. Eusebio's wife said her husband was tending the vegetables in their garden and Cordero thanked her and walked through the yard to the plot at the back of the hut, ignoring the piglet that snorted at him from behind a pen of wooden sticks.

"*Botarde, maun,*" he said, dropping any pretence of formality.

Eusebio Leite looked up from a row of sweet potatoes. Cordero was standing casually on the side of the plot, his hands in the pockets of his pants. "You again," Eusebio said and looked back down at what he had been doing.

"Afraid so. Just a few things I need to know," said Cordero and he continued before the headman could object. "Did you know what Juno da Silva and the others were up to today?"

"Juno?"

"Yes Juno."

"He's preparing the burial for tomorrow," Eusebio said, his attention focused on his digging. "Normally the mourning lasts three days but Sabu had no living relatives anyone could contact. It's tomorrow he'll be buried. Juno was organising things."

"After he and the others killed Tomas, you mean?"

The headman looked up, surprise in his eyes. "Tomas? The *bonko*?" he said. "What are you talking about killing him?"

"Well they tried," Cordero said taking a hand from his pocket and fingering the limp waxy leaves of a maize plant. "But they were stopped." He fixed his eyes on Eusebio. "Do you want me to believe that you knew nothing about the abduction of Tomas from the priest's shed, nothing of him being tied up and dragged out to the *lulik* land along the river, and nothing of the plan to kill him to avenge the death of Sabu Bada?"

Eusebio rubbed a hand across his chin, then swung it out to his side. "First I've heard of it. Honest, *maun*. The elders don't tell me everything they're up to."

"Well you can bet I'll be asking them if you were complicit." Cordero walked up the row of sweet potatoes closer to the headman. "What can you tell me about the human remains I found there along the river. Under an overhang. Pretty much straight down the ridge from Sabu's place?"

"I don't know anything about human remains. I told you, that's all *lulik* land and we are forbidden to go there. Sabu was *maka'as* about that," he said meaning extremely firm and uncompromising.

"And I suppose you knew nothing about him growing coffee on that land either?"

Eusebio was noticeably less confident now. He fidgeted with a digging stick and merely shrugged. Cordero let it go. For now.

"One more thing," he said. "The other day you told the female police officer that militiamen visited Tepia just prior to the referendum on independence." The man nodded. "You said one had an axe that had blood on it." Again he nodded. "And you told her that this man said the blood was from a person who wouldn't take orders. Is that right?"

"Yeah. So?"

"How clear is your recollection of that man and what he said?"

"I remember it. He looked silly, threatening everybody with an axe like he was a big man even though he had no other weapon. There were ten of us. Only four of them. We all had machetes. They wouldn't have lasted long if we'd wanted to cut them down. The blood on the axe was probably from a chicken or a cat he'd killed and tried to scare us with."

"But are you sure he said the blood was from *one* person who wouldn't take orders—not from *people* who wouldn't take orders?"

Eusebio thought for a moment. "Yeah, I'm sure. He said it was the blood of *one* person. Wanted each of us to imagine ourselves as that person, I guess."

"And you're absolutely positive of that?"

"You deaf?" the man asked and started digging. "How many times do I have to tell you, *maun*?"

• • •

"How do you feel now, Tomas?" Estefana asked as they entered the bedroom she had been sharing with Carter.

"I'm okay, *mana*?" Tomas told her and blinked with appreciation.

"Did you enjoy the food?"

"Oh yes, *mana*. I like rice porridge very much."

They sat facing each other on the floor, their backs against the two single beds on either side of the room. Tomas was wearing a clean but oversized T-shirt with a Ninja Turtle logo across the front and shorts frayed on the legs. She slid his cardboard box out from under her bed where she had put it until Tomas had washed, dressed and eaten, and handed it to him. "I collected your special things for you," she said, "but I didn't look at any of them because you promised to show me yourself."

Tomas took the box and smiled. "*Mana*?" he asked.

"Yes," replied Estefana.

"Thank you. For saving me. You are my best friend ever!"

"That's okay, Tomas," she said. "Now why don't you show me what's in the box?"

He looked at the box, thought a moment, then opened it and took out a shaving brush, its bristles worn. He held it in front of Estefana but pulled back when she tried to take it from him. "Sorry," she said. "Silly me. You don't shave yet, do you? Whose is it?"

"It's *amu's*," Tomas said. "He threw it out but I picked it up and kept it because he's my friend. He lets me guard his motorcycle."

"Yes, you told me that," said Estefana.

"He listens to all my secrets," Tomas added. "Like in confession. Only we talk outside of the church because people get angry and yell at me if I go inside."

Next he took from the box an old picture book of dinosaurs, the pictures fading, several pages torn. "I found this," he said. "Outside the school. Someone must have dropped it." Again he wouldn't let Estefana handle the book. "I can't read but I like to look at the pictures," he said. He turned the pages. "Look at this one, *mana*," he said and pointed to a picture of a Triceratops, although he didn't know the name. "And this!" showing her a Tyrannosaurus.

Estefana made a show of shaking all over, acting scared. Tomas giggled. Next from the cardboard he took grey-brown feathers—boobook owl, Estefana thought, from the quick glance—attached to fur and fastened to a thick twig that had been polished. "What's that?" she asked.

"I don't know," Tomas said, his brows creased. "A friend gave it to me. That's why I keep it." He put the thing quickly back in the box and took out an old fifty centavo coin. He placed it in Estefana's hand and sniffed. "Do you know where I got that?" he asked.

"No, tell me."

"From a man I saw last week." He yawned. "I'd never seen him before. He came into the village and asked directions to the new *uma lulik*." Tomas rubbed his nose. "I told him it was where the old one had been. He must have been going to the *tebedai*. He reached in his pocket and gave me the coin. That's the first money I have ever earned!"

"You should have given the man directions, Tomas," Estefana said. "After all he paid you and if he wasn't from here he may not have known where the old *uma lulik* had been?"

"He said he used to live here a long time ago," Tomas replied. "He was nice. He talked to me. Like you do. I asked him where he was from. He said the past." Tomas frowned. "What did he mean, *mana*? And he gave me the fifty centavos," he added without waiting for an answer. "Fifty, *mana*!"

He snatched the coin from Estefana's hand and placed in back in the box. He shook the box, looking at the bits and pieces he hadn't shown her and yawned again. The lids over his too-large eyes appeared heavy. "I'm tired, *mana*," he said. "Can I show you the rest of my special things tomorrow?"

"I may be working again tomorrow," Estefana said. "We'll see. No promises, okay? Why don't you get into this bed tonight. I'll get into this other bed a bit later after I've had my dinner and a cleanup. If you get frightened you can wake me up."

"Will there be rice porridge tomorrow, *mana*?" he asked.

Estefana smiled to herself. "I'm sure there will be, Tomas."

19

Cordero walked from the gate on the near side of the cemetery believing—rightly—that the hut of Tereza Silveiro lay out of sight in the trees on the other side of the graves and wouldn't be accessible by road. He walked slowly and jerked his head back at every sound—a rooster on the loose, a bird taking flight. He didn't necessarily subscribe to Timorese customary beliefs about the dead continuing to be active in the world of the living but he respected the hold those beliefs had on ordinary people, especially in remote rural areas. And walking alone through a graveyard, to the hide-away of a witch, was sure to excite ideas and feelings—however fanciful—that tens of thousands of years had implanted deep inside every Timorese person's psyche. Even his.

Tepia was a poor, under-developed village and its status showed in the cemetery the locals called *hakoi-fatin*—the place of burial. Most graves were marked by earthen mounds pointing in all directions rather than the usual Christian east-west orientation. Only a few—those of the relatively more well-off— had cement liners, fewer boasted blue and yellow decorative tiles, most of which were cracked, and the two vaults that lay side-by-side topped with a cross were old, crumbling and dedicated to long forgotten priests. Legions of nuns who had simply worn out and died in Tepia over the years were buried in a mass grave, their name markers long ago eroded away and weeds growing in their place. Buffalo skulls—animist symbols—were positioned on wooden poles at the foot of many of the graves. All the graves were concentrated in the center of the cemetery even though the space had been set on a broad stretch of cleared ground. It seemed to Cordero that those in the ground were fearful of things above it and were huddled together for protection.

He crossed through the long grass, conscious that snakes were said to favour cemetery grounds, and relaxed a little only when he'd made the other side and was in the shade of the trees. For a while the air seemed fresher, the heat more bearable. But as he neared his destination his uneasiness resurfaced. Along a barely discernible track, nestled under huge oriental plane trees, he could just make out a traditional conical hut. Thatch made from kunai grass covered the entire structure, like a tea cosy, to the stone foundations. A line of casuarina slats which formed the walls could just be made out above the stone. There were no windows and an entrance was cut into the thatch and covered only by a blanket to protect against the elements. Presumably this was where Tereza Silveiro lived. He sensed an eerie stillness about the place as though no air circulated here and no insect dare make a sound. A strange uneasiness came over him as he drew nearer to the hut.

Cordero took a deep breath, and walked to what looked like the opening. "Enter *alin*," a rasping voice uttered, addressing him by the term used for a younger sibling. "I've been expecting you."

Cordero stepped over the stone foundation and gingerly entered the hut, a hand either side of the opening to steady himself because it was dark inside. As his eyes adjusted he made out a shadowy figure seated in the center of a room. An empty hardback wooden chair was positioned in front of the seated figure and a hand that looked almost mummified motioned to him to sit. Around the walls hung clothes, tiny bells, assorted feathers and dried flowers, roots and herbs in clumps. The wax from unlit candles covered a table on the side of the seated figure and a teapot steamed idly though there was no fire. Stones and pieces of wood covered one side of the earthen floor. He detected a slight movement in the far corner above a bed. He looked up and thought he saw an owl with a watchful eye on the room.

"How did you know I would come, *senyora*?" he asked.

"Do you know how old I am, *alin*?" she asked and issued a throaty cough.

He could see her more clearly as his eyes adjusted to the darkness inside the hut. She was shrivelled in appearance as though her body had shrunk in on itself. She wore a wrap of blue, red and white stripes that covered her body, and a scarf of the same colors with feathers on her head. Yellow beads hung from her neck and her left arm was covered in bangles of bone. Cordero counted two large silver ear-rings hanging from her right ear lobe but thought there may have been more under her white hair. Her eyes were deep-set but a brilliant black and clear. Her face was gnarled, the gums sunken, and her skin was the color and texture of elephant hide. She held a corn-cob pipe between a few stained teeth and puffed on it as she spoke. He could smell the cloves that had been mixed in with the tobacco.

"Old? N-No," Cordero stuttered not knowing why. A slight breeze made the bells jingle along one wall.

"My father told me I was born when they came for Dom Boaventura in the mountains," she said, indicating a Portuguese military expedition that captured, and likely killed, the hero king of the present-day district of nearby Manufahi. Cordero raised an eyebrow. "He said I would be Boaventura's revenge." She puffed on her pipe and coughed. "I have special powers. I knew you would come." She took her pipe out of her mouth and laid it on the table. "Besides, you are a police officer and I'm told police officers are curious."

"Well, actually I am a police investi—"

"What is it you want to know, *alin*?" she said cutting him off.

Cordero let the interruption pass. "They say you are a witch, *senyora*," he said but it was a question.

"They say a lot of things, *alin*," she replied.

He noticed his shadow cast onto the back wall of the hut. He turned slightly and there was a candle burning on the floor which he hadn't noticed when he entered the hut. He paused to clear his own throat. "About a week ago the bones of several people were found in the sands of the Comoro River in Dili," he began. "When they were put together it was noticed that the bones had been burned. On what would have been these people's backs. We think these bones came from a burial spot along the river, near here, just north of Tepia, and that they washed down stream toward Dili in heavy rain." He chose his words carefully now. "I have heard it said that in other parts of Timor, when a person who is thought to be a witch is killed, their spirit is weakened by burning the body." The old woman was looking at him with unblinking eyes but she said nothing. "I came here to ask if you knew of any witch killings in Tepia."

"You ask this because you think I am a witch?"

"I ask it because you have lived a very long life and I am told that you are very wise," he replied.

She coughed again then snickered. "You don't bullshit well for a police officer," she said.

"Police inves—" he started to correct her but stopped.

"And you don't look me in the eyes, *alin*. Do you fear I will enchant you? Maybe I will turn into a beautiful young girl and seduce you. Here. Now. Is that what you fear?" she tilted her head slightly. "Or maybe what you want?"

He forced himself to look at her directly then. "No. I don't fear that. Or want that."

"Would you like tea?" she said and waved at the teapot, her bangles jangling. "Or do you think I put a potion in there?"

Cordero stared at the teapot. He hadn't noticed the two cups beside it before. He filled both, picked up his cup and sipped just a little. He put the cup back on the table. She hadn't answered his question and he tried a different approach. "This morning we intercepted a group of elders who had abducted a boy from Tepia—Tomas—and had taken him out to the same spot we think the bones came from with the intention of killing him to avenge the death of the *lia-nain*, Sabu Bada."

"Tomas, you say?" The old head nodded slowly. "The *bonko*?"

"Yes, the hunchback."

"I wondered when the village would put its troubles on his back along with his hump," she said. She picked up the pipe and sucked on it but the tobacco had burned down and gone out. She emptied the ash into a bowl on the table which Cordero noticed for the first time. Then she placed the bowl carefully on the floor, her bracelets jangling again. Outside a wind was picking up, the thatch covering of the old woman's hut began to shake a little, and the feathers on her headpiece ruffled. "There will be a storm for the *lia-nain's* burial," she said looking up. He thought he caught a smile appear on the woman's face at the thought.

"As I said, *senyora*, I am wondering if you know of any witch killings in this area," Cordero repeated.

"You like the tea?" she said leaning slightly forward and he remembered the cup.

"It's fine," he said and took another sip. She hadn't touched her cup. He heard a clap of thunder far off in the distance. "Do you— know, I mean, anything about witch killings?"

"I know a witch killing is a powerful thing, *alin*." She leaned back in her chair and sighed. "When the *bapa* were here," she said using the colloquial term for Indonesians, "they wanted things their way. They didn't know our history. They didn't respect our culture. They didn't care. They had guns like this," she said and leaned forward and gestured at Cordero with both hands pointing directly at the center of his face, "and say 'You do things our way now'." She closed her eyes, coughed, leaned back again and breathed heavily. "They say 'This is no longer your land; this is our land.' They say 'You, go! Live there. You come! Live here.'" She opened her eyes and looked at him. "You know this what I am telling you, *alin*?"

"Yes," said Cordero. "Most of my family moved to Australia during the Indonesian time but I am familiar with what happened." He thought she was referring to the forced relocation of people, partly to break local support for the resistance fighters, partly to accommodate Indonesian agricultural development plans.

"I don't know where this 'Australia' be at. Maybe east, beyond that town Baucau or south, near that one they call Suai." She closed her eyes again. "But it no matter."

She was silent. He waited. Cordero wondered if the old woman had fallen asleep. He started looking around the room— the feathers, the herbs, the owl. "People came here from the other side of the mountain," she said, resuming her account. "*Bapa* tell them to come. They come here with paper they say gives them land. Paper from the *bapa* in Railaco or Ermera. But nobody can read the paper and the land they say is theirs already belongs to people here. The people been farming it for generation after generation. You hearing me, *alin*?"

The room seemed to be growing even darker and the candle behind him was no longer flickering. Cordero heard thunder again and wondered if a storm was brewing. "They call me a witch," she said abruptly. "But I can't turn myself into a bird or a buffalo or even a mouse. I can't summon spirits from the underworld. And I can't cast a spell on you, *alin*." She breathed deeply and adjusted her wrap. "I make potions from herbs that cure illness. And I take care of injured birds," she said and gestured toward the corner where the owl was perched. He could see it clearly now, despite the poor light. He could also see that the thing was looking back at him. "I like birds, the freedom they have to go anywhere they want with a flap of their wings," she added. "They remind me of my youth, long ago." She breathed softly and shallowly.

"But they say you wander at night, *senyora*," Cordero said, turning back to the woman.

"They say many things they don't know anything about," she said. "I go at night because then I be left alone." Her tone was indignant. "To scavenge for food and other things I need. Do you see a garden here that supplies me what I need? Do you see money I can spend at the kiosk? Chickens that lay me eggs?" She coughed again. "The young ones taunt me and throw things at me," she said lowering her voice and wiping spittle from her lips. "I used to be able to chase them away but not anymore. You see I am old, *alin*."

"You pretend to be a witch?" Cordero asked. "To keep them away?"

"It's worked for a long time," she said and smiled her jagged smile.

He could see it now: the trinkets and theatrics were just a lone old woman's defence against people taking advantage of her.

"But why are you telling me about the *bapa* and the people he brought?" he asked.

She shook her head, agitated again. "People were angry their land was being taken away by the *bapa*," she said. "Robbed by the *bapa*! They were even hungrier than usual. Their children were dying!"

"Then why didn't they challenge the paper the *bapa* gave those people? At least after the *bapa* left?"

"You talk nonsense, *alin*!" she screeched at him. "No one challenge the *bapa*. Be shot dead if you do. And there are no more papers when they go. The *bapa* burn them all. No one can prove anything."

Cordero thought for a minute. The woman calmed herself, closed her eyes and wriggled as though getting more comfortable. "Are you telling me that the people with the paper from the *bapa* were accused of being witches in order to get rid of them."

"It takes you a long time to understand things, *alin*," she said and smiled, her eyes closed tight.

"How many people are we talking about?"

She didn't answer immediately. Cordero waited. "There were several families with the paper," she said and folded her hands across her lap. "But after the *bapa* go and one family disappear the rest know pretty well what would happen to them if they stay and they leave Tepia."

Maybe fifteen years ago, Cordero calculated. That would fit within the age range Brooks the pathologist had given for most of the skulls. "And who would have been responsible for the disappearance of this family?"

"You think I live this long in a small village by making trouble to people, *alin*? You work that out yourself. Who you think would have to approve someone be called a witch before others believe too and kill them?"

Cordero thought he knew the answer to that. He rubbed the back of his neck.

"One more thing, *senyora*," he said. "I wanted to ask you about a young girl. Clarita. Clarita Araujo."

But the old woman seemed hardly to be breathing at all now. "I am tired, *alin*. I must sleep before I go witching tonight. And I am out of tobacco. Bring me tobacco and we will talk about that one another time."

As Cordero left the hut of *Senyora Batibat* he noticed the air was close outside and the sun was setting bright and hot in a cloudless sky. No wind. No thunder. No sign of rain. When he peered through the afternoon glare, the hut of *Senyora Batibat* seemed to dissolve into the trees. He wondered if he had imagined his whole time talking to the old woman inside.

• • •

"I'm not certain yet," Cordero said as he poured the last of the gin into their glasses. "She told me her birth coincided with the quelling of an uprising against Portuguese rule just before the First World War. That would make her about a hundred years old." They were sitting on the verandah and he eased back down on the side of the bed he'd given over to Carter for the night. "That's old for a Timorese, very old, and it may be her way of claiming she's special, you know, being born at a providential moment in Timor's history." He took a sip of his gin. "Then she wanted me to believe she only made elixirs and cared for injured birds. But what I saw, even more what I felt, in that place makes me wonder if that's true."

"Felt?" questioned Carter. "Did I hear that right? You *felt*?"

"Yeah. It's hard to explain," he said and stared into his glass as he swivelled it around in his hand.

"You think there's more to *Senyora Batibat* than she was letting on?" she asked.

"As I said, I'm not certain. What she said about people being settled in Tepia with Indonesian land claims could be true. And that would certainly infuriate any locals whose land was confiscated."

"Enough to kill?" asked Estefana.

"Possibly," Cordero said. "With the exception of the recent skull the rest could easily constitute a family. Maybe the family who'd been brought in from elsewhere and who were killed as a warning to the others." They sat in silence a moment. "But if she was making up the other stuff about her age and whatnot she could have made that up as well."

Crickets were chirping over near the church and the iron roof of the nuns' house creaked as it cooled. Above them the night sky was awash with stars. "Tomorrow Estefana," Cordero said as he finished his gin, "I'd like you to call Dili. Most land titles were destroyed by the Indonesians when they left. She was certainly right about that. But see if there is any record of land disputes around this area, around Railaco, that might lend credence to what she said. Ask Jacobsen to check with Jakarta through INTERPOL as well. They might be more forthcoming if she tells them she's looking into illegal logging or other kind of *Timorese* misbehavior rather than anything the Indonesians did during the occupation." Estefana nodded. "Then see if Father Roque can locate any church records of baptisms. Brooks said one of the skeletons might have been a two-year-old. There's a chance the mother had that child baptised here when the Indonesians insisted on every Timorese identifying with a monotheistic religion. There just may be a church record from around fifteen years ago that could give us a family name or two we could check to see if they were recorded in the 2004 census."

"And what do you propose you and I do tomorrow?" Carter asked as they rose and stretched before retiring for the night.

"We'll go to the *lia-nain's* burial," Cordero said. "If what *Senyora Batibat* told me is true it would have been him who approved the designation of the family as witches and by extension their killing to restore customary land title. We may see something that suggests a culprit or culprits who sought revenge by killing Sabu Bada."

20

Clouds hung low and leaked rain across Tepia the next morning and the dreary weather matched their mood as Cordero and Carter made their way to the *uma lulik* for the burial of Sabu Bada. Cordero thought about *Senyora Batibat's* prediction that it would be raining today but shook it from his mind. He ached from sleeping in the back seat of their vehicle. Carter was hungry after passing on the rice porridge and making do with coffee. Estefana had gone to check on Tomas. He'd been shown the door after breakfast by Sister Felicia and had skulked off through the downpour to Father Roque's shed. Estefana would ring Dili when it was safe to assume people would be at their desks and then she would call on the priest. "So," Cordero had said when Carter settled into the SUV. She waited for him to finish but he said nothing more.

"I don't get what we're doing here or, more precisely, what *I'm* doing here," she said when he pulled up at the clearing outside the *uma lulik*.

He looked across at her. "How come? In American cop shows the police always go to the funerals of murder victims," he said grinning.

"This is about as far from an American cop show as you can get," she said ignoring his gaze. "Besides, you said there's a good chance he wasn't murdered."

"That's right. But he didn't kill himself on a whim. He had help," he said and turned back to the clearing.

"I'll grant you that but how are we supposed to identify whoever that may have been?" she protested. "We don't even know the people here. And there must be close to a hundred!"

He left the wipers on so they could get a clear view of the scene. The rain was drifting across the clearance in watery veils. The marquee erected for the *tebedai* remained standing but the thatch had been refreshened although now it was sodden. Beneath was a table draped in black with a red and blue *tais* across one end. Beside the table stood a pole on which hung the ceremonial trappings of Sabu Bada—the buffalo horned headpiece, the red chest medallion, his anklets and bracelets. His sword was missing because Cordero had confiscated it the night of his death—much to the dismay of the headman. On three sides of the marquee most of the villagers stood motionless in the pouring rain. Only the youngest children stared out, away from the *uma lulik*, wet, uncomfortable and unsure of the significance of the thing they were attending.

"When a person dies in Timor," Cordero explained, "it's important to do two things. One is to ensure that the person's spirit makes the journey to their ancestral village in the spirit world instead of hanging around to interfere in this world. This is particularly important where death comes about unnaturally because the spirit will seek retribution unless it's satisfied this will be taken care of by others." He was emphasising his points with vague movements of his hand across the scene in front of them. "The other thing is to repair the loss of that person to the community by weaving together again the social fabric. Any on-going obligations Sabu owed to his late wife's family must be cancelled through gift giving. And their acceptance of this enables the community to get on with things and is signalled by them giving lesser gifts back to his family, or his origin house in this case since he has no family here." He looked to see if she was following him. "Exchange you see—that's the foundation of relationships in this country because everyone, ultimately, depends on everyone else. Now the two exchanges should go smoothly. If either doesn't, it may give us a clue to what's going on in respect of Sabu's death, the skulls or even the girl, Clarita."

Carter nodded. She understood. She was thinking how the Navajo bury their dead with their moccasins on the wrong feet to confuse the *chindi* or ghost of the deceased should it seek to return and of the ceremonies they use to restore harmony in a community after an experience involving any kind of significant loss or trauma.

"Okay I get all that," she said. "But how are we going to know who's who?"

"We won't," Cordero replied. "We can only watch for anything unusual—anything that proves disruptive to a ritual which has been followed for hundreds, even thousands of years." He looked across at her again. "Anyway what else are we going to do today? Everyone we want to talk to is out there and they won't talk to us until this is over." He cut the wipers. "Come on, we can't be seen to disrespect the *lia-nain* by sitting in our vehicle to avoid getting wet."

They made their way to the side of the *uma lulik* just shy of the marquee. Both had pushed their hands as far as they could into the side pockets of their jackets and turned their collars up against the rain. Other than that, there was nothing they could do but accept they'd be soaked, like everyone else although no one else seemed to be paying it any mind.

A low moaning began and built into a loud wailing from the women in the crowd. On the ladder of the *uma lulik* the legs of two men appeared, unsteady at first, as they emerged bearing the bottom end of a roughly hewn coffin. Two other men made their way gingerly down the ladder carrying the top end. The four casket bearers carried the coffin to the table under the marquee and placed it down carefully. People began to comfort each other, place flowers on the coffin, and embrace it. An old man carrying a black flag on a pole whose finial was adorned with buffalo horns appeared on the ladder of the *uma lulik*. It was Balbo Fuentes and he led four drummers down and onto the clearing near the marquee. Each of the men wore a black headpiece and black shirt or T-shirt over a subdued *tais mane*. Another man on the other side of the marquee—Cordero recognised Juno Da Silva—called to men and boys sheltering under the trees and they came running carrying a bamboo frame onto which the coffin was secured with heavy ropes. The crowd shuffled into a line to process the body of Sabu Bada along the track through the trees for burial beside his wife at his hut. Balbo Fuentes led the way with the flag drooping in the rain. He was followed by the drummers beating a slow rhythm, and the men and boys bearing the coffin. Another man brought Sabu's ceremonial things. The villagers straggled along behind. Carter saw four men carrying the carcass of a pig tied to a smaller platform under a canopy of fresh bamboo shoots at the rear of the line of mourners. That would be for the ritual meal. Several women brought up the rear with sacks of rice balanced on their heads and plastic bottles of cooking oil in their hands.

The procession made its way slowly up the track. Children carried candles that had gone out a long time ago in the rain. The adults were sombre but the younger boys bearing the coffin began to kid each other as they slid in the mud. An older man admonished them and the boys appeared solemn again. Two of them took off their flip flops and pushed them up their arms to get a better grip in bare feet. Even then the casket bearers had to negotiate tight bends in the track by going backwards and forwards trying to get the right angle to turn and all the time the drummers beat their mournful rhythm.

"Do you see the gifts the women carry?" Cordero whispered to Carter. "A few *tais*, a bottle of *tua-tein*, a leather belt and tobacco. I'd say they're gifts from Sabu's wife's family. Small things, symbolic mainly, nothing too valuable and all easily buried with the body." He wiped the rainwater from his face. "I don't see anything big like a buffalo or a pony—the sort of thing you'd expect the people representing Sabu would offer back. Maybe it's his coffee equipment they'll give in exchange or maybe the hut and his land will be divided among his wife's people."

"Okay," Carter said unconvinced of the relevance of what she was being told. "What does it tell us?"

"Nothing except it confirms that he has no immediate family here. That's why this whole thing has been done in a hurry. Normally the wake would take three days and the close family would be involved in rituals for weeks, even months, after the burial. I get the feeling everyone wants this over with quickly."

On through the rain the procession ploughed for another mile. When the leading group finally came within sight of Sabu Bada's hut the drum beat became louder and more rapid. The rain had stopped falling but the yard was a field of thick mud. Cordero saw women going in and out of the hut and others breaking from the line of mourners to join them with groceries. The women with the bags of rice and cooking oil headed around the back to the kitchen. Food was being prepared to go with the pig that would be cooked for a ritual meal once Sabu was buried. Halibo was standing to one side. He saw Cordero and raised his arms in a gesture of 'What did you expect me to do now?' then the boy took a cigarette from his pocket and lit it.

The coffin was carried to a grave dug that morning beside the tomb of Sabu's wife. All but one of the drummers stopped drumming and the last one produced a solo in a furious cracking beat. On cue, all mourning and wailing abruptly ceased like the sudden silence of cicadas. When the drummer had finished, Balbo Fuentes came forward. He had exchanged his black flag for a sword with an elaborate goat's hair handle. He stood at the foot of the coffin, raised the sword above his head, paused a moment, and brought it down fast stopping just above the top in a practiced motion. "That gives Sabu protection in the afterlife," Cordero explained to Carter, "although it's usually reserved for fighters and kings."

The coffin was lowered into the grave. Sabu's anklets and bracelets were placed in as well. His headpiece and chest medallion would be handed to whoever would succeed him. Two other men carrying swords came and stood alongside Balbo. Despite their elaborate customary attire, Cordero recognised them as Braga Bucar and Fonseca Lage. Juno da Silva emerged from the shed where the coffee beans would have been dried with three large dogs on strong ropes. As the dogs barked and yelped, another man walked around the gravesite seven times reciting words that Cordero could not make out. The people closest to the grave began to edge back, turning their eyes away or clenching their hands to the breasts. The youngest of the children had been moved away behind a screen of adults. Struggling and whimpering, the dogs were manhandled in front of the men with the swords. When the circling had stopped, Balbo spoke but, again, Cordero could not make out what he said. Next, one by one the dogs were beheaded. As each was slaughtered, its blood was dripped over the grave and its carcass thrown on top of the coffin. The hole was then quickly attacked by six men with shovels. Once filled, two men positioned a large rock on top. This was to seal the grave until a false tomb could be erected above it. When the men had finished, and stood to brush the mud from their hands, there was an immediate rush of people across Sabu's yard and back down the track. Cordero and Carter watched in astonishment as the area quickly drained of mourners and only the elders, Sabu's wife's immediate relatives, and the few representatives from Sabu's origin house remained to exchange gifts over the ritual meal.

Cordero walked over to Halibo and handed him a five dollar note. "Job over," he said and the youth pocketed the money and walked off without a word of thanks. Cordero walked back, took Carter's arm lightly and gestured that they should take to the track as well. "That was interesting," he said. "Very interesting. But I need to make a call and check my understanding of Timorese burial practices before I say any more."

• • •

"That's what I thought," Cordero was saying into his cell. They'd returned to the nuns' house, rustled up bread rolls and tomatoes for lunch to go with the tuna they'd brought from Dili, and had sat down to eat when his cell had rung. He stood and paced the room. "Yeah, yeah. I'd heard one of the villagers say that nobody dies naturally here anymore. They're obviously reading meaning into it," he was saying. Carter looked across the table at Estefana who made a face as if to say she couldn't follow the conversation either. She passed the bread rolls instead. They waited. "Real fast. Yeah….That's one, yeah….No. Three….Got it. Okay. Thanks Cristorao. Owe you, *maun*." He closed his cell and sat at the table.

"That was Cristorao Guterres," he said taking a roll and tuna onto his plate. "He teaches anthropology at the university in Dili. We use him when—"

"Point being?" asked Carter dispensing with the preliminaries.

"Well, two things really." He took a bite of his roll. "First," he said, chewed and swallowed. "When one dies unnaturally it's known in traditional communities as a red death. People believe that a red death can contaminate the living, you know, certain people, their crops, maybe the whole village. They often behead a dog—or maybe a chicken—to keep the dangerous 'red' away and reinstate the 'black' which is associated with a natural death. When that's done the body can be buried and everyone can rest assured it will stay buried." He took another bite of his roll.

"And you're telling us this because?" asked Carter. Outside the clouds were breaking up and the sun had appeared in patches evaporating the damp into a light mist that hovered above the ground. The nuns were praying in the next room—the soft cadence of their voices penetrating the wall as one called a succession of holy titles for the Mother of God to which, together, they rhythmically responded 'Pray for us'.

"One dog," he said, raising a finger and ceasing to chew. "They behead one dog. But for Sabu's burial they beheaded three. I'd call that overkill wouldn't you?" Carter looked at Estefana, who shrugged her shoulders. "And then of course, well, you saw how everyone took off in a panic." They both looked at him. "What that says to me, and to my anthropologist friend, is that they're scared. Real scared that Sabu's spirit will return seeking justice. Or vengeance more correctly. Having no close relative to mourn and comfort him in his own home wouldn't help. Consequently the grave is 'hot'—spiritually potent. People ran from it as fast as they could. And they tried to 'cool' it, to keep a lid on it if you like, by offering three dogs not just one. That means it's very hot indeed."

He sat back satisfied that it was all now self-explanatory only to confront the doubt in their eyes.

"Okay but how does any of that help us?" Carter asked.

"Well it tells me," Cordero said pouring himself coffee, "that they have no idea who killed Sabu Bada or why. In a small village like this, that's unusual. And it tells me that they fear they'll never know. Look at how they buried Sabu deep into the ground rather than lay him out in an above-ground sarcophagus like his wife. They'll build a similar thing on top but only for show. They want to make sure he stays in the ground. What that all adds up to, I'm almost certain, is that the person who killed Sabu or at least was there when he died doesn't live in Tepia and that the reason for his death is not tied to any current grievance in the village. It's an old, mysterious thing." He noticed them staring at him. "Otherwise, you see, they'd be able to find out, eventually at least, who it was and why. And that means they could find a way to keep things under control." Carter nodded but said nothing. Estefana pulled a bread roll apart with her fingers as she considered the theory. "Did you find out anything, Estefana?" Cordero asked to change the subject.

"Danique Jacobsen is still checking with Jakarta but I rang the National Directorate of Land, Property and Services Registration and they told me that, yes, there are ongoing disputes about land title in this area and that many of these relate to customary claims versus Indonesian title."

"That was smart," he said finishing his bread roll and tuna and starting on the tomato. "Calling the Directorate, I mean. And that's enough to tell us *Senyora Batibat* may have been right when she told me about people being pissed off that the Indonesians were giving away their land."

"Shhh," said Carter, shooting a finger toward the room where the nuns were praying.

"Oh, sorry," Cordero said. "What about church records?" he asked in a whisper, looking back to Estefana. "Any luck there?"

She shook her head. "I'm afraid not, *maun*. Father Roque gave me what records he could find but said that they were probably incomplete and maybe even inaccurate. He said even the priests back then weren't properly trained in record keeping and Tepia was so far removed from the bishop's notice that no one was keeping much track of them." Estefana looked out of the window toward the church. "I went through the records as best I could but I didn't find anything helpful. Whole years are missing entries for baptisms, marriages, deaths. Page after page had been left blank."

"Well I can't say I'm surprised but we had to try," said Cordero. "Good work, Estefana. How's the boy by the way?"

"Oh he seems to have survived his ordeal well enough," Estefana said, her expression brighter. "The whole experience frightened him but he has been through a lot in his short life and he is strong. He insisted on showing me his special things again. I think he forgot that he showed me last night."

"Well there's nothing more we can do about Sabu or the skulls today," Cordero said, draining the last of his coffee. He rose from the table. "I'm going to keep on the case of the girl, Clarita Araujo."

"How?" asked Carter.

"I'm going to have a word with Moussi—the mechanic. Our man with all the accelerants. Father Roque told me he came back here from Dili in order to find a wife. I wonder if he did." He wiped his mouth. "And I'd be interested to know what he ended up doing if he didn't."

Carter and Estefana stood also and started out of the room together ahead of him on a mission of their own. "What are you two up to?" Cordero asked.

"As you say, there's nothing we can do today while everyone we want to talk to is either up at Sabu's place or avoiding vengeful ghosts," said Carter.

"We're going to cook dinner," Estefana finished the statement, her face cheerful. "Father Roque and the nuns will be joining us."

•••

On his way to the mechanic's workshop Cordero had to pull up sharply in the SUV to avoid hitting children who came charging out of the school grounds all over the road. After the first wave of youngsters rushed past, an older group of boys came strolling out, arms draped around each other's shoulders. Girls appeared laughing and singing as they crossed the road. Cordero was in no hurry and so he watched on patiently.

He heard a motorcycle approaching from behind and the rider honked and held up a hand in recognition as he passed. It was Rui and he carried two of the older girls who had jumped on his pillion. Up ahead he brought the motorcycle to a stop, put one foot on the ground to steady the bike, and talked briefly to several boys as the girls dismounted and adjusted their skirts. Cordero saw Rui shrug his shoulders at a question one of the boys had asked him before he signalled to his two companions to re-mount and he raced off, the girls laughing and waving, their skirts riding up their thighs even higher.

Two boys about ten years of age raced each other down the road kicking an empty plastic water bottle. It reminded Cordero of his own childhood in East Timor before his family fled to safety from the Indonesians in Australia. One of the boys wore a baseball cap backwards on his head and it flew off into a puddle as he missed a wild kick for the bottle. But the race was on and the boy didn't stop. Cordero engaged his park brake, stepped out of the SUV and called after the boy but he didn't respond. He picked up the cap. The *Real Madrid* crest on its crown was smudged with mud and he tried to wipe it clean. As he walked back to the gate of the school, Cordero was twirling the cap around on his finger. Thinking. He looked up at the school and back down the road from which all but a few children had disappeared. He placed the cap on the top of the school gate. He was confident that in Timor it would be there untouched for its owner to collect the following day.

21

Cordero heard the sound of clanging on metal as he exited the SUV and walked toward Moussi's workshop. Pulling the door aside to enter, he noticed light penetrating the tarpaulins that served as a roof and streaming through the bamboo walls. The dirt floor remained littered with tools and machinery and there were puddles from the rain. A motorcycle—the priest's—had been shifted to the center of the workshop where Moussi was squatting, examining it. The benches along one wall overflowed with assorted cans and tools. Moussi was tapping on something, his back to Cordero.

"*Botarde, maun*," Cordero called and Moussi turned but didn't return the greeting. "You didn't go to the burial of the *lia-nain* today," Cordero said but his remark carried a question.

"I was there this morning. It's finished now. I've got work to do," Moussi said. He turned back to his tapping. "What do you want?"

"A friendly chat. Nothing more," said Cordero, glancing over Moussi's back. "Is that Father Roque's motorcycle you're working on?"

"You came down here to ask me that?" Moussi said, standing and meeting Cordero's stare.

"No. But I thought I'd ask since you seem to be busy with it," Cordero said and ran a hand lightly over the fender.

Moussi dropped a ball-peen hammer he was holding to the ground, took a rag from the back pocket of his shorts and wiped his hands. "It's been here almost two weeks," he said. "The part I needed from Dili arrived when I came back from the burial. I figure *amu* will want his motorcycle." He wiped his hands even harder and put the rag back in his pocket. "There's lots of souls need saving around here."

"Why do you say that?" Cordero asked casting an eye around the workshop.

"No reason, *maun*. Making conversation. You said that's why you came here."

Cordero ignored the sarcasm in Moussi's tone. "I hear you lived and worked in Dili for a while," he said and glanced back at the priest's motorcycle.

"That a crime?"

"No. But I was wondering what brought you back here," Cordero said. "Most people seem to be heading in the other direction. Away from Tepia."

"That was three years and more now, *maun*. Strange thing to ask now."

"Nonetheless, I'm asking," insisted Cordero.

"With all those *malae* leaving," Moussi said, meaning foreigners, and specifically those who worked in peacekeeping operations with the United Nations Cordero guessed, "the work was drying up. Not many opportunities for me in Dili." He took a cigarette from a pack on the bench, lit it and inhaled. "I figure I knew enough about motors to come back here and work. No one else doing it this side of Railaco." He replaced the lighter on the bench and exhaled. The smoke drifted up through the rays of light from the tarpaulins. "Besides my father died and his property became mine."

Cordero nodded. He squatted down to examine the priest's motorcycle more closely.

"You didn't see yourself as a farmer?"

"My father wasn't a farmer. He was a *badain-besi*," Moussi said—a blacksmith. "Making tools, fixing them. Most of the gear I need was already here," he added and waved a hand around the workshop.

"No other reason you came back from Dili?" Cordero asked avoiding eye-contact.

"What other reason, *maun*?"

"Oh, I don't know," answered Cordero and shrugged. "Maybe you got homesick. Maybe you got lonely in a big place like Dili. Maybe you thought you'd come home and, you know, find yourself a nice local girl to marry." He glanced over his shoulder and up at Moussi.

The mechanic had taken another drag on his cigarette and he coughed as he laughed. "You married, *maun*?"

"No."

"Then you've saved yourself a lot of grief and worry." Again he laughed. "So have I."

Cordero stood and looked at Moussi directly. "You know a girl by the name of Clarita Araujo?"

"I know lots of girls, *maun*. But I never made the mistake of marrying one."

"I didn't ask if you married her," Cordero said. "I asked if you know her."

The smile went from Moussi's face. "Araujo huh? Clarita Araujo?" He frowned and thought a moment. "Yeah," he said and pointed the butt of his cigarette toward Cordero. "Yeah I know her but I haven't seen her around here in a long time. Over a year, I'd say. I think she went to Dili or Ermera. Like you said, most people are leaving Tepia these days." He put the cigarette to his lips and blew smoke out of his nose.

"Pretty girl was she? Clarita?"

Moussi laughed again but held the cigarette in his lips. "Pretty girls give you the most grief, *maun*." He saw that Cordero wasn't sharing the joke. "Yeah, she pretty enough. But she weird too. You'd see her eyes rolling backwards in her head and then she'd shake like she was possessed." He took the cigarette out of his mouth and pointed the butt at Cordero again. "Best leave girls like that alone, *maun*."

"And that's what you did? Leave her alone?"

Moussi gave him a hard stare. He took a deep drag on his cigarette, tossed it on the ground and stamped on it with his sandal. "Ask anyone, *maun*," he said offended by the suggestion in the question. "I said '*Bondia*', '*Botarde*' to her if I saw her. Polite like. That's it. I never touched her. Why you asking?"

"Oh, curiousity I guess," Cordero said. "It's a curse all policemen share." He smiled at Moussi, strolled over to the benches against the wall and casually examined the cans on top and underneath. "You have a lot of different kinds of fuel here," he said. "Diesel, kerosene, turpentine," he checked them off tapping each with a finger as he went. "And what's this?" He picked up a small brown bottle with a skull and crossbones symbol on its label and the black flame on a yellow background warning the contents were highly flammable. The bottle was nearly empty but he noticed two others that looked full on the ground under the bench. Cordero smelt the jar. It was a strangely sweet smell. "This is?" he asked holding the jar out at Moussi.

"Benzene."

"Benzene, eh? Very flammable I hear," said Cordero.

"Yeah. Benzene's flammable. It's also very expensive out here," Moussi said taking the can out of Cordero's hand and placing it back on the bench.

"What do you need all this benzene for?" Cordero asked.

"Why you think?" Moussi grumbled. "Lots of old motors out here, *maun*. Lots of new fuels now too. Knocking is a real problem with them motors. I mix that one in to keep them running."

"I would have thought something as dangerous as this would be kept under lock and key," Cordero said.

"Who's going to steal from me, *maun*? They steal from me, I can't fix their motors. Then what they do?"

Cordero could see logic in that and nodded. "You haven't seen Clarita for a year?" he asked.

"Over a year," Moussi corrected him.

"And you don't know where she is or where she went?"

Moussi simply stared at Cordero and grew impatient.

"Where's Rui today?" Cordero asked, changing the subject.

"Not enough work for him today. Why should I pay him to stand around? I don't know where he is but he's not here."

"Wouldn't he miss the money? Not working today, I mean," said Cordero.

"I never see that boy in any great need of money."

"How come?"

"Ask him," said Moussi. "His business, not mine."

"What can you tell me about Rui?" Cordero was leaning against the bench directly in front of Moussi.

"What you want to know?"

Cordero shrugged. "Where's he from? How long has he been working for you? What kind of boy is he?"

"You ask a lot of questions, *maun*. I don't have all day to be chatting."

"It's what I do for a living," Cordero said, making light of the complaint. "You fix motorcycles: I ask questions."

"Rui lives outside Tepia. With his mother and younger brother, I think. Father's dead. He's been working here for about two years. He likes motors. Works well. I never had no problem with him. But I don't always have enough work for him either."

"Did you ever see him with Clarita Araujo?"

"Back to her are we?"

"Yeah. You ever see Rui with her?"

"*With* her? What do you mean, *maun*?"

"You know, talking to her, hanging out with her? Maybe giving her a ride on the back of his flashy red motorcycle?"

"Case you haven't noticed people always giving other people a ride on the back of their motorcycles here, *maun*. It doesn't mean anything."

"She didn't hang around the workshop?"

"No."

"And he never talked about her?"

"With me? No." Moussi bent down and picked up the ball-peen hammer again. He turned away signalling that what Cordero had described as a friendly chat was over.

"But he does like girls?" Cordero asked before ending the conversation.

"Don't you, *maun*?" Moussi said, his back turned to Cordero. He started tapping again without waiting for an answer.

· · ·

"Do you like to cook, *mana*?" Estefana asked as she led Carter out onto the road and off to a nearby hut suggested to her by Sister Agnes.

"I don't get much chance to do it back home," replied Carter. "Usually it's precooked I buy and stick in the microwave."

"I love to cook, *mana*," Estefana said, the delight evident in her voice. "My mother and I cook together a lot. If you like, I'll show you how to do this special recipe she taught me. It's easy but delicious."

"Okay but don't keep me in suspense. What is it?" Carter asked.

"*Na'an-manu manas*. Spicy chicken, *mana*. The nun told me we'd be able to buy a chicken from the woman in the hut up ahead. Most of the other things we need I saw in the nuns' garden. Except for the galangal, turmeric and lemon grass. But this woman should have those as well. They're very common in Timorese cooking so they should be growing in her garden."

"Galangal and turmeric," Carter repeated. "Sounds good."

"And lemon grass. Better than rice and eggs, *mana*," Estefana joked. "Not to mention rice porridge!"

They strolled to the hut and found the woman sweeping her yard with a home-made wicker broom to keep scorpions away. She stopped when they approached and exchanged greetings. After a little haggling, the woman sold them a chicken for two dollars. Estefana had said that was expensive but the woman allowed her to raid the garden out the back for any herbs or spices she needed while she killed and plucked the chicken. She warned her to watch out for any scorpions she might have scared into the patch. When the woman finished preparing the chicken she offered Estefana the gizzards for no extra cost but Estefana declined, thanking the woman and suggesting she keep the gizzards herself and make soup.

Back at the nuns' house Carter took instructions from Estefana. The latter placed a large pot of salted water on the gas cooker to boil. Then she cut the chicken in half and, when the water was bubbling, took the pot off the cooker and put both halves of the chicken into it. On the kitchen table she'd arranged large red chillies, the roots of tumeric and galangal, and lemon grass stalks. These she had Carter chop finely before mixing them together in a paste.

"Do you like cooking now, *mana*?" she asked Carter.

"Beats microwaving a meal packed in plastic," Carter said. "Bet it tastes a lot better as well."

Meanwhile Estefana mixed soy sauce and tamarind paste from the nuns' frugal pantry, added small red chillies, garlic and shallots she had fried quickly over the cooker, and a little sugar. She stirred the mixture vigorously to make the sauce.

They could hear the nuns and Father Roque moving chairs around the table in the cramped quarters of the adjoining room. Cordero popped his head in the kitchen door and asked if he could help. Estefana said no but Carter gave him a handful of fresh tomatoes and told him to cut them at the table and to put them on a plate as a side salad.

When the chicken had had time to blanche in the pot of boiling water, Estefana retrieved the halves, patted them dry, and rubbed them thoroughly with the paste Carter had prepared. She began to fry the chicken halves on either side in oil in a pan. While she was doing this, she told Carter to simmer the sauce mixture in the bowl for ten minutes, stirring to make sure it didn't burn, and to boil the rice. Soon delicious odours filled the kitchen and wafted out through the rest of the house, exciting taste buds and watering mouths. In the kitchen, as the pungent capsaicin from the chillies rose from the cooker, Carter coughed uncontrollably and Estefana's eyes began to tear up. They looked at each other then and could only laugh at their discomfort.

When the chicken was done, Estefana removed the halves from the pan, cut them into smaller chunks. These she put onto a large plate and drizzled the hot sauce over each of the pieces. Then she drained the rice, put it into two serving bowls, and she and Carter took the meal out to the nuns, the priest and Cordero.

22

Father Roque stood and offered a short prayer over the table. "We thank you Father for this delicious food and for the fellowship we share tonight, through Christ Jesus. Amen." He blessed himself and sat. Cordero was seated at the other end of the table admiring Carter from the corner of his eye during the saying of grace. She had her hair pulled back in a ponytail and a warm glow in her face he hadn't taken time to study before and she sat on his right side with Estefana. The nuns huddled together next to the priest. Sister Felicia seemed to prefer a longer prayer for she kept her hands together and her head bowed after Father Roque had sat back down. They waited. And waited. Finally she too blessed herself and the others could begin serving themselves and eating.

The older nun pecked at her food like a sparrow, resentful that Father Roque had asked her to hand the kitchen over to the house guests. The younger nun ate like it was the end of Lent and the forty days of fasting and denial had finally come to an end. Carter almost choked when she put too much of the hot sauce into her mouth but quickly learned to relish the taste of organic, home cooked food. Estefana ate daintily but enjoyed every mouthful of the special meal she'd learned to cook from her mother. Cordero and Father Roque cut, tore, chewed and shovelled hungrily. The entire chicken was devoured in no time and Cordero and Carter were left to compete at picking the bones.

The remaining sauce was soaked up in the rice they scooped onto their plates, and the simple fresh tomato salad cleansed their palates. As the food quickly disappeared, the conversation just as quickly grew in intensity. "How goes your investigation, Tino?" Father Roque asked. "Or should I say your investigations—plural?"

"Well we think we've identified the girl who was killed more recently. Clarita Araujo. Do any of you know of her?" Cordero said, addressing the nuns as well as Father Roque.

Sister Felicia looked disgusted and leaned back to emphasize her repulsion. "That girl got it into her head that she was a witch," she said and sniffed. "Silly young thing. She wouldn't have anything to do with our church or with us after that." She looked at the younger nun for agreement and sounded a humph.

"Was that the girl who suffered from epilepsy?" Father Roque asked. Sister Agnes nodded on Sister Felicia's behalf. The priest shook his head. "They hear what is said about them and they internalise it, I'm afraid."

"What do you mean 'what is said *about* them'?" Estefana asked.

"No one here with the exception of present company and the nurses at the clinic would have any idea what epilepsy is or how it affects those who suffer from it," the priest explained. "Naturally— or should I say ignorantly—they'd take it as a sign of witchcraft, sorcery, possession—you name it."

"Yes," agreed Cordero, pouring coffee and holding the pot up by way of invitation to others. Estefana and Carter produced their cups and Cordero obliged by filling them. "And then the person so labelled will admit to whatever is being said about them even if they know they'll be beaten or worse as a result."

Carter sipped her coffee. "They're usually people who have lost everything—if they ever had anything to begin with," she said. "The idea that they are a witch gives them an identity at least, and it becomes important to retain it no matter what."

Father Roque nodded his agreement. "But we've not seen this girl in the village for a long time, *senyor*," Sister Agnes said, also accepting the offer of coffee, much to Sister Felicia's apparent distaste.

"We'd thought she'd gone to Dili," added the older nun, who placed her hand over her coffee cup to prevent Cordero filling it.

"What about your skulls?" asked Father Roque changing the subject.

"We're pretty sure we've found where they came from before they were washed down river," said Cordero, sipping his coffee and adding a little sugar.

"Well I can tell you I said a few Hail Mary's under my breath as we approached the spot where they were planning to—" but the priest stopped rather than alarm the two nuns. He poured himself coffee. "How is Tomas by the way?"

"He's fine *amu*," said Estefana. "It's good of you and the sisters to care for him as you do."

"We would do more if we could," said Father Roque shaking his head, "but there is a wild, feral element about that boy after years of neglect."

"But it doesn't appear that those people were the victims of a militia massacre," said Carter returning to the skulls.

"No," Cordero said, satisfied with the taste of his coffee now. "Those deaths may be connected with a land dispute going back to the last days of the Indonesian occupation. *Senyora*—I mean Tereza Silveiro—told me there were contested titles here about fifteen years ago and we've been able to establish that was indeed the case around here."

"Another one who thinks she's a witch," Sister Felicia said and again with a huff conveyed her disapproval.

"A little charity, Sister," said Father Roque. "That would have been well before my time and before the good sisters' time as well."

"We still have questions to ask the elders," said Cordero. "We'll get to them tomorrow when the burial of Sabu Bada is well and truly behind them."

"If those people were not killed as a result of militia activity our work," said Carter waving a hand across herself and Estefana, "is done here."

"Except that we can't get back to Dili without *maun*," Estefana pointed out. "And there are now two more cases he has to solve."

"Yes indeed," said the priest. "And so what of Sabu's murder?"

"I'm not entirely convinced he was murdered exactly," said Cordero.

"But surely—" Father Roque began.

"Oh there's no doubt his death was the result of a scuffle but whether his killing was intentional is the issue." He drained his coffee cup. "It may be tied up with the same dispute involving the skulls. It could go back quite a long way."

"What do the French say: revenge is a dish best served cold?" said the priest smiling. "But *that* cold?"

"As I said, we have questions to ask," was all that Cordero added. "Do any of you know Rui—the boy who works for Moussi?"

The nuns looked at each other and then at Father Roque. "Everyone knows Rui," the priest said and chuckled. "He's a gadfly around the village. But he's harmless. And no, we don't have much to do with him if that was the next question."

"How much longer will you be staying?" Sister Felicia interrupted and there was a hint of impatience in her tone.

"Another night or two and I suspect we should be ready to return to Dili," answered Cordero. "If we are no trouble, of course, and that is okay with you, *madre*."

"You are no trouble, *senyor*," the old nun replied but her expression said otherwise. "And your payment goes to support our mission here. Since the bishop stopped sending us novices, our regular income has fallen to almost nothing." Sister Felicia stood and Sister Agnes did the same like a well-trained poodle. "Thank you for the meal," Sister Felicia said bowing slightly to Estefana and to Carter. "If you will excuse us Father, we have evening rosary to say."

As the nuns made to leave the room Cordero posed one more question to Sister Felicia. "Do either of you have anything to do with the school or the school children, *madre*?"

Sister Felicia stopped and turned. "The bishop would like a proper school here in Tepia—a Catholic school. So, no, we don't have anything to do with the school." Her tone was imperious. "But the school children are another matter. The teacher there is very lazy. He often doesn't turn up and when he does he'll sit out the back and smoke cigarettes and leave the children entirely to themselves. Often we can hear a commotion at the school even from here and we know he hasn't turned up. Then Sister Agnes and I may go down and do what we can to teach the children about God and His Blessed Son." She raised an eyebrow as if to say 'Any more questions'.

"Thank you, *madre*," Cordero said. "I hope you have a good night's sleep."

"And you *senyor*," the nun replied.

When the nuns had finally exited the room Father Roque reached into his jacket which hang on the back of his chair. From the pocket he produced a bottle half full of a clear liquid. He put it on the table and went to a cabinet behind him for four small glasses. Estefana looked at Carter who looked at Cordero who shook his head. "We call this *Cachaça* in Brazil," the priest said laying down the glasses. "Distilled cane sugar. Very strong. But we don't often have guests and I think it is appropriate that we finish the bottle tonight after such a wonderful meal."

Before they could say anything he had filled the glasses to their brims and proposed a toast to the night's two chefs. Carter almost choked but she held it down, Estefana turned red in the face and fluttered her hands in front of her mouth, while Cordero and Father Roque coughed, smiled and poured themselves a generous second glass to empty the bottle.

23

"**I** don't have to tell you anything," insisted Braga Bucar.

They were sitting on plastic chairs under a eucalypt tree in Braga's yard. Cordero had decided the best approach would be to speak to them individually, starting with the two who had appeared the least comfortable about killing Tomas—Braga Bucar and Fonseca Lage. That way he hoped to learn things that could be used as leverage to open up Balbo Fuentes and the hardest of them all, Juno da Silva. Cordero imagined Fonseca Lage, with his bottle of palm brandy, to be the weakest link, but Braga's hut was on the way and they had decided to talk to him first. Estefana was translating for Carter, though with a head slightly numbed by last night's *Cachaça*. The morning was growing hotter although the sun was a ruby behind smoke from the damp vegetation farmers were trying to burn for new subsistence plots. Dark clouds were building on the southern horizon.

"I can arrest you for abducting Tomas with intent to murder him." Cordero was saying.

"You see a jail around here, *maun*? Or a judge?"

"There are both in Ermera," replied Cordero.

"You'd have to get me there."

"I have a vehicle," said Cordero growing impatient.

"You'd have to take that *bonko* as well," said Braga referring to Tomas, "and all the witnesses here who'd say I did nothing and you're crazy too." He'd been sharpening a coffee pruning knife when they'd arrived and he went back to it again. "You may think you have power here but you don't," he added studying the edge on the blade, hoping they would just go away as quickly as they had appeared. Cordero ran a hand through his hair.

Estefana translated the gist of the conversation, telling Carter that Braga was refusing to recognize Cordero's authority. "Try another approach," suggested Carter. "Appeal to what he values as an elder."

Cordero pulled out a handkerchief and wiped the back of his neck. He stood and cast an eye around Braga's yard and along the ridge that bordered it. "Good land here," he said. "Hard work clearing it and preparing it but land that rewards the effort." He glanced down at Braga whose eyes were focused on the blade he was turning in his hands. "How did you get on when the Indonesians were here? How were you able to protect this land so well?"

Braga looked up, a sullen expression on his face. He put the pruning knife down on the ground, folded his arms and cast an eye on his surroundings. "Not much they did around here," he said. "They had men in Railaco who'd come out from time to time. Patrols. But there were no *Falintil* here," he went on, referring to the pro-independence guerrillas, "and no reason to stick around. You can't grow rice on these slopes which is the only interest they had in land. They left us alone most of the time." He looked at Cordero. "Why you asking, *maun*? That was a long time ago."

"Just curious," said Cordero. "They didn't bother you?"

"No."

"Others? Did they bother anyone else around here?"

"Maybe, I can't speak for others."

A rumble of thunder threatened to bring more rain but it was a long way off and the sun continued to dominate the sky even through the smoke.

"The Indonesians were moving people around though, weren't they?" asked Cordero wiping the back of his neck again. "Timorese people I mean. You know, breaking up communities all over the country." Braga said nothing. "And when they moved people they gave them land title to encourage them to stay where they put them." He stared down at Braga. "Didn't they?"

"If you say so," Braga answered.

"I do say so because we know that happened here. There are records," said Cordero stretching the truth of what Estefana had learned from the national office dealing with such matters. "What would you—the elders, I mean—do when someone turned up and claimed land on the basis of an Indonesian title?"

"What could we do, *maun*?" Braga said and raised his arms testily. "Like I said, they'd send patrols out every once and a while checking on things." Braga lent forward in his chair. "If you protest, they'd take you away and you don't come back. We just waited."

"Waited?" Cordero asked. "For what?"

Braga looked up at him. "For them to go. For good. What else?"

"And when the Indonesians did go? What did the elders do then?"

Braga gripped the knife again and stared at it for a moment. "We put things back the way they'd always been," he said and continued his sharpening.

"What do you mean by that?" Cordero asked but there was no reply. "What happened to the people who had Indonesian title?"

Again Cordero waited.

"We dealt with it," Braga grunted.

"How? How'd you deal with it?"

"You should ask the *lia-nain*. He was in charge of things," Braga said, looking at Cordero with anger in his voice. "But he's dead."

"You're one of the elders. I'm asking you," Cordero said. But again Braga didn't answer.

"Do you know anything about the *lia-nain's* death?" Cordero asked.

Braga shook his head. Cordero could sense his tolerance for talking was draining away and changed his line of questioning. "What can you tell me about the place where you took Tomas?" he asked. Silence. "We know there are human remains near where you'd stopped. We've evidence that a number of people were buried there." More silence. "Killed, burned, then buried,"

Cordero added, emphasising each word. He waited. Nothing. "Who's idea was it to take Tomas there—to the riverbank on *lulik* land to kill him? Balbo's? Juno's?"

"You'd best ask them," said Braga standing and glaring at Cordero. "If you're going to arrest me, do it. If not, I've answered enough of your questions and I have work to do."

• • •

They sat in the SUV outside the hut of Fonseca Lage. His wife had told them that he had gone foraging in the forest for wild foods to supplement the small crop of maize and sweet potatoes their garden produced. She expected him back soon. The breeze had picked up from the south blowing the smoke away and it was cloud now not haze beginning to block the sun.

"Bucar wasn't giving too much away but his silence spoke volumes," Cordero said. "This village is up to its neck in guilt and denial. And that's just those bodies on the riverbank. And Tomas. We haven't yet got to Sabu Bada's killing or Clarita Araujo."

"What was it Bucar said, Estefana? They put things back the way they'd always been?" asked Carter who took the water bottle Cordero was holding, sipped from it and handed it back. "That wouldn't hold up as an admission of anything in a court of law but it's suggestive that they had a way of dealing with people they considered a threat." She brushed the hair from her forehead. "And that could link them to what was buried along the river."

"Let's see what Fonseca has to say for himself," said Cordero. "I see him coming now."

They confronted Fonseca in the cleared yard at the back of his hut. He was unshaven, his hair a greasy mess that hung down over his eyes. He wore shorts, a torn T-shirt, and sandals and carried a few elephant foot yams and bitter beans he had scrounged from the forest.

"We'd like to ask you a few questions, Fonseca," Cordero said, assuming introductions were unnecessary given the circumstances of their meeting on the riverbank. "Is there a place we could sit and talk?"

Fonseca didn't protest but simply gestured with the hand that held the yams to the half-finished and, by the look of the weeds running riot, now-abandoned foundations of a cement block house near his thatch and bamboo hut. He was a small man and when he sat he curled further into himself and appeared even smaller. He placed the yams and beans at his side, wiped his face, and took a cigarette from the pocket of his shorts. He lit the cigarette, inhaled, and blew smoke out into the breeze. He hadn't said a word.

"We know Juno came up with the idea of killing Tomas to avenge the death of the *lia-nain*," Cordero began. "You didn't want to go along with that, did you?"

Fonseca turned and looked up at Cordero, the cigarette close to his mouth but not inhaling. There was regret on his face and his lips quivered slightly. His wife appeared and without excusing herself picked up the few yams and beans.

"Is that it?" she said with angry disappointment in her voice. Fonseca looked at her but said nothing. "How do you expect me to feed the two of us and the grandchildren with this?" she asked. "You're useless," she said and stormed off carrying the scraps he'd collected. Fonseca stared at the ground humiliated.

"I was asking about the plan to kill Tomas," Cordero repeated. "You didn't want to go along with it, did you?"

Fonseca didn't reply.

"Come on, *maun*," said Cordero. "It's time to act and speak up. Help me. You didn't want to harm the boy, did you?"

"No," Fonseca said finally and looked away. "That boy's stupid but I didn't think he should be killed."

"But Juno and Balbo did. And they forced you. Is that right?" Cordero asked.

"Not just me. Braga too. He didn't want to kill the boy either but they said we were elders and it was our duty." He took a drag on his cigarette and waved the smoke away from his face.

"Why was Juno so insistent the boy be killed?"

Fonseca took another drag on his cigarette and let the smoke engulf his face this time.

"Why Fonseca? We're not leaving until you tell us," insisted Cordero.

Fonseca wiped his eyes and stared blankly across his yard. "Juno wants to take over as the *lia-nain*," he said. "He wants to be seen as strong, in charge, the one elder most likely to uphold tradition. He's always been the crazy one coming up with ideas and he's always thought he'd make a better *lia-nain* than Sabu."

"And Balbo?"

"Balbo would do anything Juno says. And if Juno became the *lia-nain* that would give Balbo more control over the other elders. The two are like brothers."

"So killing Tomas would show the other elders that Juno was now firmly in charge, is that it?" asked Cordero. Fonseca nodded. "Let's get back to what you said about your duty as an elder," Cordero said. "When the Indonesians left there were people here who'd come from outside the village, who controlled land the Indonesians had given them. How did the elders deal with that?" Fonseca, expressionless, remained silent. "You couldn't contest the title because all the records of who had rights to what had been destroyed. And there was no one here to adjudicate the claims. What did the elders do?" Fonseca took a deep drag on his cigarette. Sweat appeared on his upper lip and his eyes began to water. "Did the *lia-nain*—Sabu Bada— decide that someone had to be killed to set matters straight? To take back ownership and scare off the others? Is that how Juno got the idea to kill Tomas to set matters straight after Sabu was killed?" Cordero could see Fonseca's resistance shaken. "Is that why you took Tomas to the riverbank, near the overhang, because that's where you all killed the family with Indonesian title to land?"

Fonseca threw his cigarette on the ground and stood to walk away but Cordero grabbed his arm. "Who declared that land *lulik*, Fonseca, and when? Was it Sabu Bada? And who gave him the right to plant on *lulik* land? We've seen the coffee plants down the side of the ridge below his hut. Is that how he was able to pay for the new *uma lulik*? Was that the land the family you killed had Indonesian title to?" Fonseca had his back to Cordero who maintained the grip on his arm and could feel that Fonseca was no longer resisting. *He thinks he was right but he feels he was wrong,* Cordero was telling himself, *and with a little more pressure he'll want to unburden himself.* "Did you cut their heads off, *maun*? Did you burn the bodies? Did you dig the graves? Would it help if I gave you palm brandy, Fonseca?"

The man pivoted toward Cordero, anger in his eyes. "They were witches, *maun*," he spat. "The *bapa* sent them here to kill us all," he said referring to the Indonesians. "That's why the *bapa* didn't need soldiers in Tepia. He had *them!*"

Cordero was annoyed with himself for ending his tirade by insulting Fonseca's honour and forcing him on the defensive. But the truth was slowly emerging. "Kill you how, *maun*?" he asked.

"How does the *bapa* kill people? Takes their land, their food. Starves them. Those witches came here and destroyed our crops. When we dealt with them, the crops came back. I'm not sorry for what was done. We did what we had to do. No one else here to help us, *maun*. Where were you and your police officers and judges when we needed them? You talk about the state. Where was your state when our children cried all night because their stomachs were empty?"

"But you killed children too," Cordero protested. "Young girls."

"The power of the *buan*," Fonseca hissed, "passes down through the females. Sabu said they all had to go."

"And that's why you burned the bodies?" Cordero asked. "Because they were witches? And buried them out there to close off that land and keep their spirits from Tepia?"

Fonseca shook his arm free of Cordero's grip and said nothing. The sun disappeared behind a huge bank of black clouds, darkening Fonseca's yard. The breeze dropped and the first rain hit the ground at their feet.

"Is that why the girl was killed and her body burned? Because you all thought she was a witch as well?"

Fonseca looked at him, the anger replaced by confusion. "What girl?" he asked.

"Clarita Araujo. The one who was sick with fits. The one killed a year ago."

"I don't know anything about a girl who was sick with fits. And with Braga and the others and that boy is the first time I'd been out on that *lulik* land since the witches were killed. I don't know what you're talking about, *maun*."

"*Ajuda tiu!*" a shrill voice called for an uncle's help and a young boy ran barefoot from the tree line to the back of Fonseca's hut. Carter recognized him as the boy Father Roque had been talking to in the market. Juno da Silva's grandson, Ziggy. The boy saw Fonseca and the others on the side of the hut and hurried over. The rain grew heavier. "Someone is killing grandfather," the boy said and rubbed his nose. "He's gone to the clinic place because the nurses are there. There's blood everywhere. All over his face, his chest, in his mouth, in his eyes. It's awful. Grandmother told me to get you. You must come. Quickly!" and Ziggy began tugging on Fonseca's arm.

Fonseca summoned his wife to take care of the boy. As soon as the grandchildren appeared at the door and caught Ziggy's attention he ran to them to recount his exciting news. Fonseca moved forward then back, patting his pants' pockets, unsure of where to go or what to do. Cordero put his hand lightly on Fonseca's shoulder. "Come, *maun*. We'll drive you," he said and gestured toward the SUV. The rain was now a downpour. "Come on. Get in front." As he drove the SUV out of Fonseca's yard, Cordero turned to him. "One more question, *maun*. Do you know anything about Sabu's death?"

"Sabu. And now Juno," said Fonseca, his expression morose and his hands clasped. "I know it's those witches come back to get us. I've feared it all these years. Now they're here!"

24

Balbo had taken Juno to the clinic and he was now waiting outside under an awning smoking a cigarette and trying to dry out. Rain poured down. Fonseca ran from the SUV straight to Balbo. Cordero, Carter and Estefana hurried inside the building. There was a trail of blood across the tiled floor to a small side room where Juno had been taken. A nurse appeared, the one they had spoken to days earlier—Sefa Soares—and she was going about her duties with calm efficiency. When she saw them she put a tray on a bench near a sink, wiped her hands, and came over anticipating their questions.

"He'll be fine," she said before she was asked. "He was hit with a machete but with the flat side, not the sharp edge." She demonstrated using her hand to represent the machete. "After we cleaned him up we noticed a cut above his eye that required stitches and his nose is broken. That's why there's so much blood." She picked a clipboard up from a table in the center of the room. "We'll keep him here for a while and keep an eye on him. He's not a young man after all."

"Why would anyone hit you with the flat side of a machete?" Cordero wondered out loud.

"Ask him?" said the nurse. "He doesn't seem to want to tell us very much at all." With that she walked off staring down at what was written on the clipboard.

The window was closed to keep out the rain—making it an airless as well as cramped room. Juno sat in a chair to the side by the door while a nursing assistant was attending to his nose. Fresh stitches protruded above his right eye and flecks of blood

197

had dried and crusted in his eyebrow. A table and a bed occupied the room as well as Juno and the nurse leaving little space for Cordero, Carter, and Estefana to all take up positions inside. "I need to make a phone call, *maun*," said Estefana excusing herself, and Carter said she would wait outside the door.

"*Deskulpa, mana*," Cordero said apologising to the nursing assistant for interrupting. He turned to Juno without waiting for a response. "What happened, *maun*?"

"The *asu* damn near killed me," said Juno sucking air through his mouth. He had referred to his assailant as a 'dog'—which is a deeply offensive censure among Timorese and not used lightly. "That's what."

"Who, Juno?" asked Cordero. "Who tried to kill you?"

"How would I know? Probably the one who killed Sabu!"

With great patience the nursing assistant was trying to affix gauze to Juno's nose with adhesive tape but he was agitated and kept moving his head and knocking her hands away.

"Can you describe him?"

Juno tried to sniff but made a face at the pain. "Young man, thin, hair unwashed, dirty T-shirt and jeans." He stared out the window, breathing fast and his jaw set hard.

"Calm down," said Cordero, "and tell me what happened from the beginning."

Juno took a deep breath, the nursing assistant saw an opportunity and worked the gauze in under the tape. Cordero threw a leg over the table in the center of the room.

"I was working in my garden," Juno began. He went to sniff once more, grimaced, put a hand to his nose but thought the better of it. "He grabbed my machete and started asking me questions. He threatened to cut my head off!"

"But he only hit you?"

"Isn't that obvious!" complained Juno.

"And you've never seen this man before?" Cordero asked.

"No. Never."

"What was he asking you?" Juno went quiet, a furtive look in his eyes. "What questions, *maun*?" Cordero asked again.

Juno looked away. Cordero rose, gently ushered the nursing assistant aside and faced Juno. "That nose of yours looks very painful, *maun*," he said. "I don't think the nurse here has re-set it properly. Let me have a go. But I must warn you, I won't be as gentle as her," and with that he raised a hand as if to grab Juno's broken nose.

"He wanted to know where they're buried," Juno said raising his hands to protect his nose.

• • •

Estefana figured her best chance of getting cell coverage in a storm was at the health clinic. She moved just inside the front door and tried her luck. On the third attempt she got through to her friend Dado Ramon in Dili.

"Dado? *Botarde maun*," she said. "It's Estefana dos Carvalho. *Diak ka lae?*"

"Hey Este! *Diak mana. Ita fali?*" an eager voice asked how she was doing herself.

"Yeah, I'm well too, Dado. It's been a long time. How's the new job in Dili?"

Dado had a job as a data analysist at the Ministry of Agriculture and Fisheries.

"Been here twelve months now, Este. I miss Suai but Dili's great. There's going to be a movie theatre opening here soon. Imagine that—big screen, bigger sound! Can't wait. Oh, and, yeah, I like the new job. Nice crowd. Steady income now I'm a father. I heard you moved to Dili too. With the cops. That right?"

"Yeah, I'm seconded to work with INTERPOL for the next few months," Estefana said. "I moved about a month ago and I'm still finding my feet."

"I know what you mean," Dado said snickering. "It's a bit like that in Dili. A lot bigger than Suai, eh? We'll have to get together. My boy Lopo is ten months old now and you haven't met him. Adelina would love to see you as well. What are you doing tonight?"

"I'm not in Dili right now, Dado. I'm in Tepia." She was pacing the front room of the health clinic and she looked at the rain cascading from the awning outside.

"Tepia?"

"Yeah," she said. "It's a small village on the west side of the Comoro. Almost parallel to Aileu."

"This cop business? Car broken down? What are you doing out there, *mana*?"

"On a case. That's why I'm calling you." She gave him a moment to focus on that. "Most of the farmers here grow coffee to supplement the usual stuff they get from their gardens. I need to know if there were any major crop problems in this area about fifteen years ago. Around the time the Indonesians were packing up and leaving or just after they'd gone."

"Gee *mana*, I'm not sure I can help you. The Indonesians destroyed all the records they'd kept, their militia buddies got rid of most of the rest in the turmoil before the referendum, and the transitional authority was too busy trying to keep the peace to worry about agricultural production. They just, you know, brought food in from outside."

"I know that, Dado," Estefana said.

"Well, we didn't start compiling records until seven, eight years ago and they're pretty basic because extension workers are learning how to do it. You should see how bad the reports can be."

"I don't need accurate records, Dado," said Estefana. "I just need to know if anything was going on at that time. Anecdotal stuff would do. There must be a colleague you can contact from Railaco, Ermera or Aileu who was alive at that time and remembers what was going on around here."

Dado made a doubtful sound and fell silent.

"Dado? You there, *maun*?"

"Yeah sure, *mana*. I'm thinking." Estefana could hear Dado umming and ahing on the other end of the call. "There is a guy— Bepi. He's from Aileu. Bepi must be sixty years old at least. Was a farmer along the eastern side of the Comoro until a few years ago, I think. He's with us at the Ministry now. Says it's a lot easier working a computer keyboard than a patch of ground at his age."

She heard Dado muffle a laugh. "You're asking about that general area right? Eastern and western side of the river?"

"Well I'm on the western side and that's my main area of interest."

"About fifteen years ago?"

"Yeah."

"Okay, I'll ask him. I think I saw him in the office earlier. Can you ring back in ten minutes?"

• • •

"And what did you tell him?" Cordero was asking.

Silence again and Cordero motioned his hand toward Juno's nose.

Juno flinched. "I told him they were out along the river. In the *lulik* land down from Sabu's place," he said. "He wanted to know precisely so I told him where on the riverbank."

Cordero noticed that the nursing assistant had stopped collecting the bloody wipes she had used to clean Juno's face and was listening intently to the questioning no doubt to spread it through the village that evening. "You can go now, *mana*," Cordero said. "Thanks for your help and keep anything you've overheard to yourself, please. This is a police matter." He waited until she had left the room, disappointment showing on her face. "How did he know about them?" Cordero asked.

"He found out from Sabu." Juno pressed his lips together and pointed them up at Cordero. "Before he killed him."

"And you told him because you thought he'd kill you too?"

"He had my machete raised above my head, *maun*! What would you have done?"

"He didn't say who he was?"

"No."

"Or why he wanted to know where the bodies were buried?"

"No and I didn't ask."

"Then what happened?"

"Then he hit me with the machete and ran off." Juno looked equal parts pained and angered. He looked around the room at nothing in particular, agitated. "I called out to my wife who called Balbo and he brought me here."

"He take your machete when he went?"

"Yes."

"You're the one who claimed they were witches, aren't you? Don't try to hide it. I've got witnesses."

"They *were* witches, *maun*! Things were dying all around. They'd cursed the land and they'd cursed us!" He grimaced and for a second time went to touch his nose but stopped. "Besides. Sabu agreed they were witches and he was the *lia-nain*."

"And a *lia-nain* would lend credibility to such claims," said Cordero. "Who did the killing?" Juno remained tight-lipped. "I know you're handy with a machete—saw that when you were going to kill that boy out there. Was it you?" Juno said nothing. "*Maun*! I asked you: who did the killing?"

"The elders!" Juno admitted in a temper. "Sabu, me, Balbo, all the others!"

Cordero waited for Juno to calm down again. "And it was an entire family that you killed?"

"Hmm."

"What?"

"Yes," he admitted. "It was all of them. They were all witches."

"Even the children?"

"Witches have no age, *maun*. They can be any age they want."

"What were their names?"

"I don't know, *maun*. They'd come from over Viqueque way. The *bapa* brought them. No one wanted to know them. No one talked to them. They'd taken our land!" Juno stood, a little unsteady on his feet, and grabbed the chair for support. "If I knew their names, I wouldn't repeat them anyway or I'd be inviting them back to harm me."

"Why bury them under the overhang?"

"It was wet. You can see how it rains here." He waved a hand at the window where the rain was being blown against the pane. "We had to burn the bodies. We did it under cover."

"Why burn the bodies?"

"I'm telling you; they were witches! And they sent a witch back to kill us!"

"But he didn't kill you, did he, Juno? He only broke your nose and cut your eye when he could have cut off your whole damn head. And I'd say the cut was probably an accident." Cordero turned to leave. "We'll talk again, Juno."

• • •

Cordero gave Carter an abbreviated version of Juno's account as Estefana walked over from the front door of the clinic to join them. "He's gone out to the riverbank," Cordero said. "I'm sure of it. And if we move fast, we'll find him there."

"*Maun*, I learned something that could be important," said Estefana.

"Not now, Estefana. We've got to move quickly." He turned to Carter. "Father Roque has a canoe. If you two take it along the river there's a good chance you'll get to the overhang before him. I'll drive up to Sabu's and come down the ridge. That way we should catch him in the middle."

"*Maun?*" Estefana tried again.

"Listen to what she has to say," insisted Carter and Cordero reluctantly did as he was told.

"I rang my friend Dado Ramon. He works in the Ministry of Agriculture. I asked him to find out if there were any major problems with crops in this area ten or more years ago." She had Cordero's attention now. "He said something attacked the coffee cherries about fourteen or fifteen years ago. They think it might have been coffee berry borer."

"Coffee berry borer?" asked Carter.

"It gets into the berry and eats the bean. Destroys the entire crop," said Cordero. "It's a major hazard for coffee growers across the world." He pondered that a moment.

"Dado says the bettle comes from Africa," Estefana said. "If that's what attacked the coffee berries it would have been a mystery to people around here. That might make them believe it was the work of witches."

"Witches working for the Indonesians to ruin Timorese," added Cordero. "And due to the general mayhem at the time there'd be no one coming out to tell them any different or to deal with the infestation. It all fits. Good work Estefana."

"There's more, *maun*." He looked at her. "Dominique Jacobsen had called, and I rung her back. She had no luck getting information about land titles out of the Indonesians. But she said if we're not dealing with a war-related crime any longer, *mana* and I should head back to Dili immediately and be assigned to another investigation."

"Good luck with that," said Carter.

Cordero raised an eyebrow. "You don't seem to have a lot of respect for authority," he said.

"I just hate being told what to do," she said and headed for the door. "Like you. Come on!"

25

They dashed through the rain across to the SUV, ignoring Balbo and Fonseca, and climbed in. Cordero worked the ignition, threw the vehicle into gear then promptly stalled it. He swore under his breath. "I heard you tell Juno to calm down," Carter said shooting him a sideways glance. "*Kalma* right?" He studied her, bemused. "My Tetun teacher uses it with me all the time. Says you have to let language grow from inside you and not force it out. Well, police work is much the same and you need to calm down now."

He noticed her grinning, started the SUV again and let the clutch out with greater care. "It's just that the pieces are falling into place," he said by way of an excuse. "But you're right—*kalma!*"

He started up the road to the church and Father Roque. Several women were running home to get out of the rain; a few men ignored the downpour and only ambled along to wherever they were going. "Thanks to Estefana we know why they were killed—the destruction caused by the coffee berry borer and the panic that would have put through a community already hostile to newcomers who'd been given land," Cordero said. "We know who killed them—the elders. And we know why they were buried where they were—away from the village in order that their spirits would not haunt the place."

"And no one would go messing around the burial site," Carter added.

"Right," said Cordero. "It was a case of superstition mixed in with tragedy and ignorance aided by opportunism on Sabu's part. He saw a chance to use that land to strengthen his standing in the village."

"We don't know the name of the family," Carter pointed out, "because they were outsiders parachuted in by the Indonesians who no one wanted to get to know."

"And that made them easy targets," added Estafana from the back seat.

"Right again," said Cordero. "And that's the one piece of the puzzle we're missing. Who were they? What are their names?"

"That and who this guy is who attacked Sabu and Juno," Carter pointed out.

"Hopefully we'll soon know that," said Cordero. "Maybe he's a member of the family or a family friend. Juno said they killed the entire family but since no one seems to have bothered to get to know them we can't be sure."

"Or he could be an Indonesian who regrets the trouble they caused," Estefana offered. "There were Indonesians who opposed the invasion and more than a few have come back to Timor-Leste and worked as volunteers. Maybe he came back and argued with Sabu and the elders because of what they did to that family."

"That's true," agreed Cordero. "Whoever he is he appears to be an outsider."

"He can't be too much of an outsider," said Carter, "or how would he know who Sabu and Juno were?"

Cordero changed into a lower gear to turn into the churchyard. The SUV sloshed through the mud up toward where Father Roque lived. "Well whoever he is I don't see him as a killer—yet. I'm not convinced that the *lia-nain's* death was intentional. If whoever was with Sabu when he died was a killer, he could easily have killed Juno as well but chose only to immobilize him in order to take off and not be followed." He pulled up at the front door of the priest's house and cut the engine. "But he does have a machete and he is on the run. So be careful."

"You too," said Carter as they left the vehicle.

Cordero knocked on the door. No one answered. He knocked again, more insistently as the others joined him under the narrow portico out of the rain. Again there was no response. He tried the door. It was unlocked. "Roque!" he called. "Father Roque!

Anybody there?" Nothing. They huddled together considering their next move. Cordero began to rattle the keys to the SUV in his impatience. "Why don't I head—" but they heard a motorcycle come spluttering up the road and into the churchyard.

Father Roque rode into his shed, dismounted and lifted the motorcycle onto its stand. "Rui brought my bike back," he said taking off his helmet. "I gave him a lift back to the workshop because of the rain. I noticed your vehicle outside the clinic on my way. Is everything okay?"

The priest looked from one to the other for an answer. He was soaking wet but it didn't seem to bother him. "Juno da Silva's been attacked," Cordero said. "Same guy responsible for Sabu's death we think."

"Juno? Is he badly hurt?"

"Broken nose and injured pride," said Cordero. "He'll be fine."

"Shit," said the priest. "How can I help?"

"We're going after the guy who attacked him. We think he's headed out to the *lulik* land along the river. On foot. You said you had a canoe. If Carter and Estefana take it I think there's time for them to head him off. I'm driving up to Sabu's place to come down the ridge behind him and cut off any escape that way." Father Roque nodded. "Can they borrow the canoe?"

"I'll do better than that," Father Roque said slipping his helmet back over his head. "I'll paddle them myself. I think I know where this fellow will be heading and I know the river." He swung the motorcycle off its stand and kicked it to start. "Get on," he said to Carter and Estefana. "There's enough room on the back if you squeeze tight. The canoe's down by the water."

"I don't see Tomas, *amu*," Estefana shouted as she climbed on behind Carter.

"No," he shouted back across the sound of the engine. "Ever since the abduction, Sister Agnes has warmed to him and Sister Felicia has found him useful. He'll be at their house doing chores they've found for him."

26

Across from where the canoe lay on the riverbank, the main channel was fifty yards out, connected by a runnel oozing seepage from the slope. Father Roque brushed loose vegetation from the canoe, dragged it across the sand and gravel, and slid it into the water. Estefana, the smaller of the three, was told to get in first, at the bow. She had never ridden in a canoe before and remained nervous about venturing into *lulik* territory. She lost her balance, fell, and landed on her backside in the water. She crawled into the canoe on all fours and sat, her trousers soaked. Carter was also unsteady. She put a hand out to Father Roque for support and managed to get into the middle of the canoe with only a wet left boot. The priest cast off gracefully, ankle deep in water.

Rain continued to fall. So much had fallen over the last few days it had washed soil and loose vegetation into the shallows turning them into a muddy sludge. The main channel was steel grey under the heavy cloud cover. Where the water washed over submerged rocks it produced ripples the size of small waves. "We'll head for the center," Father Roque called from the back. "The current is strong there and it'll take us down fast." He pushed back hard on the paddle. "Just hold on to the sides and try not to unbalance the canoe. We're likely to get pushed around a bit."

As water began splashing over the bow Carter noticed the white on Estefana's knuckles as she clutched the sides of the canoe with a mixture of determination and trepidation. "Do you have many parishioners down river, father?" Carter shouted over her shoulder to break the tension.

"Down river, no," the priest shouted back, moved the paddle to his other side and pushed back hard again, settling into a rhythm. "There's about a dozen families upstream I see from time to time. Keeps me fit all this paddling." His attempt to joke seemed to have little calming effect on his companions. "But I don't get down here very much at all."

The eastern side of the river was thick forest with a few small clearings where subsistence plots appeared to have been cleared but on which nothing had been planted. A few water buffalo lay motionless in the shallows oblivious to the rain and a cormorant was balanced on the back of one, scanning the water for fingerlings. A little beyond where Tepia aligned with the river they paddled passed primitive huts whose thatched roofs covered them to the ground. Smoke from cooking fires flattened out above the huts in the rain. Further along, passed the last of the huts, Carter noticed a stream flowing into the river. It was a sizable tributary running a jagged course around large boulders and it was easy to see why people might regard it as a barrier dividing two quite distinct patches of the riverbank. The boundary to the *lulik* land, Carter imagined. If they'd gone this far already they were making good progress and might be ahead of their quarry.

• • •

As Cordero drove toward the hut of Sabu Bada he kept thinking he was no closer to finding whoever killed Clarita Araujo. Why was she buried in the same place fifteen years or so after the original killings? Coincidence? He didn't think that likely. Why was her body burned like the others? Was it because she was considered a witch or because someone wanted to suggest that she was? And why use accelerants rather than twigs and leaves like the others? Was her killer one of the people who killed the alleged witch family, which would make him one of the elders? If that was the case what would be the motive since none of them professed to have known much about her? Something linked the most recent killing with the early ones. Of that he was sure. But what was it?

The SUV shuddered over the rockier parts of what passed for the road and slid sideways through the watery mud that the rain had produced. Cordero had to keep firm control, especially at the speed he was going which he knew to be too fast for the conditions. Carter, Estefana and Father Roque were sure to get ahead of the man they were after via the river but he couldn't afford to be far behind them. As he had warned, the man was on the run and armed with a machete. After attacking Sabu and Juno he was nearing his goal—whatever that might be—and might not stop now at killing or seriously injuring anyone in his way.

His mind came back to Clarita. She had been a pretty girl which could suggest a sexual crime or jealousy as a motive for her killing. But that would render an elder an unlikely suspect. Eusebio was young enough perhaps but the others were in their sixties or seventies. If sex was the motive could that suggest Moussi? Or Rui? Clarita had also been an outsider who was considered a witch because she suffered epileptic seizures. Clearly fears about witches were common throughout Tepia. But witch killings were not random acts. They had to be approved and their approval required they be connected with a clear problem—like the widespread inexplicable ruin of the coffee cherries. Nothing they had uncovered that had happened in the village or to a particular villager would explain what had prompted a witch killing twelve months earlier except that the previous *uma lulik* had burned down around the time of her death.

He stopped speculating as he neared Sabu's hut where he would leave the vehicle and hurry down to the riverbank in order to close off any escape route for the man who had attacked Juno. But on a sharp turn he over-corrected, slid off the side of the track, and buried the back wheels in the sludge. He tried to edge forward, changed gears and reversed but the wheels only whipped up slush and the SUV wouldn't budge. He jumped out to examine the problem. The back wheels were half submerged. He stood in the rain cursing the ground, the vehicle and himself. The SUV was stuck and he'd have to finish the last five hundred yards on foot.

• • •

Although they had drawn parallel to Sabu's hut, they could see no sign of his coffee plants through the heavy foliage on the side of the ridge. Keeping the coffee trees low to the ground not only made harvesting more manageable but obviously helped conceal the fact that Sabu had planted them on *lulik* land. A little further on Father Roque steered the canoe out of the river's main channel and in toward the bank. He pulled in downstream of the overhang where they could not easily be seen by anyone approaching from the village side.

The priest stabilised the canoe while a much-relieved Estefana stepped out and Carter followed her on to firm ground. The rain had stopped and the rush of the river was the only sound. They dragged the canoe onshore and covered it with branches from a nearby casuarina to conceal it.

"Stay here, Father, and leave this to us?" suggested Carter, but Father Roque would have none of that.

"It's fine," he said. "I may be a priest but I am also a man, you know. Let me help."

They squatted behind the far side of the overhang and waited. Estefana seemed troubled by the grit and water in her boots from getting in and out of the canoe. After a few minutes she took off her right boot, drained it, slid her foot back in and retied the laces. The water she had shaken out had rebounded from the rock in front of her and splashed onto her face. Without thinking she took off her left boot and heaved the contents further out toward the river. The movement alarmed a mixed group of herons and egrets and they took flight. At that moment Carter heard someone slashing through the shrubs and grasses along the riverbank with a blade. The man heard the birds rise suddenly from near the overhang. He stopped in his tracks. Carter waited a moment then took a peek. The man saw her and began to step away. He noticed Estefana and Father Roque, and tore back the way he'd come.

Carter was up and after him before the others. Father Roque followed quickly while Estefana struggled to get her boot back on.

Fifty yards along the riverbank the priest slipped and fell. Carter ran on but the man was light on his feet and he added thirty yards to the gap between them. Estefana slowed when she came upon the priest struggling to get up. "I'm okay," he said. "Go after the American." Carter was losing ground as the man started up the ridge.

She lost him momentarily as he headed through the coffee trees and she took a wrong turn as a result. Estefana was behind her at a distance. Carter stopped, scanned the coffee trees, the eucalypts, caught a glimpse of the man and took off. But he was too quick and he could chop his way through undergrowth where she was impeded by it. She lost him for a second time. When Estefana finally caught up with her, Carter was looking for movement, hands on hips, sucking air into her lungs. "I've lost him," she said. "I hope Cordero is coming down from up top. Come on!"

• • •

Cordero had finally reached Sabu's hut, taken a breath, and begun down the slope. He couldn't see the others but trusted they'd made land and blocked any chance of the man they were after running north along the riverbank. The ground was slippery and coming round a bend in the rough track he made to get a foothold to pivot on a rock only to discover it was bark covered in mud. He slipped and fell onto his backside. He cursed, regained his feet, and heard heavy panting coming toward him from below.

The man looked up and saw Cordero. His eyes shifted from side to side. He raised the machete in an attempt to force his way passed. Cordero dived at him, tackling him around the waist. The machete flew from the man's hand and was lost in the undergrowth. They fell toward the river and slithered down through the coffee trees. When they came to rest the man was on top. Cordero tried to grab the man's hands and link his own legs around the man's back to restrict his movement but this opponent was wiry and Cordero couldn't hold him. The man freed himself from Cordero and kicked him so that he slid away in the mud, then turned and charged up the slope.

Cordero was trying to get a firm foothold when Carter and Estefana reached him. "There," he shouted and pointed and they left him to stumble and flounder for a footing. As they cleared the coffee trees and came onto the clearing around Sabu's hut they could hear a motorcycle being kick-started. First attempt: nothing. Second attempt: same. Silence, probably working the choke. They ran. Third attempt: nothing. Carter had almost made the side of the shed. Estefana was on her heels. Fourth attempt: the engine rumbled. He revved it hard. Carter almost reached him but had to jump clear and he was gone in a spray of mud and exhaust smoke fishtailing down the track toward Tepia.

Carter noticed Cordero struggling up the ridge, covered in mud. "Where's the SUV?" she yelled but he gestured that the pursuit was over. "What?" she shouted as he approached.

"Bogged," he said, bent over catching his breath. "The SUV's bogged down the track." He waved a hand half-heartedly in the direction of the stranded vehicle.

"Bogged! For fuck's sake Cordero." She looked back after the motorcycle. "We've lost him."

Father Roque appeared on the side of Sabu's hut, also covered in mud and limping slightly. "Did he get away?" the priest asked. "How?"

"Sabu's bike had the key in the ignition," Cordero said straightening. "No one thought to take it out."

Carter, Estefana and the priest looked hopelessly in the direction the man had gone.

"Well that's it," said Carter. "We'll never catch him now."

"He'll be back," said Cordero. "He came to see that burial site." He took a few steps forward and turned to face them. "For whatever reason that's why he was here. And we stopped him from doing that." He turned away and stared down the track. "He'll be back."

27

"You know, back home—my home in the States, not yours—Hopi Indians are big believers in witches," said Carter. They had walked back to the churchyard, leaving the SUV and the canoe for another day. They had cleaned themselves up, Cordero using Father Roque's wash basin while Carter and Estafana shared the washing facilities in the nuns' house, and were now sitting on the veranda waiting for dinner to be served. There was no *Cachaça* or gin left to drink and they had to settle for tea instead. After the rain, the water, and the mud, hot strong tea was a balm and there were no complaints. The rain had stopped long ago and a few stars were twinkling in the breaks that were opening in the clouds. "But they don't believe in confronting witches," Carter was saying. "They believe the best way to deal with a witch is to live a good life, to act according to the best Hopi virtues. Witches not only explain unusual events and ill-fortune. They function to encourage good, moral behavior. Here the opposite seems the case."

Cordero nodded and sipped his tea. Estefana shifted uneasily.

"I don't know anything about American Indians," said Father Roque, "but I do know that here the whole witch thing is connected to the continuing strength of the animist worldview." He put down his cup and waved a hand across the churchyard and beyond to the village. "You see very little sign of modernity here," he said. "The school is six or seven years old but the teacher is poorly trained and irregularly paid. Adults can't read and have not been educated at all. There are no radios or television sets to expose them to the outside world. Trucks come, occasionally to pick up coffee beans or to drop off supplies and there's a microlet service to Railaco, Ermera and Dili but only once a week and rarely taken by anyone more than thirty years of age. Most people here have not travelled more than ten miles from Tepia in their entire lives. The health clinic is modern. Foreign donors even paid for solar panels to be installed recently to provide power. But its very modernity is a reason for villagers to be suspicious of it. Things have not fundamentally altered here in generations."

"There is the Church," said Cordero.

"Of course the Church likes to extend its influence whenever and wherever it can," the priest replied. "But as I've pointed out to you, Tino, the faith doesn't penetrate far into the thinking of these people. They weave its stories, symbols and rituals into the beliefs they've held for generations."

"And the witch thing?" asked Carter.

"There is a body of thought that argues primitive people lack the ability to think abstractly," said Father Roque. "They can only count using concrete things like fingers and toes, for instance, as I'm sure you have discovered. After they exhaust their hands and feet their calculations become vague. 'A lot'…'many'…but no real idea. 'How far is your hut from here?' you'll ask. 'Two cigarettes', will come the reply meaning the time it takes to smoke them with no idea of distance." He picked up his teacup from the floor of the veranda. "According to this argument they don't understand categories because a category is an abstract concept. Have you heard anyone talk about a forest? No, they talk about particular trees. A crop? No, it's the coffee plant or the maize plant. They live in a world made from a collection of singular objects." He took a sip of tea. "Are you following me? Am I boring you?" he asked.

"No please go on," said Carter before the others could answer.

"Okay they can't explain natural events because they have no capacity for natural laws—again, abstract things. And so the natural world is not an inanimate, impersonal thing. If it were, they could not control it in any way. To them it is alive with spiritual forces. They project their own emotions onto these. You know, lightning must be a god expressing his anger. That sort of thing. And since the world is comprised of unique individual things, each one has its own personality which means each also has its own particular power." He finished his tea. "When a buffalo dies it's because its spirit is unhappy. When a thing happens that can't be explained in those terms," he spread his hands to indicate the unknown, "it must be the result of a malevolent being." He looked directly at Carter. "A witch, for instance."

"You seem to know a lot about these things, Father," said Cordero finishing his tea.

"We Jesuits are well and widely educated," the priest said. "Our superiors say it's so we can better understand the nature of God." He smiled ruefully. "Our critics say it's so we can better understand the nature of men and control them."

"You said that this idea of people lacking the ability to think abstractly is one body of thought," said Carter.

"Oh yes," replied Father Roque. "There are other approaches now that regard what I have just outlined as a European conceit. Many anthropologists regard what we call primitive people as, in fact, highly imaginative, highly intellectual but in ways different to rational thought as it developed in Europe. Think of the richness of primitive symbols and metaphors. Think of the Mayan calendar." He paused for a moment. "But then unlike the Timorese the Mayans were living in cities almost three thousand years ago."

"Well Timorese don't have a monopoly on superstition," said Carter. "Last I heard, forty percent of Americans think the world is only 10,000 years old and two percent think the earth is flat. That alone is about six million people. Many more won't walk under ladders and just about everyone gives their pets, their vehicles, even their lawn mowers and leaf blowers human names and talks to them like they were talking to a friend."

"Primitive leftovers that persist because they answer a need," said Cordero.

"But witches are real," protested Estefana. "I know people who've died because a witch put a spell on them. They weren't sick, the doctors said so. They couldn't find anything wrong. The people just died. It happened when I was young but it happens even today." She stood impulsively, her face flushed. "The man we chased today—what brought him back? Why does he want to go to that place? It's because of the witches who are buried there and whose spirits remain there. It's *malisan*—the curse!"

"You're right, Estefana," said Father Roque. "Witches are real. They are real because people believe they are real. And I'd guess that the man we chased believes that and may be seeking power he believes lingers in that place. That could make him especially dangerous."

Sister Agnes called from inside the house in a high-pitched voice that dinner was ready. Estefana waited for Father Roque to head inside and followed behind him.

"She's sensitive to this talk about witches," Carter said to Cordero while they lingered on the veranda.

"Scratch the surface of just about any Timorese and this kind of thinking is there," he said. "It's been there for thousands of years after all and you could say is part of the DNA."

"Even part of yours?" she asked.

"Scratch me and you'll find out," he said and walked inside.

After they had finished the sex, Rui and Clara lay next to each other while they caught their breath on the grass in the clearing near the new *uma lulik*. Rui's motorcycle was parked nearby but out of sight from anyone who might pass in the night. They had laid out their clothes beneath them to keep away the damp. He rummaged through his jeans, retrieved a cigarette, lit it and inhaled.

Clara raised herself on her side and began to stroke Rui's bare legs. "Do you love me, Rui?" she purred, and brushed back her hair.

"Of course I do *doben*," he replied. "Why do you have to ask all the time?" He took another drag on his cigarette.

She grabbed his flaccid penis tightly in her hand. He caught the smoke in his lungs, held it there, startled. "Because I heard you were seen with Concetta Luana! That bitch!" The purr turned to a growl. "If I ever hear that you slept with her I'd tear this *manu* off," she said, using the Tetun slang for penis.

Rui's body was tense. "She means nothing to me, *doben*," he protested delicately, afraid to move. "Today that one thinks she's my girlfriend. Tomorrow she thinks she's Moussi's girlfriend. Next week it'll be the priest. It's all in her head. You know that."

She let go of his penis. He blew out the smoke and relaxed. "Then you do love me," she said stroking his leg again. "And only me!"

Crickets were chirping in the clearing and off in the trees a night bird called out to its mate. "Of course, Clara," he said. "You're my only girl. Promise. Just you." She lay back down beside him and they gazed up at the stars.

"What are we going to do, Rui?" she asked after a while. "Now that the *lia-nain* is dead, I mean?"

"Don't worry about that, Clara," he said to reassure her. But her question had altered his train of thought to more practical concerns and he stubbed out his cigarette, rose and slipped his trousers back on.

"How will we get the money to go to Dili now?" she persisted.

"Dili?" he asked, momentarily puzzled.

"Yes Dili," Clara said. "We are going to Dili, aren't we Rui?" The voice became insistent again. "You promised, remember?"

He hated the way girls always wanted to talk after sex. Why couldn't they just put their clothes back on, get up, and leave, like men do? And she wasn't getting dressed like he was. Clearly she was thinking they'd lie there like that a lot longer. Maybe even hours. And just talk. Shit.

"Yes *doben*. Sure. We're going to Dili. I haven't forgotten what I promised you." He was going to have to get out of this, he thought to himself. Clara was getting far too serious, far too possessive. He tried to think of how many times she had used the pronoun 'we' tonight but gave up on the count. Apart from becoming irritating she was also becoming irrelevant now Sabu was dead—except every now and then for sex when he couldn't find another girl eager and available in the village. "Don't worry your pretty self about it, *doben*. I'll think of something." He reflected on his options for a moment, gazing out through the darkness over the clearing. "Like maybe growing weed. You know, ganja. Marijuana. We could sell it around here. And in Railaco. I can get seeds. There's a friend there who can get them for me. No one will want to be hanging around Sabu Bada's place now. Not with his ghost chasing whoever killed him out there. I could plant it on that land."

"Ghosts don't bother you, Rui?" she asked.

"Not as much as having no money," he said. Rui realized a Plan B was taking shape. He smiled to himself. He was in control again and thus happy. He looked down at Clara, kneeled, and began to stroke her naked thigh.

•••

"Did you hear that?" he said sitting bolt upright. "Shoosh. Listen. A motorcycle coming this way. Who's out at this time of night?"

"I don't hear anything, Rui," Clara said. "You're imagining things. Come and finish what you started."

He shifted his head slightly and cocked an ear. "There it is again," he said. "It's pulling up over there in the trees."

"For fuck's sake, Rui," she said. "Let it go. Whatever it is it's nothing."

He waited a moment and lay back down but his senses were alert to things other than her body. He was pretending to be interested, kissing, fondling, but he knew someone was out there. The question was why and what did it mean for him.

He sat up again. "If anyone touches my motorcycle I'll kill them," he grumbled.

"You're being silly," she said. She was annoyed now. "You're looking out there and your motorcycle is back this way."

"Shh!" he said. "Listen."

She tried to coax him back down but he slapped her hand away. "Do you smell that?" he said.

"Smell what?"

"That smell. Something burning."

"I don't—"

"Shit! Look! Under the *uma lulik*!"

Heavy white smoke was swirling from the foundations and shrouding the building. He tightened his pants, stumbling in his haste, regained his balance, slipped on his shoes, and grabbed his T-shirt. "Come on!" he shouted. "The *uma lulik* is on fire!"

He ran toward the building while Clara fumbled with her clothes. At the foot of the stairs, leaves and kindling had been piled up and lit. But because of the rain everything was damp— forest litter, beams, and most importantly the *uma lulik's* thatched roof—and the fire smouldered and smoked rather than roared into life. Rui quickly soaked his T-shirt in a puddle of water and began slapping out the flames. "Stay back!" he shouted to Clara as she approached.

"But Rui there's another fire!" she cried. "There!" and she pointed to the other side of the building.

Rui scattered the embers beneath his feet and ran to where she had pointed. He began swatting his T-shirt on that pile of burning sticks and leaves. It, too, was more smoulder than flame and he'd soon stopped it. That's when he glimpsed a figure running through the trees in the direction from which he'd heard the motorcycle. He caught the sound of the rider kick-start but fail to ignite the motor. "Run to the nuns' house and get those cops!" He shouted at Clara. "Now girl. Now!"

Rui sprinted toward where he guessed the motorcycle to be in the darkness. There was another attempt to kick-start the motor and another failure. *That sounds like Sabu's motorcycle*, Rui thought to himself. He'd had to work on it several times in the past few months and kept trying to persuade the *lia-nain* to buy a new starter motor. The stubborn bastard would only say 'In time' and just kept kicking at it. If he remembered rightly two more attempts before it started.

And he heard the third attempt ending like the others.

• • •

Clara noticed a small light on the veranda of the nuns' house and ran toward it. Cordero was sitting on his bed, closely examining a tiny object under the beam of a flashlight.

"*Maun*! Come quick, *maun*. It's Rui!" she shouted.

"What?" said Cordero, annoyed his concentration had been interrupted.

"Rui, *maun*! And the fire!"

The girl was hysterical. "Calm down a minute and make sense," Cordero said. "What's happened to Rui and what fire, where?"

Clara was almost out of breath and she stopped speaking to fill her lungs. She almost collapsed in the process and Cordero had to reach out and steady her. "Take it easy," he said. "Who are you? Tell me what's happened."

"I'm Clara. From the school. I help the teacher. We were in the clearing near the *uma lulik*." She was speaking quickly but now chose her words carefully. "You know, just talking. Rui heard a noise and then he could smell smoke." Her excitement started getting away from her again. "He's gone after him! Poor Rui. Come *maun*, hurry!"

"Gone after who, Clara? Why?"

"The man who set fire to the *uma lulik*," the girl said as though explaining the obvious to a child. "Rui was putting out the flames when he saw the man and ran after him. They're fighting. He might kill Rui!"

Carter and Estefana had been woken by the noise and had popped their heads around the frame of the door. "What's going on?" asked Carter, stifling a yawn.

"It's Rui—" the girl began but Cordero shut her down.

"Seems to be an argument that's turned ugly over at the *uma lulik*," Cordero said in a weary voice. "I'll go over there and take a look."

"We'll come too, *maun*," Estefana offered. "We'll just get dressed."

• • •

Rui jumped the man just as he was revving the motorcycle a fourth time and they both slammed into the ground. Rui was up first and weighing his options depending on what the man did next.

"What are you up to, *maun*?" Rui yelled at the man on the ground. "You trying to burn down that building? Why?"

The man kicked out at Rui's legs but Rui had considered that and jumped clear. Before the man could strike again Rui kicked him with his own foot, in the head, and stunned him. He stood over the man, fists clenched. "Don't try that again, *maun*," he said. "I'm warning you."

Rui saw the man glance at the handle of a pruning knife that stuck out of a saddlebag on the motorcycle. Rui grabbed it before the man had a chance. "This what you're looking for, *maun*?" Rui said, pointing the knife at the man's chest. "Why don't you sit there quietly until the cops arrive?"

The man shook his head to clear it from the kick and rubbed his eyes. Rui studied him closely. He'd never sent the man before. The clothes were torn and filthy, the hair unwashed, the slumped shoulders a glimpse into a haunted soul.

"Who are you, *maun*?" Rui asked. The man only stared back then looked away at the figures emerging through the darkness. He put his face in the palm of his hand and seemed to sob.

"What's going on?" Cordero asked. Carter moved to the other side of the man on the ground.

"This crazy guy was trying to burn down the *uma lulik*," Rui said. "Can you believe that? And he must have stolen Sabu's bike. It's over there," he said and pointed with the pruning knife.

"You stopped him?" Cordero asked, taking the knife.

"Sure I stopped him, *maun*," boasted Rui. "What do you think?"

Clara had been standing back from the fray, biting her fingernails. When she saw it was safe she ran to Rui's side and hugged him. "Oh Rui," she cooed. "I was so worried."

"Nothing *doben*," said Rui soaking up his moment of glory. "What you going to do with him, *maun*?" he asked Cordero.

"We're going to sit down and have a talk about things," said Cordero and he helped the man to his feet. "Estefana, could you bring that motorcycle across to the churchyard please?"

"What you mean, *maun*, sit down and talk?" protested Rui. "This guy tried to burn down our sacred place. And he tried to kill me! Ain't you going to tie him up, lock him up, you know, bash him? You're a cop ain't you?"

"Not tonight, Rui," Cordero said. "I'm off duty."

Cordero and Carter started to walk back to the nuns' house, the man between them. Estefana wheeled the motorcycle. Rui glanced at Clara and noted the expectation in her eyes.

"Hey *maun*?" he called after Cordero.

"What?" Cordero asked without looking back.

"Don't I get a reward?"

29

"I didn't mean to kill that one," the man was saying, eyes downcast, shoulders hunched, his T-shirt and jeans covered in mud. "It wasn't my fault."

"I believe you," said Cordero. "Why don't we start at the beginning?"

They were sitting on the veranda in an attempt to minimize the disruption at this time of night and Cordero had lit a kerosene lamp. Father Roque had been woken by the commotion and came across wearing a *tais mane* and an old T-shirt adorned with the green and yellow shield of *Seleção Brasileira de Futebol*—Brazil's national football team—on the front. He sat next to Carter who, with Cordero, was facing the man. Sister Felicia had stirred when they came back to the house but Estefana, who stood at the back of the man, had apologised, told the nun everything was just routine police work, and to go back to sleep. Apparently nothing ever disturbed Sister Agnes in her sleep. It was after midnight, pleasantly cool, and beyond the roof of the house a riot of stars now glittered in the sky.

"What is your name, *maun*?" Cordero asked.

"My name?" the man repeated. He looked exhausted, sapped of all the energy it took to concentrate on saying who he was. "My name?" he repeated.

"Ask him when he last ate, drank," Carter said and Cordero did as she suggested.

"Ate?" the man said and paused a moment. "I, um—there were scraps left after the burial. I scooped them up when the others left."

224

Cordero turned. "Estefana—" he began but she anticipated the rest.

"I'll see what I can find, *maun*," and she went inside the house.

"We'll get you something to eat and drink but you have to tell us your name," Cordero said.

The man paused again and rubbed his face and the back of his neck. He looked up at Cordero. "Vitor," he said. "My name is Vitor Coval."

"Thank you Vitor," said Cordero. "Can you tell me where you are from?"

"From?"

"You don't have to keep repeating my questions, Vitor. Save your strength. Just give me the answers."

"Yes, of course. I'm sorry," said Vitor. He seemed to search his memory a moment. "I've lived in Ermera a long time."

"Ermera. Okay. And before that?"

"Well," Vitor said. "I was born near Ossu." He looked at Cordero. "You know it?" he asked.

"Yes, it's near Viqueque. Over in the east."

"That's right. Near the mountains. The guerrillas were hiding in the caves. The Indonesian military made a lot of families move from there. Said they were giving food and information to the guerrillas. We were sent here. To Tepia. Along with others."

"How long ago was this, Vitor?"

"How long?" He considered. "I was maybe eight, nine years old. I'm not sure."

"How old are you now?"

"Twenty-three or twenty-four I think."

"You *think*?"

"I don't have papers, *maun*."

"And so you came here with your family?" Cordero asked.

"Yes," Vitor said as though the answer was obvious.

"Can you describe your family to us, please?"

"What do you mean?"

"Well, did both your parents come with you? Brothers? Sisters? What ages? That kind of thing," Cordero suggested.

Vitor looked down again struggling with a memory. "There was my mother and my father," he said and stopped. Again he rubbed his face. After a moment he continued. "And I had three sisters. I was the oldest. My sister Anata was about six or seven when we came here. Amivi was maybe four. Celina was a year or two younger." He smiled and looked at Cordero again. "And I think my mother might have been pregnant with another but I'm not sure. She didn't talk about such things with us."

Estefana returned. She had managed to find bread rolls, two cold fried eggs, a few small tomatoes, and a thermos of tea that the nuns always left in the dining area in case anyone awoke and strayed out during the night. She placed the food in front of the man and gestured for him to eat. He looked from her to Cordero and then to Carter and the priest and began shovelling the rolls and eggs into his mouth. He smiled up at Estefana in appreciation with his cheeks full of food.

"A family of you, two adults, three other children and possibly a baby," Cordero said in English for Carter's benefit, easing back and glancing at her.

"Fits the profile of the skulls perfectly," she said and turned to Estefana who nodded that she'd drawn the same conclusion.

When most of the rolls, eggs and tomatoes had been devoured Cordero resumed his questioning. "What did your family do in Tepia, Vitor?"

"Do?" he said, then realised he was repeating a question again and apologised. "They farmed. What else could they do here?" He took the thermos of tea and drank greedily.

"Whose land did they farm?" asked Cordero.

Vitor waved the thermos. "The Indonesians gave them land along the river. Near where you chased me." He attacked the last bit of food, drank more tea and placed the thermos on the floor of the veranda. A second time he gestured his thanks in Estefana's direction and smiled weakly. She noticed that the color in his face had returned.

"And what did the other villagers think of that?" asked Cordero.

"The other villagers?" Vitor stared out into the darkness. "They hated us. They hated all the people the Indonesians made come here." He looked back at Cordero. "But it wasn't their fault! They never wanted to leave their own homes in Ossu."

"The reaction from the villagers here must've made life hard for you and your family, Vitor," Cordero suggested.

Vitor covered his face with his hands. "There was nothing here then. Nothing. No school, no clinic. Even the church was closed up. Everyone relied on everyone else for everything." He picked up the thermos again but didn't open it. "But no one would help us." He paused. "When I became ill my father had to send me to people he knew in Ermera. No one here would help." He looked up at Cordero. "Their coffee was failing and they blamed us. I was too young to understand what was going on but I knew that they'd started to say there hadn't been a problem until we came to Tepia." He looked at Estefana, Carter, the priest. "Then they started to say we *caused* the problem."

"You went to Ermera because you were sick?" asked Cordero.

"Yes. I don't know what it was. No one did. I felt very weak. Fevers, headaches. At times it was hard to breathe. I don't remember how my father arranged it—a man, I think, who went back and forth to Ermera with goods to sell. An aunty who had been a nurse a long time before cared for me. I was in bed for months."

"And you stayed in Ermera after you were well again? Why?"

Vitor looked Cordero directly in the eye and he was holding back tears. "Because they killed them, *maun*," he said. "All of them. My sisters, my father, my mother. All my family!"

Cordero waited a moment and then eased the thermos from Vitor's hands least he break it with his grip. The man didn't resist. He wiped the back of his hand across his lips, his eyes, and regained his composure. "My aunty heard about it. I don't know how. Maybe the same man my father paid to take me to Ermera. I don't know. But she said I could never go back or they would kill me too." He hugged himself and began to rock back and forth. "And I've stayed there ever since."

They waited. It was a serene night only disturbed by the chirp of a few crickets in the yard and the hoot of an owl far off in the distance. Cordero lent forward. "Why did you come back now, Vitor?"

Vitor stopped rocking. He rubbed his eyes.

"When I first heard about my family being killed I was young. And sick. And scared. What was I going to do?" He looked at Cordero as though answering an accusation. "My aunty told me it was best to forget my family. My life was in Ermera, she said. With her." He stared blankly for a moment. "But I couldn't forget them. I had to find out what happened to my parents, my sisters, and who did it. For months they'd been coming to me in my dreams, asking me, begging me, to come. I had to find where they are and honour them in the right way. It's my duty, and until I do they will find no peace." For a moment he seemed lost in thought. "Word of the new *uma lulik* in Tepia spread to Ermera. It was said the *lia-nain* built it and was holding a ceremony for its opening. I didn't know anyone in Tepia by then but I saw this as a chance. This was an important man—he would know what happened to my family. I came looking to meet him." He sniffed. "At the ceremony."

Estefana fidgeted and lent forward. "*Lisensa maun*," she said, asking Cordero's permission to interrupt. He nodded. "Was it you who asked a small boy in the village where to find the new *uma lulik* and gave him fifty centavos when he told you?"

"Yes. It was the only coin I had in my pocket," Vitor answered. Estefana lent back and was silent again.

"And you went to the *tebedai* a few nights ago?" Cordero resumed his questioning.

"Yes, I went."

"And you met this *lia-nain* at the ceremony," said Cordero.

"Yes."

"Tell us what happened."

"At first I didn't know who the *lia-nain* was," Vitor began. "But I saw a man come out with the buffalo horns and dance. He wore a large medallion on his chest and carried one of those ceremonial swords, you know, a *surik*. I thought this must be him." He folded his arms tightly against his body again. "I watched until he finished dancing and then followed him. Just to talk to him, you understand." Vitor looked quickly from one to the other of them.

"Followed him where?" asked Cordero.

"He went to the back of the *uma lulik* and took off the horns, medallion and anklets and bracelets he was wearing. He put them in a bag. He spoke to a couple of men. I heard one offer to give him a ride on his motorcycle back to his hut but he said no, he'd walk, and he pointed to a track he was taking. I managed to get ahead of him and when he was clear of the *uma lulik* and the other people I stopped him on the track." Vitor wiped a hand across his face. Despite the mildness of the night a thin veneer of sweat had appeared on his forehead and top lip.

"Where was the stuff he carried—you know, the buffalo horns and *surik*?" Cordero asked.

"He carried a bag in one hand and his *surik* in the other." Vitor took a sip of tea from the thermos. He feel silent.

"Okay. Go on," said Cordero.

"I told him my name was Vitor Coval and that my family had come from Ossu but had been killed years ago in Tepia. I told him he must know about that if he was the *lia-nain*. I asked him why they had been killed and where they were buried."

Once more he stopped talking.

"And what did he say?" asked Cordero.

"He repeated the name," said Vitor. "'Coval. Coval,' he kept saying. Then he remembered. 'The witches!' he said. I didn't know what he was talking about. I said 'No, my family. My mother and father and sisters' but there was a look of anger and, I don't know, disgust on his face. 'You should be dead too,' he yelled and he raised his *surik*. I shouted at him that I just wanted to know what happened to my family but he came at me." Vitor was shifting his body and waving his arms as if reliving the experience.

"And you managed to grab the *surik* from him?"

"Yes. I was angry now. I pushed him to the ground and pointed the *surik* at his throat. I asked him who had killed my family and where their bodies were buried. He was scared, you know, shaking, and his hands were out pleading for his life. I pushed the *surik* hard against his throat and demanded an answer or I said I'd kill him. But I didn't mean it." Vitor looked up at each of them in turn. "I just wanted him to tell me who had killed my family and where they were buried. That's all."

He stopped talking and cast his gaze back down. "Go on, Vitor," Cordero urged him. "What happened then?"

"He mumbled and I thrust the *surik* harder. He pleaded for his life and said I needed to talk to an elder—Juno da Silva—to find out what I wanted to know. I threw the *surik* to the ground and turned to walk away. Honest! I didn't want to hurt him."

"But what—things got out of hand?"

"He sprang to his feet, grabbed the *surik* in both hands, raised it over his head and came at me again. I dropped to the side and kicked his legs out from under him. He stumbled and fell, maybe tripping over his bag, I don't know, but came down with the end of the blade in his chest. I turned him over. There was blood everywhere. He was dead. I was sure. I panicked. I remember my aunty saying that if I went back to Tepia they would kill me and this man saying I should be dead like the rest of my family. And I left him there and ran." Vitor shook his head forlornly. "I didn't mean to kill him."

Cordero acknowledged the account with a nod and rubbed his hands along his thighs. "Tell me about your meeting with the other man, Juno da Silva," he said after a moment.

Vitor rubbed his hands together. "I ran up the track at the back of the *uma lulik*. I ran and ran. I didn't know where I was going but that's where the *lia-nain* was heading and there was only the one hut at the end. I thought that must be his. There was no one there. I had looked around." He glanced up at Cordero with the trace of a regretful smile on his face. "That's when I noticed the motorcycle with the key in it. But I didn't take it." His expression hardened. "I came back into the village the next day and picked up from conversations I'd overheard that he was being buried alongside his wife. I'd seen her tomb at the hut. I went back for his burial. No one had seen me arguing with him the night he died and no one knew who I was. No one took any notice of me. After the burial I saw a man approach the grave with three dogs. I heard another say 'Look, Juno da Silva'. They killed the dogs over the grave and I hung around and followed that man to his hut."

Vitor took a deep breath and his shoulders slumped as though a weight had been taken off them.

"What happened when you caught up with Juno?" Cordero asked.

"I hid in the trees until he came out by himself and went into his garden. He was carrying a machete and I thought of the *surik* again and was nervous. I waited a long time while he hacked at the brush and weeds. Then he put the machete down to collect the off-cuts. I crept up behind him and grabbed the machete. He turned around in shock. He looked at me, then at the machete, and I think he knew that it was me who killed the *lia-nain*." He fell silent again.

"And?" Cordero urged him on.

"He put a hand out, stumbled back and said 'Don't' like he thought I was going to kill him. But I didn't want to kill anyone. I just wanted to know why my family was killed and where their bodies were buried. I asked him. He said he knew nothing. I said I knew he was lying and told him what the *lia-nain* had said. I could see the fear on his face and I raised the machete to scare him even more. Then he said that the *lia-nain* had declared my family witches who had to be killed and he ordered the elders to do it. He said they were buried down along the riverbank where I ran into you." Vitor nodded at Carter and the others.

"I wanted to get to that place fast. I knew that everyone would be after me because this man could describe me. I had to make sure he wouldn't call people together and follow me. That's why I hit him with the machete." He turned back to Cordero. "But I didn't want to hurt him too much. I slapped the side of the blade into his nose. I might have broken it because a lot of blood came out and he cried in pain. While he was moaning and swearing I ran until I was down on the riverbank. I don't know why I took the machete. I wasn't thinking." He looked again at Carter, Father

Roque and Estefana. "But I never made it to where my family is buried because you stopped me and I had to run away." Vitor fixed Cordero with a stare. "When I got away from you," he said, "I ran to where I had seen the motorcycle. It was there, untouched. I took it and rode away." He dropped his gaze again to the floor of the veranda.

Cordero paused before asking: "Why did you try to burn down the *uma lulik*?"

Vitor lifted his head, anger in his eyes. "They killed my family, *maun*!" he said, his voice shrill. "The elders who use that place! And when I was running from these three I saw the coffee growing on the land my family farmed. My mother and father didn't grow coffee. They grew sweet potato, cassava, beans. This *lia-nain* had called them witches, had them killed, taken their land and planted coffee trees. And the elders helped him do it!" He rubbed the back of his neck. "Besides," he added when he had calmed down, "I wanted to go to where my family is buried. I thought if the *uma lulik* had burned down you'd be busy with that and wouldn't go back to the riverbank." He sighed. "I planned to go again tomorrow."

Cordero blew out a deep breath and stood. He looked at Carter. "Well this began as your case," he said. "You have questions for him?"

She shook her head slowly. "I've got all I need to know," she replied, her eyes on Vitor. "We've established it wasn't a war crime, therefore Estefana and I have no official interest in the case." She held off a moment. "What are you going to do?" she asked and turned to Cordero. "You've got several men involved in so-called witch killings and one man here implicated in a possible manslaughter."

Cordero looked down at the fugitive and back up at Carter. "I'm going to think about it," he said. He squatted to eye-level with Vitor. "I'm sure we have handcuffs or failing that we could secure you with a bike chain and lock you in the shed where Father Roque keeps his motorcycle. Or," he said and looked up at the others to solicit their support, "you could give me your word you won't run away and we could fix up a bed here on the veranda for you tonight and talk again tomorrow. Which is it going to be?"

• • •

Father Roque walked with Cordero who carried his pillow and blanket to the SUV for another night of broken sleep.

"A tragedy that boy's life, isn't it?" said the priest.

"It has been and his tragedy has now engulfed others," Cordero said.

Father Roque said nothing for a moment. "Strange the way our lives turn out, isn't it?" he asked.

"Maybe it's fate, Father," said Cordero. "Or the hand of God or the spirits."

"Oh, I think by and large we make our own fate," the priest said. "Vitor could have stayed away from Tepia altogether. He could have confronted Sabu in daylight, with other people present. He could have gone to the elders and appealed for information."

Cordero stopped by the SUV and looked at the stars. "But not everything's in our control, is it Father?"

"What do you mean by that?"

"Emotions. The way you feel rather than the way you think. That's what drove Vitor. Grief, loss, regret. Others are driven by tenderness, beauty, desire. But you can't always make people do what you want them to do, can you? You can't always count on them to be reasonable, to see things the same way you do, especially when their experiences are different to yours. You can't count on others to be part of your plans." He blew out a deep breath. "And so our fate is not entirely of our own making."

Father Roque suspected that Cordero's comments had a personal edge to them. He lent back against the SUV for a moment, thinking.

"You're half right," he said and pushed himself upright again. "But we can always give people good reasons to choose to do what we would like them to do. Good night, Tino." And with that he walked off to his own bed.

30

Cordero had thought to leave the SUV where it was—stuck fast in the mud—claim it had been written off, and make the office provide him with a *newer* vehicle when he returned to Dili. But his conscience got the better of him and he decided to retrieve it. He borrowed a shovel from Father Roque, walked down to Moussi's workshop, and asked Rui to take him on the back of his motorcycle to the SUV. By the time they arrived it was quite hot. Cordero dismounted the motorcycle and stripped to the waist. He threw his T-shirt into the cab of the SUV, and started digging mud and slush from around the wheels. Rui watched him, smoking a cigarette. Neither spoke. When Cordero needed a break, he gave the shovel to Rui and told him to dig—which he did at half Cordero's pace. As the area around the wheels was cleared, they packed it with sticks and stones to provide traction. Cordero told Rui to push the back of the SUV while he worked the accelerator and gears—not because having him push would make much difference but because Cordero liked the idea of getting Rui's body—and ego—covered in mud and dirt. After a few attempts forward, in reverse and then forward again—Rui yelling obscenities at the back continuously—Cordero managed to manoeuvre the SUV onto the hard surface of the rough track. Rui emerged from the back of the vehicle spotted with mud. "Look at me, *maun!*" he protested. "I'm covered in this shit! I'll have to jump in the river to get it off and my clothes'll be wet for hours."

Cordero ignored the complaints. "That man you caught last night," he said stepping out of the SUV, "was the one who fought with Juno and with Sabu. He was trying to find his family. They were killed here years ago. People said they were witches. They were buried out along the river. That man survived because he was ill and had been sent to Ermera."

"What do I care, *maun*? I told you he was guilty," said Rui trying to brush the mud from his clothes but only smearing it further. "That's why I should get a reward. Who cares about witches and dead families buried on the river, *maun*? Nothing to do with me."

"No, I'm sure you're right," said Cordero. "Even so, there's one piece of this puzzle I can't figure."

"Yeah? What's that, *maun*?"

"You see Sabu planted coffee trees on the land that man's family had farmed," said Cordero. "Lots and lots of coffee trees. That's how he was able to pay for the construction of the new *uma lulik*. But Sabu lived alone. His sons had gone to Dili a long time ago. Who harvested his coffee cherries, washed them, stripped them, roasted the beans?" He stared at Rui. "Last I knew a cherry harvester made five dollars a day for a ten-hour day. That's quite a lot out here. But what if Sabu managed to get his coffee work done for less? Far less. What if someone helped him organise for that to happen and he was paid, say, two dollars fifty cents or three dollars a day per worker in return? Sabu gets his beans picked and processed without having to compete for laborers and he saves himself a lot of money." Rui started shifting his feet about. "The guy who organized it all would make a handy amount of money for doing very little." Cordero caught Rui's eyes. "But who would pick cherries all day for next to nothing?" he asked. "Any ideas?"

Rui said nothing.

"Then I thought what if the cherry pickers were children? You know, like the children who go to that school in Tepia, the one where the teacher often doesn't show up and your girlfriend Clara works occasionally? Children who wear baseball caps, like the one I saw in the dirt out at Sabu's place or the one I saw outside the school? You'd only have to be nine or ten years old to pick cherries and Sabu's plants were always pruned low so a small kid could reach the top or pull them over with a stick. Washing doesn't take much skill either." Cordero kicked at a stone to suggest he was thinking things through. Rui remained silent. "What do the children get I hear you ask? Well, they get a day out of the boring school room. They get told how important they are by someone they look up to. And maybe—just maybe—they get sweets from the kiosk." Cordero took his T-shirt from the cab of the SUV and slipped it over his head. "Or maybe, just maybe, the deal was that the ones who went to Sabu's received no wages but avoided having to sit through a day at school when the nuns come to talk about Jesus. You following me, Rui?" He waited a moment. "You say you deserve a reward for capturing that man last night. You're right and I'll tell you what your reward is going to be: I won't arrest you or your girlfriend for extortion, kidnapping and child slavery offences. Sound fair?"

With that Cordero climbed back into his SUV, made a seven-point turn to avoid the mud and drove off back to Tepia. Rui, dumbstruck, shouted after him: "That's the thanks I get for helping you get that vehicle of yours back on the road? Fuck, *maun!*"

• • •

Cordero drove to the kiosk in the center of the village, bought a bag of loose light brown tobacco, and headed up to the cemetery. He had asked Carter and Estefana to walk back to the overhang on the river with Vitor Coval so he could visit the burial place of his family. Cordero was confident Vitor posed no threat and, in a sense, Vitor and the remains of his family constituted a problem they, not Cordero, originally had been charged with investigating. At the cemetery he parked the SUV and walked through the graves and the trees to the hut of the woman known as *Senyora Batibat*. What name stuck in Cordero's head—*Senyora Batibat* or Tereza Silveiro—he wasn't yet sure. But he'd come for answers to the last out-standing questions: who was responsible for killing the girl who had turned up in Dili as the first skull they had to deal with and why was she killed?

She was sitting in the same chair, wearing the same clothes

and with the steaming pot of tea and two cups next to her on the table when he entered.

"You took your time, *alin*," she said.

"I had things to do," was the only explanation he gave. He looked around the inside of the hut. Everything seemed the same except he couldn't make out the owl in the corner of the ceiling.

"Where's your owl?" he asked.

"What owl?" she replied.

"The owl that was sitting up there last time I was here," Cordero said and pointed.

"You've been seeing things, *alin*. Why would I keep owls in my hut?"

He let it go, reached into his pants pockets and produced the tobacco. He placed it on the table. Her eyes lit up. She picked up a tin off the floor behind her chair and when she opened the lid he could smell crushed cloves. She took a generous handful and placed the mixture in with the tobacco.

"You seem—"

"Quiet!" she reprimanded him. She mixed the tobacco and the cloves and when she was satisfied put a clump into her pipe and lit it. She inhaled deeply and immediately broke into a wet, throaty cough. Her face went red. Her hands shook and she almost lost control of the pipe. Then she lent back, closed her eyes and said: "Ah, I missed that."

Cordero poured tea into the two cups but neither drank. "We caught the man responsible for Sabu's death. Vitor Coval. From Ermera. Ever heard of him?"

She ignored the question.

"When I found his body, Sabu Bada's eyes were open even though he was dead," Cordero continued and the lids on her own eyes parted like a snake's. "He was in shock, I guess, because he had managed to kill himself by falling onto his own sword." He paused, allowing the information to sink in. "I noticed a smudge running from above his right eyebrow and across his eyeball," he said and traced the line across his own face. "The smudge had been put on after he was dead because the bit on the eyeball had not spread or dissolved." Again he paused. She sucked on her pipe and let the smoke drift from her nose. "I took a sample and examined it closely last night. It was the ash of cloves mixed with tobacco just like that mixture you're smoking and just like the ash you keep in that tin beneath this table." She closed her eyes again. "I know that people use the ash to cast spells. Witches use it that way. You used it that way, didn't you?"

There was silence and stillness in the room for a long time. Cordero thought that maybe the old woman had fallen asleep. He leaned in to check just as a raspy voice said, "He had a black heart. He was an evil one."

"Who? Sabu Bada?" Cordero asked.

"Yes. The *lia-nain*. He liked to control people in this village with the traditional knowledge he claimed to know. He had the elders wrapped around his finger. Everyone feared him. And he killed my people."

"Your people? You mean the family that was burned and buried along the river?"

She opened her eyes and came forward in her chair. "Why do you think their bodies were burned? They were witches like me. *My people!*" She coughed again and leant back heavily. "I put that spell on him so his spirit would not come back to haunt this village," she added.

"What were you doing out there at that time of night?"

"Darkness is my cloak," she said. "In it I can do what I want, go where I please."

"Did you see anyone or anything that indicated how he had died when you came upon his body?"

She inhaled through her pipe and closed her eyes. Smoke flowed out of her mouth with her words. "No. Nothing. I just saw his body. I was happy to see it lying there like that. I heard children yelping in the trees as children do and so I put the spell on him and left. His death had nothing to do with me. As I said, it was his spirit I was concerned about."

"Let's talk about you for a minute," Cordero said. "How often do you have seizures?"

She looked at him through her snake eyes again. "I don't have seizures. I go into trances. In trances I see things that other people don't see. I speak to spirits and they speak to me."

"Do you often feel dizzy, sick in your stomach, your lips and throat numb? How often do you wake up on the floor not knowing how you came to be there?"

She held his gaze but said nothing.

"There is a compound in cloves called eugenol. Consume too much of it and it leads to all of these things in your body. Usually the mix of tobacco to cloves is two parts to one. That can be dangerous enough. But I notice you mix almost one to one. And you smoke a lot and have been doing it for many, many years," Cordero said.

She puffed on her pipe as if to defy him. "What are you saying, *alin*? That I'm a sick old woman not a witch?"

"I'm just saying there are ways to explain things you may be feeling."

"You don't know what I feel, *alin*," she said. "But I know what you feel. I know you are drawn in one direction but pulled in another. I know your heart is torn."

Cordero was surprised by the comment and shifted uneasily. "Let's talk about what you know of Clarita Araujo," he said changing the subject quickly.

The old woman relaxed into her chair once more and closed her eyes. "She was a beautiful girl that one. A free spirit. And she had powers. That's why they feared her."

"That's why who feared her?"

"Everyone," she said. "Everyone in the village. Even her own family would have nothing to do with her. Said she was possessed." She chuckled at the absurdity of that idea.

"Did anyone in particular fear her enough to want her dead?"

"When people are afraid they tend to run away, *alin*. They don't attack. You said yourself it wasn't a person from Tepia who killed the *lia-nain*. It was an outsider. From Ermera, you said. One who had no fear about confronting him. So no, I know of no one who feared Clarita so much they would want to kill her, which is what you are really asking, isn't it?"

"Clarita lived with you—"

"She stayed with me," the old woman corrected him. "Often. But she didn't live here. She didn't really live anywhere. Not here in Tepia. That's why I told her she had to go."

"Go? Go where?"

"Home. To Dili. To live with Margareta."

"Margareta?" Cordero asked.

"The sorcerer," the old woman said helpfully. Cordero began to recall newspaper accounts of a mild panic in parts of Dili caused by the sighting of an alleged witch called Margareta.

"You mean the witch people claimed they saw flying over Dili a few years back?"

"Margareta is a sorcerer, not a witch. There is a difference although it would probably be lost on you like it's lost on most people."

"But why her?"

"As I said, Clarita had powers. She had to learn to use them."

"What do you mean by powers?"

"Clarita could see things in her trances and talk to spirits like me," she said. "And when she fixed her eyes on you, you could think you were looking into the next world. Do I have that effect on you?" She opened her eyes and giggled again. "I didn't think so. I'm too old to leave. This is my birthplace, my home, and soon my grave. She was young. She wasn't tied to this place."

"When you told her she had to go to Dili what did she say?"

"At first she ignored me. Made excuses. But as the trances got deeper she understood. And finally she agreed to go."

"When was this?"

"About a year ago."

"How was she going to find Margareta?"

"I gave her a charm. Like that one there," she said and pointed her pipe toward an object hanging off the wall. Cordero rose from the chair and walked over to get a better look in the dim light of the hut. It was a talisman made of brown feathers—probably owl, he thought—bleached bone from a small animal and both affixed to polished driftwood with a blue twine.

"Just like this one?" he asked, his back to her.

"It's a special charm for finding your way. It has to be like that or it doesn't work. Just like that."

"And when did you give this charm to her?"

"The night before she left. It was a Tuesday. The microlet to Dili leaves Tepia very early every Wednesday morning."

"I think that's all I need for now," he said turning to face her. "Thank you, *mana*."

"There is more you need to know, *alin*," she said puffing on her pipe. "Much more. You need to know which direction to take."

"I know my way back," he said.

"I'm not talking about *back*," said *Senyora Batibat*. "I'm talking about forward. I'm talking about the foreign woman."

Cordero stood rigid for a moment. He looked at her, said nothing, and left.

31

Cordero fixed Carter with a stare he couldn't immediately break.

"Anything wrong?" she asked, puzzled by his expression.

"What? No nothing. Where's Vitor?" he said.

"Father Roque came with us. You know, the canoe. Vitor offered to help him paddle it back."

Cordero nodded. "How did it go out there?"

Carter brushed the hair out of her eyes. "It went well enough I think," she said. "On the way out, we told him about the remains washing up in Dili. Estefana assured him that now we had names for the people they'd be buried by the state with a marker. He wanted to go to the overhang and pay his respects. We were happy to leave him alone although I think it worked out well that Father Roque was there to sit with him while he did whatever it was he needed to do." Estefana came into the room with a pot of tea. Cordero found three cups. "How did you go with the witch?" Carter asked.

Cordero lay out the cups. "She put that smudge you found across Sabu's eye. Said it was a spell to keep him from bothering anyone anymore. But she didn't see anything to confirm or contradict Vitor's account of what happened." Estefana poured the tea and they each took a cup.

"Did she shed any light on Clarita?" Carter asked.

"Not really," Cordero answered, sipping his tea. "Said she was an outcast. People suspected her of being a witch. Scared of her, you know, but Tereza couldn't think of anyone who'd kill Clarita. She claimed Clarita had powers, but it was all a little vague. Said she encouraged her to leave Tepia and find a sorcerer in Dili. Margareta." He drank more tea. "Few years back people in Dili claimed they saw a witch they called Margareta flying around over Comoro, near where the skeletons were found. Nothing came of it of course but Tereza claims Margareta is real and that Clarita had to find her to be taught how to use those powers she had."

"And what did Clarita do?" Carter pressed him.

It was late afternoon now and the sun was setting behind the trees atop the ridge. Its rays shot out in brilliant beams through the low smoke from farmers again trying to clear land by burning it on the northern side of the village and the cloud linings low on the horizon to the south were turning from ochre to pink to red.

"Tereza said she finally convinced her leave. Gave her a charm of owl's feathers tied to bone and driftwood. Told Clarita that would lead her to Margareta and she—"

Estefana was raising her cup to sip the tea but she stopped. "*Maun*," she said.

"—gave it to her the night before she was due to leave and hasn't seen her since," Cordero finished.

"*Maun*," Estefana repeated.

"You need to take note when a woman is trying to get your attention, Cordero," Carter said. "Didn't your father ever teach you that? My father used to say that a man who ignores a woman's approaches will live a long but lonely life."

Cordero looked at her uncertainly for a moment. "I'm sorry, Estefana," he said. "What is it?"

"I think I have seen that charm," she said.

He put his cup aside and straightened in his chair. "You do? Where?"

Estefana put her cup gently on the table. She clasped her hands and looked from Carter to Cordero. "In Tomas's box of special things," she said.

• • •

It was agreed that Estefana was the person to approach Tomas in the first instance. She had spent more time with him than either of the others and had seemed to have earned his trust. Cordero gave her as detailed a description as he could of the charm he had seen in the hut of Tereza Silveiro and had even drawn it to the same scale he remembered on a piece of paper Estefana put in the top pocket of her police shirt.

She was a little apprehensive when she left the nuns' house and found Tomas out the back weeding their small, overgrown vegetable garden in the dying light of the day.

"*Botarde, maun*," she said as she approached and noticed his box of special things on the ground by the plot where he was kneeling.

"*Botarde, mana*," Tomas said, a smile breaking out on his face. "You scared me. But just a little. Sister Felicia told me to weed her garden and she said she would give me eggs and rice to eat for dinner if I did."

"That's good," Estefana said. "But could we talk for a few minutes, Tomas?"

"Well, I have to finish the weeding first, *mana*," the boy insisted pulling out more things from the garden.

"Sister Felicia won't mind if it's not finished today," said Estefana. "You'll still get your dinner tonight, I promise."

Tomas looked from Estefana to the garden bed and back. "Okay then, *mana*," he agreed and stood up awkwardly. "Where do you want to go to talk?"

"How about we sit on the veranda?"

Tomas picked up his box of special things and they headed across to the veranda. Estefana sat down, he snuggled up beside her, the box secured on his lap. He looked at her with a satisfied expression on his face. "Do you mind showing me your special things again, Tomas?" Estefana asked.

"Oh no, *mana*. You're my friend," he said.

He opened the box, excitement on his face, reached in and took out the book with the pictures of the dinosaurs. He flipped the book open.

"This—" he began but she interrupted him.

"I'd like to see that," Estefana said, pointing to the charm.

"That, *mana*?"

"Yes, that," she said smiling back at him.

"What about this one?" he said laying the book aside and picking the fifty-centavo coin from the box.

"No, that one," Estefana insisted.

Tomas looked doubtful for a few seconds. "Okay," he said and took the charm out of the box. She went to take the charm, he pulled the hand back that held it. She smiled and put her hand out palm up. He relented and handed the charm to her. She had listened carefully to what Cordero had told her about the charm he'd seen in Tereza Silveiro's hut and had memorized the picture he had drawn for her. She turned the charm over in her hand, examining the feathers, the bone, the driftwood, the blue twine. It matched exactly what Cordero had described.

"What is this, Tomas?" she asked.

He bent over her hand and looked at the charm as though studying the thing for the first time. "I don't know, *mana*, but I think it brings you luck."

"Who gave it to you?"

Tomas grew edgy. He took back the charm, put it in his box along with the dinosaur book and the fifty-centavo coin, and shut the lid.

"Who Tomas?" The boy said nothing but kept his eyes on Estefana and rubbed a hand roughly under his nose. "Do you know a girl by the name of Clarita Araujo?" The boy broke eye contact. "You are not in any trouble, Tomas. I just need to ask. And we are friends, you can tell me. Do you know a girl by the name of Clarita Araujo?"

Tomas rubbed his hands hard down the side of his legs. He looked back at Estefana and out again across the churchyard. He worked his tongue around his lips.

"Tell me, Tomas. Do you know her?"

"She was my friend," he said.

"Was?"

"I haven't seen her for a while."

"How did you come to be friends with Clarita?" Estefana asked.

He rubbed his hands on his legs again. "No one would play with me. No one would talk to her." He looked back at Estefana, the big cow eyes watering. "And we became special friends. We would meet, you know, and talk. She'd tell me what she was doing and I'd show her my special things."

"Do you remember when my friends and I came to get you out on the riverbank? When those bad men had taken you there?"

He nodded, holding back tears.

"You looked at me and said 'I didn't mean to do it' when one of the men was holding you. Do you remember that? What did you mean?" A tear streaked down his face. "You like your special friends very much, don't you, Tomas?" He nodded, more tears. "And that's why you didn't like it when Clarita, your special friend, told you she was leaving Tepia and going to live in Dili, did you?" He shook his head. "Is that when she gave you the charm?"

Again he shook his head. "I told her she couldn't go! I told her no one would talk to me if she went! But she took that thing out of her bag and showed me and said she had to go where it led her." He was crying now, his nose was running, and he struggled to breathe.

"Calm down, Tomas," Estefana said. "There's nothing to be scared of."

"I'm n-not scared, *mana*," he insisted. "I'm sorry!" Estefana put her arm around his shoulders and across his hump.

"What are you sorry about, Tomas?"

"We were s-sitting on the wall of the cemetery. It was d-dark. She said she had to go and was leaving the next d-day. I said no. But she wouldn't listen! She was going to leave me and I got angry. I picked up a r-rock and hit her." He was crying uncontrollably. "Then I took the charm. I didn't mean to hurt her, I promise!"

32

"What I can't figure is how Tomas managed to get the body of Clarita Araujo all the way out to the overhang," said Estefana.

They were sitting on the veranda—Estefana, Carter, Cordero, and Father Roque—drinking coffee. They'd packed and were ready to drive back to Dili. Tomas was in the nuns' vegetable garden finishing the weeding. He seemed well on his way to becoming a fixture around the place. Cordero had released Vitor Coval to go back to his aunt's place in Ermera. He could see no point in taking him to Dili to relive his story over again only to be told by a judge that he had no case to answer. Vitor had walked down to the health clinic to wait for the microlet that would take him away from Tepia for good. Between the two of them Cordero and Father Roque had managed to make him look a little more respectable by giving him clean clothes as well as some money to get by. Vitor had told them he hoped to visit his original home in Ossu one day.

"But he didn't. Did he, Father?" Cordero said. The priest held his cup mid-sip. "You had a canoe which made it easy to transport a body. And you knew where to take it, didn't you? I know you did because when you left to take Carter and Estefana to head off Vitor you didn't ask where you had to go but you pulled in at the overhang where the Coval bodies had originally been buried. And, of course, you knew how to get your hands on accelerants because your motorcycle had been in Moussi's workshop often enough that it was like a second home to you."

The priest put his cup down beside him on the veranda. "And Tomas told me," recounted Estefana, "that you were his friend and

247

he told you everything." Father Roque smiled slightly and nodded. He put his hands together as if in prayer.

"Everything you say is true," he said. "That night Tomas came running to my house from the cemetery. He woke me in a terrible state. Said he'd hit Clarita Araujo with a rock and thought he might have killed her. He begged me to come. I went with him. There was nothing I could do for her—she was dead. The issue was what to do for Tomas." He ran a hand through his hair, picked up the coffee cup but didn't drink from it. "I wasn't going to hand him over to the elders. You saw what they were capable of. And there were no police here." He stifled a laugh. "Even if there were, what would they have done? You've seen Tomas. He's no killer. The occasional outburst of frustration, yes, but nothing more. There is no hate or jealousy or lust in that boy's heart. And what would become of him if he was sent to prison? Each of you is a police officer. I don't have to paint pictures for you."

"You decided to get rid of the body and make it look like another victim of the witch killing if anyone ever found her," said Carter.

"Exactly," the priest said and looked at her directly. "As I said there was nothing to be done for Clarita. No family to grieve for her. No friends. She had long been an outcast. She would never have been allowed to be buried in the cemetery because the villagers thought she was a witch and if there were ever a marker on her grave anywhere else they would have burned it."

Each of them stared into their cups. Only the occasional sound of Sister Agnes cleaning the plates from breakfast broke the silence. "Wasn't she entitled to recognition?" Carter asked. "A commemoration of who she was?"

"You sound more like a priest than I do," Father Roque replied. "She was dead. Tomas was alive. I had a choice to make and I made it."

"How did you know about the overhang?" asked Cordero after a short while.

"One of the elders told me in confession," Father Roque explained and smiled. "When death is nearing even the most hidebound have been known to hedge their bets. I couldn't break the seal of the confessional and divulge what I knew but I could use the information in my own way. And I did and I'm not sorry for that."

"You seem to be selective in what you choose to take seriously from your priesthood," Carter said. "You're prepared to compromise on some things but not on others."

"Only eccentrics refuse to compromise and I'm not an eccentric," the priest said.

"Matter of opinion," quipped Carter.

"You may not be an eccentric but you are an accessory after the fact, Father," Cordero said. "And you've also hindered a police investigation. Had you told us what you knew, we may have been able to wrap this up days ago. These are serious offences."

"I am also the killer of Clarita Araujo," the priest said sitting upright. "I will not allow that boy to be held accountable for her death. I will insist I did it, not him. I will insist that I am the guilty one and I know enough about how she died to sound convincing."

"In my country we call that taking the fall," said Carter. "That's a very dumb thing to do."

"The Bible refers to the scapegoat," Father Roque said and smiled. "It's a necessary and honourable role at times and if this be one of those so be it."

• • •

"You don't look happy," Cordero said to Carter as he drove out of the churchyard and turned for Dili in the opposite direction to the way they'd come. "The rice porridge again?"

"You call that a good outcome?" she asked, ignoring his attempt at humour.

"As good as we could expect. Why?"

"For starters, no one paid a price."

"I'd say everyone paid a price," answered Cordero. "Sabu Bada got greedy. He's dead. Juno was ambitious. The other elders will regard him now as one who makes silly decisions and can't be trusted to keep his mouth shut. He'll never be a *lia-nain* and may even be booted out of the *uma lulik*. Vitor Coval has paid his price. He lost his family to superstition. And Tomas—well he's paid a heavy price all his life simply for being born the way he was."

"And Father Roque?" asked Carter.

"I think Father Roque is juggling the fire of faith in the cold hand of reason. He's inviting martyrdom of some kind as his release. None of us should envy him." Cordero paused. "Maybe there is a curse on that village after all."

Carter shifted in her seat to face him. "That's my point. None of what you say about the outcome owes anything to us—the police, the law. We've left them as we found them. Stuck in the past."

He checked the rearview mirror rather than look at her directly. "Maybe you're in a too much of a hurry to change things."

"And maybe you're too willing to leave things as they are."

Cordero adjusted the mirror ever so slightly. "As Roque said that night we were drinking gin, you can't rush things when it's been woven into your DNA for millennia."

"My people didn't come down in the last shower, you know. Call us Americans but we can trace our ancestors back millennia as well, Cordero."

"Okay and you've developed a sense of justice and a system of laws." He waved a hand at the mountains in the distance. "These people have theirs as well. What did you tell me that first time we walked along the riverbank? On the *lulik* land? You said you'd become sensitive to the beliefs of Navajos and Apaches. Sensitive. That's the word you used. But sensitivity isn't respect. Your sensitivity didn't stop you interrupting rituals and violating sacred taboos. You admitted that. It's all part of the job, you said. Well I'd say that's giving the job much more importance than the communities it's meant to serve."

"Where would we be without—" she began but he stopped her.

"The job? Your country is awash with firearms, drugs and broken families. Communities have lost control. You rely on a system—what you call the job—and when it doesn't work you rely on it even more." He looked across at her. "People call that insanity except when it becomes policy: repeating the same practice knowing it will fail but still hoping for a different outcome."

She held her stare for a moment then turned and peered at nothing in particular out her side window. "And you?"

"Me?" he said, surprised at the lack of come back from her. "I think what good would it do to put Juno or Tomas or Father Roque in jail? We could feel good about ourselves that the bad guys were punished but the villagers would say three of their own were taken from them. There's no healing in that, only more damage and pain." He took a deep breath. "Look, there's well over two million people in jail in your country. That's twice the population of East Timor. What damn good does it do? The numbers just keep going up and up."

"And what about the dead?" she asked.

"The dead are always with us," Cordero said and glanced across at her. "Like the father you are always quoting."

She was silent a long time as the SUV juddered this way and that until they reached a slightly more substantial link road at Rihiu. Maybe some at least of what he said was right. The contrast between policing in East Timor and policing in the US could not have been more stark. But here in this quaint backwater of a country the outcome of investigations seemed generally to put matters to rest in a satisfying fashion—however unorthodox the way they were arrived at. There were times back home when she felt the law, the courts, the police were struggling just to be taken seriously as order broke down in so many places and people retreated into the safety of their homes or took to the streets to vent their rage. And certainly, Cordero was right about her father: there wasn't a day went by she didn't feel his presence in some way. Perhaps there was something in his comment about the dead as well.

"I'm learning a lot about policing from you, Cordero," Carter said as he turned toward Railaco. "None of it good," she added with what might have been a smile.

"What will we tell our superiors, *mana*?" Estefana, who'd listened quietly to the conversation from the back, asked to change the subject.

"We'll tell Jacobsen the truth, Estefana," said Carter. "There was no evidence of a war crime but signs to indicate the human remains were victims of a witch killing the person responsible for which is now dead."

"And I'll tell my superiors," Cordero chimed in, "that I uncovered the identity of the sand digger's skull but couldn't find a compelling motive for her murder or an obvious suspect to charge. There are a hundred ways to explain away a crime in Timor-Leste," he said. "And more than one way to pursue justice."

They drove on in silence again for several minutes. "Henri will be glad when you're back," Cordero said, his tone a little awkward.

"Hmm. I haven't given him much thought," Carter said, looking out of the SUV as the last of the huts with bare dirt yards and small gardens gave way to an olive-green wall of forest.

Cordero sniffed. "Well maybe we could go out for a celebratory drink and dinner then." He hesitated. "You know—you, me, and Estefana of course."

"Josinto will want to spend time with me, *maun*. And I will want to spend time with him," Estafana insisted.

"What about your friend the nurse?" Carter asked. "Won't you want to spend time with her and vice-versa?"

"That's a hard one," Cordero said and winced. "She's caring for my sister, Ana, while she's recuperating from the appendix operation. Visits her at home. But she wants to become a police officer. Wants me to help her prepare for the entry exams next week. That night I went with her from the hospital? It was to visit her mother who's blind. The mother kept telling me how much it would mean to her daughter if I helped her. Good thing she never turned the lights on at night or my reluctance would've showed. On and on the woman went. I'd hate to think what she'd be like if she knew I wasn't going to help. The girl's a good nurse, you see, and I don't want her to leave Ana until she's completely well again."

He glanced sideways and this time definitely noticed a smile appear on Carter's lips. "What?" Cordero raised an eyebrow. "The next entry exam is only six months away. I'm happy to help her then."

About the Author

Chris McGillion is a regular visitor to East Timor where he has been involved in media development initiatives and conducted research into the communication of agricultural science in remote mountain communities. He is a former journalist whose work has been published in Australia, the US and the United Kingdom and has taught politics, philosophy and communication skills at four universities in Australia. He has authored or co-authored a number of non-fiction books on subjects as diverse as US-Cuban relations, clerical sexual abuse, and religious sociology. He lives in the Blue Mountains west of Sydney, Australia.